To Jerry Raskin: For fight[illegible] in the skies over [illegible] for being my cousin and for being the good guy you are!

all the best!
Dick Rittenband
6/22/10

A Capital Murder

State vs. Governor David Roberts

by Judge Richard Rittenband

This is a work of fiction. Any similarity to anyone living or dead is purely coincidental.

ISBN: 1-4392-4738-2
ISBN-13: 9781439247389
Library of Congress Control Number: 2009906404

Visit www.amazon.com or www.booksurge.com to order additional copies.

to Rhoda, my wife and best friend

1

"You may cross examine the witness, Attorney Roberts."

"Thank you, your honor." David Roberts' tall, lanky frame seemed to unfold as he arose from his chair.

"May I approach the witness?" Roberts asked.

"Certainly," Judge Robert Hollander replied. A veteran criminal court judge, he was presiding over the trial of State of Connecticut versus Troy Duncan. He put his hand over his mouth and stifled a yawn as he watched Roberts walk toward the witness. The overhead light reflected off of Roberts' thick red hair. *He likes to use his height and his personality to overwhelm the witness-to show him he's in charge*, Hollander thought.

Roberts stopped in front of Ronald Aiken, a short middle-aged man who looked at Roberts expectantly.

Roberts stood a little to Aiken's right, being careful not to block the view of the jury. He did partially block Aiken's view of the defense table.

"Good morning, Mr. Aiken. I'm David Roberts. I represent Troy Duncan. I just have a few questions for you" he smiled at him.

Aiken shifted nervously in his seat, looked up at Roberts and replied hesitantly "Good morning."

“When we took a recess Mr. Aiken, you had just identified Mr. Duncan as the man you saw hold up the gas station. Is that correct?”

“Yes.”

“Now, we’re talking about the same gas station aren’t we?”

Aiken seemed to have gained a little confidence. “Of course. It was the Mobil station at Farmington and Troutbrook in West Hartford” he said proudly.

“I was using the self-service pump, when I saw your client go into the store.”

“And it was at night?” Roberts asked.

“Yes. It was dark, but there were plenty of lights. I could see him clearly.”

“I notice you wear glasses, Mr. Aiken. Were you. . . . .”

Aiken interrupted. “Yes, and I was wearing them that night when I saw him.

“Are you near sighted or far sighted?”

“Near sighted, but these glasses are for distance.”

“They’re not bifocals?”

“No, I told you. I’m near sighted, not far sighted.”

“Are you sure you didn’t take them off to see the numbers on the pump?”

“Of course, I’m sure. I know what I saw, Attorney Roberts. You can ask me questions all day, but it was your client I saw that night. That’s him sitting right over there” Aiken said smugly as he pointed at the defense table.

Roberts wasn't smiling now. He looked unhappy.

"Are you absolutely sure?" he asked.

"Of course I am. He wasn't wearing a shirt and tie or a jacket but that's him. I remember the mustache."

"All right, Mr. Aiken. Just one more question. I want you to look around this courtroom. Look at everybody. Then point to the person you saw robbing the store."

What's he trying to do, trick me? He must think I'm some sort of dumb dumb. Aiken quickly looked around the courtroom. There were thirty spectators plus court personnel.

"I've looked, and the man is the same one I pointed out before; your client sitting right over there." He pointed again to the defense table.

"Do you need more time? Do you want to take another look?"

Aiken was becoming angry. Perspiration surfaced on his upper lip. He squinted at Roberts and leaned forward. "No and no!" he almost shouted. "I'm positive. That's him sitting right over there." he pointed again.

Roberts stepped back and turned toward the audience. "Will the defendant Troy Duncan please stand up?"

The courtroom was quiet except for a few nervous giggles. The jury looked in amazement as a man in the audience wearing khaki pants and shirt stood up. He had blonde hair and a blonde mustache.

"Will Michael Burton please stand up?" The man at the defense table rose. He paused and then took off his blonde wig and dark brown mustache. His head was bald, and he was grinning.

Roberts turned to Aiken whose face was now flushed.

"Thank you, Mr. Aiken for your keen powers of observation." he said as he walked back to the counsel table.

Some spectators were talking, a murmur ran through the audience, and the jury members looked astonished as Duncan replaced Burton at the defense table.

Judge Hollander banged his gavel for order.

Equally stunned was Assistant State's Attorney Frank Smith who had been sitting at his table quietly. Now, he rose to his feet and shouted "Objection, your honor! This is just showmanship; theatrics that has no place in a court of law." He glared at Roberts. "I move to strike the entire cross-examination and ask the court to instruct the jury to disregard this spectacle" he said heatedly.

Judge Hollander, who was hiding his silent laughter with his hand, nodded at Roberts.

Roberts stood up: "Your honor. I don't know why the state's attorney is so upset. After all, a trial is a search for the truth. It's still the truth no matter how we get to it."

Smith started to speak, but Hollander waved him down. I've heard enough, Mr. Smith. The defendant is entitled to a good deal of latitude in cross-examination, in testing the credibility of the state's witnesses. Your objection is overruled. The motion to strike is denied. Do you have any further questions of this witness, Attorney Roberts?"

"No, your honor. I'm satisfied."

Hollander turned to Smith. "Any redirect examination, Attorney Smith?"

Smith started to walk forward, thought better of it, shrugged his shoulders and replied "No, your honor," as he sat down.

Late that afternoon, Roberts and his friend Attorney Brian Kelly, were seated in a corner of the Hartford Club, celebrating Roberts' victory.

Kelly raised his glass. "Congratulations, Dave. I was watching from the back. A sterling performance as they say in the theater reviews. You know, Smith wasn't all that wrong. It was theater, very effective theater, but still theater."

Roberts took a sip of his martini. "Thank you, I think. Aren't good trial lawyers often dramatic in their presentations? We're advocates. What's wrong with a little theater if it brings out the truth? And, I might add, you're well known yourself as having a flair for the dramatic."

"True. True. You certainly created reasonable doubt. No wonder the jury returned so quickly with a not guilty verdict."

"Then justice was done." Kelly rattled the ice cubes in his glass of scotch. "That's good. The only downside is that you've made an enemy of Frank Smith. He wasn't very happy losing, particularly the way he lost."

"That's too bad, Brian. I was representing my client. He shouldn't take it so personally. I realize he has a big ego, but . . ."

Kelly laughed. "Big ego. That's the understatement of the year. He's an arrogant little bastard. He may look stupid with that little mustache of his, but he's very ambitious. Just watch your back, Dave. He could be dangerous."

Roberts nodded. His eyes shifted downward. "O.K." he said in a weak voice.

"What's bothering you, Dave? You should be on a high right now. Why so glum?"

Roberts leaned back, closed his eyes and sighed. "Annie and I broke up last night."

"What? How did that happen?" Kelly looked incredulous. He looked almost as stunned as Frank Smith had. "I thought you and Anne Tremaine were a perfect match. You had a hot and heavy one going."

"True," Roberts replied, "But that's all it was, apparently, an affair; and affairs end."

"You still haven't told me why it ended."

"Annie wants to try her luck in Hollywood. You know how beautiful she is. She's been a model, Miss Connecticut and all that. She wants to go now before she gets older and loses some of that beauty."

"Did you try to change her mind?"

Roberts paused and raised his eyebrows. "Yes and no. I didn't ask her to marry me if that's what you mean. I'm not sure we're right for each other over the long haul. I did urge her to stay and give us more time, but she said no. I have to do what's best for me she told me. We'd had a few drinks and the argument became somewhat heated." He paused. "Actually more than somewhat. I asked her if there was anyone else. She wouldn't answer me."

"How heated did it get?"

"I became angry. I shook her trying to get her to answer. I felt betrayed."

"Did you hurt her?"

"I don't think so, although there were probably some bruises to her arms. I was holding her so tight. I almost lost it, Brian. She's hard to give up."

"How did it end?"

"When I let her go, she slapped me in the face pretty hard. I'm sure I deserved it. Somehow I got control of myself. I left. I was afraid of what I might do."

Kelly tried to cheer him up. "You know what Yogi said? It ain't over 'til it's over."

Roberts managed a weak smile. "No, this one is really over. She's leaving in a few days. I don't think she's coming back."

"Dave, you look as if you're going to cry. Maybe it's partly the booze. Let's order something to eat. Maybe you'll feel better."

Roberts nodded.

Kelly continued. "I'm also a philosopher. I don't know who said it, but if it wasn't meant to be, it wasn't meant to be. Besides, you won a big case today. Forget about Annie. As another philosopher said, "You win some you lose some."

"I know, but it hurts to lose. Now, I have no one."

Kelly wanted to change the subject, he signaled for the waiter. "You'll get over it. Think of what you've got going for you. An All American at

Penn; from Air Force ROTC to a pilot in Vietnam. You came back a war hero. You've been a federal prosecutor. You may only be a State Senator now, but with that background you could go as high as you want; and think of that Roberts' charisma. I've seen you charm the pants off an audience, particularly when they're mostly female" he chuckled.

Roberts leaned forward. "What about my divorce?"

"No problem" Kelly said. "You've got plenty of company. More than half the adult population is divorced."

Roberts started to smile.

"Besides, I'm buying dinner tonight. What more do you want?" Kelly grinned.

2

Eight Years Later

Anne Tremaine was lying on her bed with a man on top of her. Her thin light blue negligee was fully open, exposing her breasts and lower body. But, this time the man was fully clothed. He was wearing winter gloves. Instead of caressing her with his bare hands as he usually did, they were clutched tightly around her throat choking her. She could barely breathe; and instead of a face filled with warmth and desire, his expression was one of rage, his cheeks growing redder as his anger increased and his hands tightened. She tried to get up, but with his knees straddling her right leg, it was impossible.

He had surprised her as she was coming out of the bathroom. After a heated argument, he had knocked her back onto the bed with a hard slap on her cheeks.

He was shouting at her. She tried to answer him, but his hands were so tight, she could barely manage to gasp for breath, much less say anything. His mouth was open. He was so furious that he seemed to be spitting at her. He continued to shout at her, but his voice was getting lower. Her head felt dizzy. She couldn't make out the words.

Desperately, she reached for the clock on her night table to hit him. Suddenly, the pressure on her throat eased as he knocked the clock out of her hands; and just as quickly his hands again tightened around her throat. She couldn't breathe; she felt terrible pain in her head. She dimly saw his head inches away closing in on her; then darkness, then nothing. The door slammed, but she couldn't hear it.

Anne Tremaine's long blonde hair was spread out on the pale blue blanket. She looked as beautiful as she ever did; except for the bruises on her throat; and her beautiful blue eyes which stared vacantly at the ceiling. Christmas morning, 2005. It was Anne Tremaine's worst Christmas. It was also her last.

3

Snow flurries were swirling around the Governor's mansion as Ben and Becky Brown walked toward the main entrance. It was the early afternoon of Christmas day and the site of Governor David Roberts' annual bi-partisan Christmas bash. Invited were members of the Legislature which was to convene the first week in January and a variety of others, including neighbors, members of the Administration, the attorney general, the commissioner of public safety and the mayors of Hartford and West Hartford. It was the "in" place to be that afternoon if you were in politics or government.

Benjamin "Ben" Brown was a state representative from Litchfield in the Northwest corner of Connecticut and Republican leader in the House. His wife, Rebecca, "Becky", Brown was a veteran state police lieutenant recently turned private investigator. They had met while Ben, a criminal defense attorney, cross-examined Becky as a witness for the State. Becky pulled the fur collar of her dark coat closer around her neck as the cold wind whipped through the driveway. Ben lifted his scarf up to cover most of his face. It was 28 degrees with a wind chill factor of 20 degrees. Six inches of snow had fallen three days ago giving everyone a White Christmas.

"Come in out of the cold." Cindy Roberts, Connecticut's first lady and a state senator from Hartford, greeted Ben and Becky as they came through the door to the lower foyer. "Welcome." she said. "Happy holidays to my good friends." she smiled as she and the couple exchanged kisses. "Alex will take your coats, and then we can go into the living room so you can stand in front of the fireplace and get warm. That's where David is. There's also egg nog and cider with cinnamon to warm you inside, especially if you choose the alcohol added kind." she laughed.

"How have you been?" Ben asked.

"Wonderful." Cindy replied. "I love this time of the year. New Year's day will be our second wedding anniversary."

They greeted several members of the General Assembly as they made their way toward the fireplace. Frosty the Snowman was playing in the background as the conversation usually heard at political affairs filled the room. There were brightly lit Christmas trees in the living room, library and sun room.

Governor Roberts noticed them approaching and called out: "If it isn't my leader and my favorite tennis partner." He smiled as he shook hands with Ben and embraced Becky. Ben and Becky warmed their hands as they stood by the crackling fire. Roberts, 58, was in his third year as Governor. At six foot four with red hair he was an imposing figure.

"It's a day to celebrate." Roberts said. "Here, join me in some egg nog." Roberts filled the cups with the spiked egg nog. "Becky, this should warm the cockles of your heart, and, Ben, this should put some hair on your chest." He grinned: "I got that right, didn't I?" He asked. "I wanted to be both politically and anatomically correct."

"Perfect, as usual." Ben retorted. "You never miss."

Roberts lifted his cup, touched the others in a toast and proclaimed: "Happy holidays and good health to all. I think that was also correct." He smiled.

"Speaking of health", Becky said. "Are you up to some tennis?"

"Don't worry." Roberts replied. "I'll hold up my end. How about next Saturday morning? You and I against Cindy and Ben at the West Hartford Racket Club. I know Cindy's available. What about you two?"

"You're on!" said Ben.

The closeness between the Governor and his leader in the House of Representatives had produced a social friendship between the two couples which had grown stronger by their mutual enthusiasm for tennis. During the warmer weather they played on the courts at Elizabeth Park nearby. In the winter they played at the West Hartford Racket Club.

The Governor moved on to greet other guests. Ben and Becky, who knew most of the guests, circulated among them throughout the first floor to the tune of White Christmas, Christmas carols, the clinking of glasses and refills of egg nog and cider.

Becky and Ben were soon separated, and Becky found herself standing alone in the upper foyer. She looked up and saw State's Attorney for the Hartford Judicial District, Frank Smith, walking toward her quickly with a big grin on his face. She started to wish him a Happy holiday when he suddenly put his arms around her and kissed her on the lips. When he tried to open her lips, she pushed him away. Flushed, she raised her voice: "Frank, what the hell do you think your doing?"

Smith pointed to the mistletoe hanging from the beam above them. "Oh!" Becky said, "but you didn't have to kiss me so passionately!"

"Sorry, Becky, I got carried away. You know how much you turn me on, pretty lady."

Again raising her voice Becky said: "Well, the feeling is certainly not mutual!"

At this point people were staring at them. Ben walked up to Becky: "Everything all right here?" he asked.

Becky sighed: "It's okay, Ben. Frank and I just had a little misunderstanding."

Calmer now, Becky turned to Frank and asked: "What are you doing here, anyway, Frank. I thought you didn't like the Governor."

"I'm a neighbor. I live one street down on Terry Road right behind here." Smith replied.

"But you don't even like him." Becky said.

Smith looked at Becky a little more intensely. "I don't have anything against him personally. I can try to overlook his two marriages and his escapades of the heart he had in between. He's hardly a role model for what a governor should be, but it's his policies I don't like. He's too soft on crime!"

"That's nonsense." Becky replied. "What are you talking about?"

Smith turned to look at Ben as well. "You two are in law enforcement although on different sides. I'm talking about Roberts' support for the exclusionary rule that lets guilty people go free." Smith said.

Becky frowned. Smith said: “You don’t understand it? Ben, you’re a high paid criminal defense attorney who is used to standing in the way of justice. Why don’t you explain it?” he smirked.

Ben ignored Smith’s comments and turned to Becky.

“I’ll try to give you the neutral version; also the short version.

The law in our State today makes inadmissible in court any evidence resulting from a police search that’s based upon false or inaccurate information, even though the evidence clearly establishes the defendant’s guilt. The evidence is excluded. Hundreds of criminals have gotten off because of this technicality.” Ben said.

Becky interrupted. “Now, it’s coming back to me, but isn’t there an exception to that rule?”

“There you go.” Smith broke in. “The exception is that a search would be allowed if the officers acted in good faith; that is, without knowledge that the information was false or inaccurate. It’s known as the ‘good faith exception’”.

“Then, what’s the problem?” Becky asked.

Smith shrugged. “The Connecticut Constitution does not allow for a good faith exception even though Federal law and most states do; so we need a Constitutional Amendment to permit it. Your defense attorney husband is in love with the State Constitution. He and your mamby, pamby Governor are opposed to an amendment.”

“What do you mean?” Becky asked.

Smith looked at her: “You really don’t keep up with the news, do you? Last year Jim Spaulding, your State Senator from Litchfield, introduced just such an amendment. Roberts was able to muster enough votes at the Capitol to defeat it. It's going to be introduced again next month. Becky, you've been in law enforcement. You know how important this is. If you have any influence at all with Roberts, you should persuade him to support the amendment. Stiffen his backbone if that's possible."

"That's what Mr. Gangbusters here wants." Ben interrupted. "But, there's more to it than that. David Roberts is not soft on crime."

Smith started to speak but was interrupted by the ringing of his cell phone. "Excuse me." He said.

He put the phone to his ear, "Smith here." He paused.

"Slow down, Sergeant Phillips, and tell me what happened." Smith listened, his eyes widening. "Okay, Sergeant, pick me up at the Governor's Mansion; radio ahead. Tell them not to let anyone in except the forensic team."

Smith walked over to the Governor with Ben and Becky and pulled him aside. "Governor, I have to leave. The Hartford Police just found a body in a condo at River View. Looks like a homicide. I think you know the victim, Anne Tremaine."

Roberts seemed stunned: "Annie?" he said. "Of course, I know her. We're old friends." He leaned against the wall and ran his hand through his hair. "I understand." he told Smith. "Go ahead but keep me informed."

4

Anne Tremaine, Smith thought as he gazed out the window of the state's attorney's car. *He had seen her often when he was at the Capitol pushing his anti-crime legislation; she was a real beauty. They would speak on occasion.*

Smith was seated in the front seat next to Sergeant Phillips, his regular driver. Phillips interrupted his thoughts: "Who is this Anne Tremaine?" he asked.

"She's a lobbyist at the Capitol." Smith replied. "She represents or, I guess, did represent, several trade groups, banks and solid waste companies in the legislature. She was very successful and very well connected." Smith said.

"How did she get into being a lobbyist?" Phillips asked.

"She started out as secretary to State Senate Republicans. She was born in Litchfield, was graduated from Trinity College in Hartford, and then got a job running the New Britain office of the Congressman from the 6th District before she worked for Senate Republicans. She went to law school at night, but instead of taking a job as an attorney, she went right into lobbying."

Phillips persisted: "What made her a good lobbyist?"

Smith sighed: "She was a natural in that position; with her knowledge of the legislative process, her good looks and personality, her education and intelligence and her friendship with many of the members of the General Assembly. This is one woman who stood out in a crowd. She was not only all that, but she was also very close to the leadership of both parties."

The black Crown Victoria sped south on Hartford's Main Street, took a left onto Charter Oak Avenue and headed toward the Connecticut River. When it reached the I-91 barrier, it turned south again onto Van Dyke Avenue past the Colt Firearm building arriving at the River View Condominiums complex overlooking Charter Oak landing and the Connecticut river on the northwest side of the Charter Oak Bridge.

The words Charter Oak originated from an exciting event in Connecticut history. In 1662 Britain's King Charles II granted a Royal Charter to the colony of Connecticut permitting its people to elect their own officials and make their own laws. His brother and successor, King James II was not so democratic. To reassert dominance over the colony he sent Sir Edmond Andros and 70 soldiers to Hartford to retrieve the Charter. While Andros and Connecticut officials were arguing the night of November 1, 1687, the candles were suddenly snuffed out. Captain Joseph Wadsworth grabbed the Charter and put it in a secret hiding place, a hole in the trunk of a huge oak tree located on the edge of what is now Charter Oak Avenue. The British never found it, and the people continued to govern themselves under the Charter through the American Revolution.

Sgt. Phillips turned into a driveway at a sign that read "River View Condominiums", drove up to a circle and pulled in behind a Hartford police car parked in front of one of the condos. In the center of the circle was a fountain set upon grass with a flower bed around it. There were several police cars parked around the circle as well as mobile TV units. An ambulance was pulling away. Several reporters were standing on the grass in the circle.

Smith and Phillips got out of the car and walked toward the building entrance. Smith, on the inside, was somewhat shielded by the taller Phillips.

Smith moved quickly on a short, wiry frame and talked rapidly. His brown eyes seemed to sparkle when he spoke, sometimes with enthusiasm, other times defiantly. His dark moustache matched his dark brown hair. People called him a "ball of fire" and a "human dynamo". The former FBI agent was considered a pro-active state's attorney who often rode at all hours to the scene of a crime. He liked to compare himself to Thomas E. Dewey, the former New York racket busting district attorney who went on to become governor of New York and a two time presidential candidate.

The reporters spotted him and rushed forward. Smith was outspoken and usually provided a good comment or sound bite. He was popular with the press.

"Frank, Frank" called out Channel 3. "Is the victim really Anne Tremaine?"

Smith slowed a little. "Too early to tell" he replied. The reporters groaned. Smith continued, "I do have one comment. Don't step on the flowers." He smiled and waved as he entered the building.

A police officer greeted them with "Upstairs." They started to climb up. The two story condo was covered with plush blue wall to wall carpeting. It overlooked the Connecticut River and the jogging trail on the water's edge. Down the hall on the second floor was the master bedroom with a balcony facing east toward the river.

Smith was met in the bedroom by Inspector Anthony "Tony" Cassella of the State's Attorney's office. "What have we got, Tony?" Smith asked as they walked over to the bed.

"She's a beauty" Cassella said, as they looked down at the body of Anne Tremaine. "If it weren't for her eyes and the red marks on her neck, she'd look like a centerfold in Playboy."

"I know who she was." Smith replied. "She used to attract a lot of attention up at the Capitol. What a waste."

Cassella looked up at Smith. He was a little shorter than Smith and much heavier. An allstate wrestler in high school, he looked the part, thick arms and a short neck with a heavy black beard no doubt designed to obscure the neck. His left eye sometimes twitched when he talked. He was in his early fifties, having been a Hartford police officer for 20 years before his last ten with the state's attorney's office.

"Well," Tony said, "according to the M.E.'s preliminary estimate the cause of death is strangulation. She's been dead about 8 hours. That would take it back to about 7 o'clock this morning. That fits with the time on the broken clock on the floor over there." Cassella pointed at the clock which had stopped at 7:15.

"Who found her?" Smith asked.

"Her sister, Jean Beaumont. She and her husband and their two kids were supposed to have Christmas dinner here. We found a turkey in the refrigerator, cranberry sauce and other trimmings. I guess she didn't get a chance to start cooking. When her sister got no answer, she let herself in with an extra key. She called 911 from the telephone on the night table.

We've only done a quick look around the place. But we've found two very interesting items, both in the bathroom. The glass over the sink has the seal of the governor of Connecticut; and there's a letter to Governor Roberts from Governor Malone of Massachusetts.

Maybe we have the governor of Connecticut as a suspect."

"Are you kidding?" Smith replied. "Roberts doesn't have the guts to do something like this."

He looked closely at his chief inspector. "Don't say anything about this; and make sure the police, the M.E. and the criminalists keep their mouths shut. I don't want any leaks to the media. This case is already big news because of the victim. Let's not blow the roof off by having the governor's name mentioned," Smith said.

Smith and Cassella had walked out onto the balcony. They looked down on the jogging trail.

"See if you can find someone who was jogging early this morning. Let the M.E. and the criminalists do their jobs. Tell them to be super thorough and careful" Smith said. "This is a case made for the media; and we don't want any screw-ups; whatever you do, keep the place guarded. I don't want to see the murder scene on tonight's news."

He looked north towards the state Capitol. He could see the gold dome of the capitol with the afternoon sun on it. "This is a beautiful view of the capitol." I guess she'll never see that again."

Smith and Phillips hurried downstairs.

As Smith stepped outside, the television cameras were turned on. "Hold it," Smith said with a grim look on his face. "I can't hear you all at once. The victim is a woman by the name of Anne Tremaine."

"The lobbyist?" Channel 30 asked.

"That's right," Smith replied. "Preliminary reports, and I want to stress the word, preliminary, indicate she was strangled sometime this morning.

That's all I have to say at this time. I won't take any questions."

Phillips helped him push his way through the crowd. Cassella joined them. They got into the car leaving the TV cameras to film them as they drove away.

5

"I have a brief statement, then, I'll take your questions."

Governor Roberts was standing at the podium in the old Judiciary Room at the State Capitol. This was the eighteenth news conference of his administration, and although it was the day after Christmas, there was a good turnout of the state media. The late afternoon conferences were designed to dominate the evening news programs.

"I intend to propose to the legislature when it opens next month a one percent increase in the state sales tax. This is expected to bring in an additional $350 million in annual revenue which is to be used solely for drug education in our school system starting in kindergarten.

We must dry up the demand for illegal drugs. We must develop effective programs to indoctrinate our young people as to the dangers of using drugs.

We have to begin at the kindergarten level so that starting with that generation the use of such drugs can be dramatically reduced. When the demand dries up, the suppliers will go out of business.

These drugs are like a cancer in our society. It is the cause of much of our crime problems in Connecticut. Drug addicts turn to robbery and burglary to obtain the money needed to feed their habits. Addicts can't work, so they go on welfare. Drug addiction causes a breakdown in family life, an increase in divorce, and in family violence; and drug addicted mothers sometimes give birth to drug addicted babies. We must stop this cycle of dependency and despair.

I recognize there are other causes of the ills of our society. But most of these problems have been with us for years. The scourge of our society in the second half of the last century and the beginning of this one has been the dramatic increase in drug dependency. While we take steps to resolve these other problems, we must strike hard at the problems of illegal drugs which today transcend all other problems.

Now, I'll take your questions."

"Ralph."

"Governor, does this mean a de-emphasis on other aspects of the war on drugs?" the Associated Press asked.

"Not at all," Roberts replied. "Drug rehabilitation and law enforcement both remain a high priority; but, no matter how well they're doing, it's not enough. Drug use continues to grow. We often hear and read news announcements about the big drug busts in our state. Law enforcement has done a good job but these drug busts just scratch the surface. Drugs continue to flow into our state.

Interdiction at our country's borders, which is a Federal response, hasn't really stopped illegal drugs from pouring into this country.

Some have suggested the death penalty for drug kingpins, the major suppliers. These people aren't worried about that. They're more worried about being gunned down by their competitors; and even if you do eliminate them, there are others ready to take their place. So long as huge profits can be made, so long as the demand is there, people will find ways to sell drugs and people who have become addicted will find ways to buy them."

"How do you think the Legislature will react to a 1% increase in the sales tax?" Channel 3 asked.

"No one wants to raise taxes," Roberts said, "but I think if the members of the General Assembly reflect on the need for drug education, and the impact it will have, they will support this proposal; and in the long run, it will pay for itself. A substantial decrease in drug addiction will lessen the financial burden on our law enforcement agencies, the court system, our prison system and our welfare system. The present drug problem is costing millions in these areas.

Sure, it's going to cost money initially; but we are drowning in drugs, our social problems are overwhelming us. When we're in such a crisis, money has to take a back seat to the survival of our society. This expenditure will be an investment in our children's future. We cannot let this opportunity pass us by."

"Why are you proposing this now?" Channel 8 asked.

"Because time is running out. We must act now before the problem becomes insurmountable.

Why today, during Christmas week? Because it's a slow news time, and I want the people of this state to think about what I've proposed, then contact their representatives and senators and urge them to support this proposal. Also, it gives the legislators time to reflect upon this proposal. I hope the legislative leaders will schedule hearings to take place shortly after the legislature convenes and take action as soon as possible. I hope that this program will be part of the school curriculum by next September, if not before."

"How do you propose to implement this program?" the Hartford Courant asked.

"If the legislature approves my proposal, I will immediately appoint a blue-ribbon commission to develop effective and realistic educational programs. It will be an action commission that will develop programs to put in place as soon as possible. I intend to appoint to this commission educators, psychologists, psychiatrists, advertising specialists, sales experts, people from the television and movie industries. I want the finest minds in the nation on this, some of whom live right here in Connecticut. The educators and psychologists can develop the message, and the media people can develop the means to deliver the message effectively. The advertising and entertainment industries are experts at persuading young people to buy products. I'd like them to use that same expertise to persuade young people not to use drugs.

"Governor," WTIC news said. "as you know, State's Attorney Frank Smith and Senator Jim Spaulding have both said your approach to crime is too weak; that you tend to coddle criminals. They've criticized your opposition to the good faith search warrant exception. Do you think they'll criticize this proposal for drug education as another weak response to the crime problem?"

"Well, Mr. Smith and Senator Spaulding can speak for themselves, of course. As to the search warrant, apparently, I have more faith in the constitution than they do. Concerning the drug education proposal, they and others have to understand that law enforcement alone is not doing the job. We have to try innovative approaches to this problem."

"Do you expect either of them to run against you for governor in the next election?" Channel 30 asked.

Roberts smiled. "I can't predict what they're going to do; I haven't even decided whether I'm going to run for re-election; but it would be an interesting race. Both of them and I have differing views on many subjects. Perhaps, such a contest would be a referendum on these ideas. Let the people choose. That's what democracy is all about."

"Governor, you said this is a slow news time," the New Haven Register said. "Did you know that Anne Tremaine was found murdered yesterday?"

Roberts looked startled. His face became a little pale. "Yes, Frank Smith told me last night. I'm sorry. She was a fine person."

"Governor, you seem shaken by the news about Anne Tremaine. Is that because you and she had an affair a few years ago?" the Register persisted.

Roberts face turned red. "My relationship with her is none of your business" he said.

"But the people have a right to know, don't they?" WPOP radio news, followed up.

"No, they don't" Roberts replied. "Anne and I were good friends; my private life before I became governor is nobody's business; and let me tell you something, Mr. Bauer; I don't appreciate your implying something wrong here. She died just yesterday. Don't you have any decency?"

With that, Roberts strode quickly out of the room.

6

Roberts walked quickly past the hall of the House of Representatives on his way back to his office. Bob Sweeney, his press secretary, was so much shorter than Roberts he could hardly keep up with him. "You shouldn't have ended like that," the former political reporter for the Stamford Advocate said. "It will draw editorials accusing you of putting a chilling effect on the First Amendment. I'm sure you've heard that before."

Roberts smiled, slightly. "Yeah, I know, but it's too late now. I'm still ticked off at their insensitivity. Annie hasn't even been buried yet."

The governor was greeted by his Chief of Staff, William "Bill" Donovan as he entered his office. Donovan was a 32 year old attorney who had been legal counsel to Senate Republicans before signing on with the Roberts administration.

"Bill, I want to be left alone for a little while. No appointments, no phone calls for 20 minutes or so. I'll let you know."

The governor walked into his private office and closed the door. He poured himself a scotch on the rocks, took off his jacket, loosened his tie and sat down in the large chair behind his desk. He took a sip of his drink and swivelled around to the window that overlooked the grassy area on the south side of the Capitol building. Much of the grass was showing despite a snow fall four days ago. The temperature was nearly 40 degrees that morning and much of it had melted by 2:00 p.m.

The grass reminded him of the meadow that stretched out to the west from the window of Anne Tremaine's former condo in West Hartford, a view that was part of the beginning of their relationship. They both lived in the same condominium complex, where he had purchased his after his divorce. He had first gotten to know her following his election to the State House of Representatives. They had lunch during the legislative session several times, they had been at parties together and political banquets. There were always other people there. They hadn't had a formal date. The spring had been crunch time at the Capitol as the session was moving toward adjournment. Late hours for the representatives and covering his law practice the rest of the time left him no time for a social life.

The legislature adjourned on the mandatory date of June 6th, and it was the following weekend that he finally got to relax. It was a hot Saturday afternoon when he strolled to the outdoor pool to take a swim. Anne was there in a brief red and white striped bikini which showed off her gorgeous body; large breasts that seemed about to burst out of her top; smooth skin, flat stomach and beautiful legs. She wore high heels that made her look taller. Her blonde hair was piled on top of her head. They swam together in the pool, splashed around a little and then sat on chairs under a table with an umbrella. He had been captivated by her during the session. She had a warm, outgoing personality. Her blue eyes sparkled when she talked and she tilted her head a little to the side sometimes when she smiled. Now, seeing her at the pool and being so close to her made his blood run faster.

They talked about the legislative session and what a relief it was that it had finally ended. As they laughed over a story their hands touched, and he began to feel an intimacy toward her that he hadn't felt before.

"You know, it's getting late" Anne said. "Why don't we go up to my place and have a drink to celebrate the end of the session." He took her hand as they walked toward her condominium. She showed him around the living room and dining room, a family room with a large TV set, a stereo system with speakers in every room. They were all tastefully decorated. All the rooms had deep plush carpeting, blue in the living, dining and family rooms and pink in the bedroom. The floor to ceiling drapes were the same colors as the carpeting and they were all open. She showed him the bedroom with the large picture window overlooking the meadow. "What would you like to drink?" she asked. "Scotch on the rocks would be fine" he replied.

"Good choice, two coming right up. Take in the view, I'll be right back."

Roberts stood looking out at the sun setting in the west partially hidden by clouds causing part of the meadow to be bathed in sunlight and the remainder to have a darker look.

The stereo came on playing soft dance music as Anne returned with the drinks.

"To the end of the session and the beginning of a good friendship" she said as they clanked glasses.

She had turned so they were both facing the window. He was very conscious of being dressed only in a bathing suit and of her being in only the skimpiest of bikinis. He was about to turn and kiss her when she said "Tell me about your future political plans."

He told her that he was planning to run for governor someday after serving a few terms in the senate; what he planned to do as governor; how he intended to use the power of the governor's office to produce programs that would benefit the state.

She smiled at him; "I've heard that political power is the ultimate aphrodisiac!"

They put their glasses down. He pulled her toward him, put his arms around her and leaned down to kiss her lips and mouth. She kissed back, pressed against him and put her arms around his neck, her left hand caressing his hair. It was a deep, passionate kiss.

They stumbled onto the bed. They stayed there all night halting their lovemaking only to order some pizza.

This was the start of a torrid affair. They were together constantly. Although they didn't move in together, they slept together every evening, either in her place or his. This was the physical and emotional intimacy that seemed to be missing in his marriage to Carole.

The relationship cooled down a little during the next legislative session probably due to the time commitments of the legislature and his law practice. The passion was there, but somehow they weren't comfortable with each other intellectually, and in their discussions about the future. Perhaps, she wanted him to propose to her. But, there was something missing between them, and maybe it was too soon after his divorce two years earlier for him to begin a married life again. A little more time with Anne might have done it. Maybe they would both be ready in a short time. But it wasn't to be. She insisted upon trying her luck in Hollywood. He wanted her to stay even though he wasn't ready for a commitment. They could both be explosive on occasion. A few days before she left was one of those occasions. They had argued bitterly.

Anne returned two years later. Their attempts to rekindle their relationship didn't work. *What was it they say*? mused Roberts. *Love is like a cigar. If it goes out, you can light it again, but it's never the same.*

Ah, Annie, what might have been! Roberts thought. His eyes became moist as he leaned back in his chair and covered them.

7

The Governor's official Town Car pulled into the driveway of the Executive Mansion at 6:15 that night. It was already dark, and it was cold. The temperature was 24 degrees. The governor got out and greeted the state trooper at the entrance as the car pulled away.

The Executive Residence is a nineteen room Georgian Colonial located on six beautifully landscaped acres on Prospect Avenue, overlooking the city of Hartford on the dividing line between Hartford and West Hartford. The residence is located on the Hartford side. The furniture and decorations are 18th century originals and reproductions. Both of the recent governors had some of the building refurbished. Built in 1909, it wasn't purchased by the state until 1943. It was first occupied as the Executive Residence in the fall of 1945.

Roberts greeted his wife, Cindy, with a big hug and a long almost passionate kiss. Then, he held her close, and whispered into her ear. "I'm so lucky to be married to you. I love you so much."

Cindy stood back with a look of surprise. "I love you, too darling, but what brought on this display of affection?"

"I'm not sure, but let's go into the library. I have something to tell you."

They walked into the library which was adorned with Persian rugs, dark maple walls with bookcases on both sides of the fireplace, comfortable leather chairs and a couch. It was also where the bar was located. Cindy started to make the drinks, a martini on the rocks for her and straight up for her husband. "Don't forget, very dry," he said.

Cindy Stevens Roberts was average height with blonde hair and blue eyes. At 48, she was a native of West Hartford who graduated from the University of Connecticut and its Law School. Cindy joined a downtown Hartford law firm and at the same time went to work as a volunteer for the Hartford Democratic Party. A striking woman, she reminded several people of Anne Tremaine.

She had married Andrew Douglass, an attorney from her law firm with whom she had a son, Barry, who became the center of their lives. Andy was driving Barry home from a Christmas lighting ceremony in downtown Hartford a few years later when they were hit head on by a drunk driver going the wrong way up an exit ramp. Andy and Barry died instantly. Cindy had stayed home working on a legal memorandum due in two more days. For years, she felt guilty for not having gone with them. *If I'd gone along*, she thought, *the timing would have been different. We wouldn't have been at the ramp at the same time, and there would have been no accident.* Later, Cindy resumed her maiden name to try to put the tragedy behind her and moved to an apartment in Hartford's West End.

She met David Roberts when she was a state representative from Hartford and Roberts was state senator from West Hartford. They shared similar views on education and crime but remained in opposite political parties. She started to date Roberts, they became engaged and were married on New Year's Day, 2004.

"I watched the news at 6," she said to her husband, as they sat next to each other on the couch. "There was a lot of news. Anne Tremaine's murder, Frank Smith's comments, some of his speech to the Chamber in which he criticized you, surprise, surprise; and, they reported on your afternoon news conference. They showed the drug education proposal and, of course, your remarks criticizing the media. There hasn't been enough time for the media to criticize you back.

Now, do you want to tell me why you're so upset?"

David turned toward Cindy.

"Well, as you know, Anne and I were once very close. I've told you about our affair which started and finished long before I started dating you. It was primarily a physical attraction. Even though we broke up, I still considered her a decent person. I have fond memories of her."

Cindy took his hands.

"Wait, there's more. I didn't tell you about this because I didn't want to upset you; and it was really nothing; but, now it will probably come out, so I want you to hear it from me.

Remember when you were in Lake Tahoe for the Conference of Legislative Leaders at the beginning of the month?"

Cindy nodded.

"That Thursday I was taking my morning jog along the river. Ray, Trooper Wilson, was with me. The jogging path goes right by Anne's condominium. She must have seen us go down river because as we were coming back, she called to me from her balcony. She invited us up for a cup of coffee. It was pretty cold out, so we accepted. Ray and I had coffee, and then she said she wanted to talk to me alone. Ray went up to the boat launch area to get the car. As soon as he left, she started coming on to me. She wanted to renew our relationship. I told her that I thought we had had something special before she left for California, but by the time she returned I no longer felt the same way. I told her that I still had strong feelings for her, but now, only as a friend. I had moved on by then, I told her that I loved you, and it just wouldn't work between her and me. She started to kiss me. She said that she would change my mind. I told her that I would always remember the passion we shared and that I would always be her friend, but it would have to be a strictly platonic relationship. I said I was sorry and then I left.

That's all there was to it. However, now that she's been murdered, I can't deny seeing her if it comes up.

And, there's more. As you know, I was jogging Christmas morning in the same place, but I didn't go up to the condo. The last time I saw her was that Thursday morning the first week in December."

"Are you planning to go to the wake?" Cindy asked.

"Yes, I'd like you to go with me, but under the circumstances you might not want to."

Cindy stood up. "No, I'll go. I knew her as a lobbyist. It might look strange if I didn't go."

“Do you have any idea who might have wanted to kill her?” she asked.

“Not a clue” David replied as he got up. “She was an active lobbyist as you know, but nothing controversial enough for anyone to kill her.”

“Well, don’t worry about it” Cindy said as she took his hand. “Lets have some dinner.”

They walked toward the dining room. “I’ll be just a minute” Cindy said as she headed toward the kitchen.

What an honest man she thought as she ran water in the kitchen sink. *I guess that’s what first attracted me to him; when he spoke on the floor of the State Senate, when he held news conferences, he was always candid and direct. He took unpopular positions at times. He always stood up for the Constitution. She admired him, and once they were dating, she called him the last honest man in politics.*

He was easy to talk to she remembers. *A good listener*. There were nights after the 2001 legislative session had closed for the day and everyone had gone home that they talked for hours, either in the Senate Chamber or his office in the Legislative Office Building. It took time, but he gradually helped her to overcome both her grief and her guilt. He told her that he had lost his children, not by death, but because his ex-wife had turned them against him after their divorce. He hadn’t seen them since the divorce in 1991. David and Cindy started going out to dinner together. They talked about many things, politics, issues in the legislature, their hopes for the future, his desire to run for governor, hers for the state senate. Cindy had come out of her shell although the memories of Andy and Barry were still there. Soon they were laughing together. What was a friendship became a romance in early 2002. When the session ended in June, they took a trip together to Nantucket Island off the Massachusetts coast. David had rented a house near Surfside on the eastern side of the island overlooking the Atlantic Ocean. Cindy knew what it meant to go with him. She was a little nervous anticipating their first night in bed together. The day they arrived, they took blankets to the beach. She pointed out to sea, and said "If we take a sailboat straight across the ocean, we'll land in France."

"France!" he replied. "Straight across would probably take us to a Norwegian fijord. That would be nice. All the girls are blonde, beautiful and blue-eyed like you. French, Norwegian, whatever. You're prettier than all of them," he said as he pulled her close. They were both wearing Bermuda shorts and sweatshirts. Next, they were holding each other under the top blanket. It was windy and starting to get cloudy. The beach was nearly deserted. As David kissed her and held her close, his hand slipped up under her sweatshirt. She sighed and responded by nuzzling his ear and putting her hands underneath his shirt. She could feel his muscles and his ribs. Jogging had really kept David in shape.

"Not here" she said. They got up, grabbed the blankets and ran to the house, holding each other's hands. As they reached the second floor, they stopped for a moment to kiss. The blankets were left behind on the porch. They rushed into the bedroom and quickly took off their clothes. They tumbled onto the king sized bed. It had gotten much windier. The windows were rattling. The waves were crashing onto the beach below, but Cindy didn't hear them. All she could hear were David's words "Cindy, I love you. I love you." Her heart was pounding. She had difficulty talking. All she could do was nod, but she finally managed to whisper "me to, me to."

It was more than passion Cindy thought. They were content to hold hands and just look at each other without saying anything, even in a restaurant. They were so in sync that they completed each other's sentences and sometimes said the same things in unison.

That fall, they went their separate ways, each campaigning for their respective offices. Since they were of opposing parties, they rarely met in public.

David was sworn in as governor in January, 2003 and Cindy to her third term as state senator from the 2nd Senatorial District in Hartford. A few months into the session, after Cindy was firmly in place as President of the State Senate, they formally announced their engagement with their wedding scheduled for the following January 1st.

8

"Governor, your 11 o'clock appointment is here."

Governor Roberts walked out into the reception room. "Gentlemen, good morning."

"Good to see you again, Governor." Inspector Cassella of the state's attorney's office said. "Let me introduce Detectives Brian Shaw and Mark Hopkins of the Hartford police."

Roberts shook hands with them. "Nice to meet you, Gentlemen. Come in, come in."

The three detectives followed him into his private office, and took the three large chairs forming a semicircle around the front of the desk. Roberts sat down behind his desk in the large blue swivel chair with the high back. All of the chairs were light blue leather with mahogany arms. The Governor's chair had an imprint of the seal of the State of Connecticut on it.

"Governor," Cassella started off. "We appreciate your seeing us on such short notice. We'll try not to take too much of your time."

Roberts nodded.

"We're checking with everyone who knew Miss Tremaine to try to get some lead on her murder. How well did you know her?"

"Well," Roberts cleared his throat and leaned back. "I knew her as an effective lobbyist over the past few years; prior to that, she was secretary to the senate Republicans. I also had a very close relationship with her, but that was over years ago."

"When was the last time you saw her?" Shaw chimed in.

"December 3rd, about 7:30 in the morning. As you probably know, I jog every morning, or at least try to do it every morning, along the jogging trail in the south end of Hartford by the river."

Shaw nodded as Roberts continued.

"Annie's condominium faces the jogging path. On December 3rd, I checked the date this morning, she was on her balcony and invited me and Ray Wilson, my bodyguard, up for coffee. That was the first and only time I've been to her condo, and it was the last time I saw her."

"How did she seem to you that day?" Hopkins asked.

"Normal, cheerful, friendly as if she didn't have a care in the world. You can check with Ray on that."

"Do you have any idea why she was murdered or who might have had reason to kill her?" Cassella asked.

"No, as I told Cindy last night, I don't have a clue. She was pleasant, courteous, with a warm, friendly personality. She didn't have a nasty bone in her body. She was a lobbyist, and the bills she was either working on or against could be somewhat controversial; but nothing she worked on was controversial enough to get anyone mad enough to kill her. She never got involved in such issues as abortion, right to bear arms, or even the death penalty. She was simply representing commercial clients or associations. You might check with her clients to see what they know. Perhaps, there was some controversy, but I doubt it; as for her personal, family or social life, I know nothing about that."

"Did anyone on your staff know her well or have any reason to go to her condo?" Cassella went on.

"No," Roberts replied. "Not to my knowledge. Anyone would have known her as a lobbyist around the Capitol whom they would see on occasion. You can check with them, if you like, but her lobbying was done mostly with the members of the General Assembly. She was quite good at that."

"You're sure you haven't been back to her condo since December 3rd?" Cassella asked.

"I'm sure" Roberts replied.

Cassella's expression changed, he seemed to turn a little hostile and his voice was accusatory.

"But, you were there Christmas morning." Cassella challenged him. "Right about the time of the murder."

Robert's face flushed. *How the hell did he know about that?*

"You asked me if I'd been to her condo." Roberts answered. "I didn't go near the condo. I did my usual morning jogging along the river."

Cassella looked at him skeptically. "You didn't think it was important enough to mention it?"

Roberts made an effort to appear relaxed. He even smiled hoping to win Cassella over. "It must be my legal training. As I used to tell clients, don't volunteer anything, only answer specifically what you've been asked."

"Isn't that the advice you gave to people who had something to hide?" Cassella pressed him. "Or people who had been arrested or been about to be arrested?"

"Look, Tony, I have nothing to hide. I should have volunteered it. I'm sorry." Roberts said.

"I'm sorry too" Cassella said as he stood up. "I didn't mean to push you. It's just that we're very frustrated at this point as to who might have killed her."

Roberts also stood up and came around the desk. "That's okay, Tony," Roberts said. "I understand and no hard feelings."

"I apologize if I offended you in any way, Governor." Cassella said.

"That's all right, Tony." Roberts said as he put his arm around Tony's shoulder and escorted him to the door. "You're just doing your job. Come back any time if you think I can be of help."

9

The Miller-Simpson Funeral Home was located on South Main Street in West Hartford. The Governor's Lincoln pulled into the parking lot a few minutes before 7:00 p.m. Roberts helped his wife out of the car and headed toward the door. There were already a few people in line. One of the attendants offered to take the Governor and Cindy to the head of the line but Roberts said no. "We don't want to be treated specially, but thank you."

He and Cindy each signed the book. The woman in front of them turned towards Roberts. "Oh, isn't this a tragedy, Governor? She was so pretty and so young. Who could have done such a terrible thing?"

"I don't know." Roberts replied. "You're right though, it is a horrible tragedy."

One woman said "My, don't you make a wonderful first couple." Cindy smiled and said thank you.

The casket was open. Anne Tremaine lay there with her hands folded on her stomach. The bruises around her neck had been covered up. As Roberts stood next to the casket looking down at her, he thought, *She's even more beautiful in death. What a waste. Annie, if you can hear me, I wish you the best. I hope God will take you to him and comfort you; and that in heaven you find the peace and joy you couldn't find here. I did love you once.* He moved on to the family. "Mr and Mrs. Tremaine, I'm so sorry" he said. Anne was a wonderful person. He clasped their hands.

“She thought the world of you, governor.” Lilly Tremaine said. “She was a wonderful daughter” Ed Tremaine said. They both thanked him for coming. He introduced Cindy to them and moved on to Anne’s sister and her husband, Jean and Larry Beaumont.

He expressed his condolences. Jean held his hand, stepped back and pulled him closer. “She really loved you.” Jean said quietly.

“I know” Roberts replied.

“She told me that she saw you in her condo in early December; she told me that although you told her it wouldn’t work between you, she hadn’t given up hope.”

“I know. She told me she’d keep trying, but I told her it was over. It’s too bad it had to end this way.”

Jean looked startled, then let out a sigh and thanked him for coming.

As they were walking out the front door, the crowd had grown larger. People called to him. A few complimented him on his drug education proposal. “I’m with you on drug education, Governor.” a few of them shouted. “Good luck.”

Roberts said thank you, and waved to everyone; then he and Cindy got into the car. “Let’s go home, Ray.” he said.

“What was that all about with Anne’s sister, Jean?” Cindy asked.

Roberts sighed wearily, “Oh, that. She told me she knew about Anne’s attempt to renew our relationship and my reaction. I told her what I told Annie. She seemed to think that Annie hadn’t given up. I don’t know why. I certainly made myself clear to her. Well, it doesn’t make any difference now.”

Roberts put his arm around Cindy and pulled her close. “Besides, you’re the love of my life; and that’s the way it should be.”

10

The four men were meeting in the State's Attorney's office. Frank Smith was seated behind his desk in a large judge's-type chair, rocking back and forth. There was a conference table against and perpendicular to Smith's desk. Inspector Cassella sat on one side, Hartford Detectives Mark Hopkins and Brian Shaw on the other side. It was 5:30 in the afternoon.

His intercom buzzed. It was Pat, his secretary, letting him know she was leaving for the day. "Leave the lights on but lock the outer doors. I don't want to be disturbed," he replied. "I'll lock this door." He motioned to Cassella, who turned the lock. "Have a good night, Pat," Smith said, and hung up the phone.

He turned to the others, "Now, what do we have on the Tremaine murder?"

Cassella put down his cigar and leaned forward eagerly. He looked at Smith, "Quite a bit" he grinned. "We place Roberts at or near the scene through the testimony of Mr. and Mrs. Tedesco who met Roberts Christmas morning jogging near Tremaine's condo. We have their statements. Roberts admitted he was on the jogging path at the time, a point he didn't think was important enough to tell us. When I confronted him with it, he tried to weasel out of it. He became angry as if we'd caught him in a lie."

Smith nodded.

"There are two glasses with the Governor's seal on them and both with his fingerprints on them; one found in the bathroom and one with the other glasses in the kitchen cabinet" Cassella said.

"Time of death was approximately 7:15 a.m. This comes from the broken clock located on the floor near the night table. It also matches with the medical examiner's estimate. He knew she had been dead about 8 hours so it had to be Christmas morning. That's the best we could do with the length of time the body had been there. We know it wasn't the day before that because her mother Lily Tremaine called and talked with her late Christmas eve. Roberts met the Tedescos at 7:25 Christmas morning on the jogging trail near the victim's condo.

And here's the real icing on the cake. We found a letter to Roberts from the Governor of Massachusetts dated December 22nd and stamped at the Governor's office here on December 24th. Roberts' fingerprints are on the letter which clearly places him there no earlier than the 24th. He was there either the 24th or the 25th. He lied about when he was there. He admits he was there the first week of December, but says that was the last time he saw her. He told that to all of us. This letter makes him a liar."
"we found it in the bathroom, must have fallen out of his pant's pocket."

Smith held up his hand, "Wait a minute. Couldn't someone else have left the letter there, say someone from the Governor's office?"

Cassella shook his head. "The only prints on the letter are Roberts' and his secretary. She has an alibi for all day and all night Christmas eve and Christmas day; so do all the others in the Governor's office including the janitor. The only one near the scene at the time of the murder was Roberts. Don't forget, he tried to cover-up that he'd been there Christmas morning."

"What about motive?" asked Smith as he started to walk around the room.

"Everyone knows he had an affair with the victim before he married his present wife. He admits being there the first week in December in the morning. The glasses with the fingerprints were used for alcohol which means he was probably there sometime other than in the morning. Maybe the affair started up again. Robert's wife was away a lot. Maybe, Roberts tried to break it off and she threatened to expose him; or maybe she threatened to expose him anyway if he didn't do what she wanted. Maybe, she was blackmailing him. She's had a lot of success in lobbying, and maybe all of it wasn't because of her personality or her knowledge of the legislation.

Then, there's the statement by the victim's sister, Jean Beaumont. She spoke to Roberts at the wake. He admitted Anne was trying to renew the relationship; that he had said it was over; that she told both Roberts and her sister that she would keep trying. The sister was upset by what he said next."

"What was that?"

"He said, 'It's too bad it had to end this way.'"

Shaw spoke up, "Couldn't that be taken more than one way? It's not necessarily a reference to his killing her."

Smith turned on Shaw and pointed his finger at him. "That may be, but that's for the jury to decide. Let him explain it, if he takes the stand."

He looked at Cassella, "How about eyewitnesses?"

Detective Hopkins entered the conversation. "We scoured the area talking to neighbors, paper boys, delivery people. No one saw anything. We split up the neighbors. I talked to some; so did Brian and so did Inspector Cassella. We had to come back a few times. Some of them weren't home but, we finally reached them all. We came up empty."

Smith leaned forward, "I think we have enough for a warrant now, but I'd still like to pin it down with a witness. After all, this is the Governor we're talking about. I don't want a judge to chicken out on this. We need a very strong affidavit to be able to convince a judge to sign an arrest warrant for the Governor of Connecticut.

Well, that's it for now, gentlemen. Give it some more thought, and if you think of anything let me know right away; and keep looking for that witness."

They all got up to leave.

"Thanks fellows, let's be in touch," he said as they left.

Cassella remained behind. Smith stared at him, "Tony, we must have another witness. I want this tied up so tight that even Roberts can't wiggle out of it. Tony, drop everything else and get me someone who saw Roberts at the condo." He smacked his hands together. "We've almost got the son of a bitch."

He put his arm around Cassella. "I expect you to deliver on this, Tony."

"Got you, boss. I'll get right on it."

11

"Are you almost ready?" Cindy called out from the bedroom.

Roberts was in the bathroom. "I'm almost finished" he said.

They were going to the University of Connecticut women's basketball game against the University of Tennessee at Gampel Pavilion on the UConn campus at Storrs. UConn had defeated Tennessee in the NCAA championship game last season, and the Lady Vols were seeking revenge. Roberts' daughter "Bobbie" was a senior and at 5'8" the leading scorer for the defending national champions.

Their driver and Roberts' bodyguard, Ray Wilson, was in civilian clothes. He, too, would attend the game.

As they leaned back in their seats, Roberts closed his eyes and thought of the time he had told Cindy about his estrangement from his children. They were on a four day weekend in New Hampshire. They had taken the train to the top of Mt. Washington and were seated on a rock overlooking the White Mountains. It was a very hot day, but the view was spectacular, and the wind helped to cool them off. David and Cindy had been dating long enough to see something permanent ahead, and although she was a member of the opposite party, David trusted her completely.

"We became estranged a few months after my divorce from Carole in 1991. Bobbie was eight and Mark was six. The root of the problem developed upon my return from Vietnam in 1973. I told you of my experience as a P.O.W. Well, in February 1973, we were finally released. The last few months, in December of '72 and January '73, B-52 bombers had carried out several heavy raids on Hanoi and Haiphong. It looked as if there would be a peace settlement, so the torture stopped and the food became better. The North Vietnamese didn't want us to look emaciated when we returned. Despite that, I had lost 65 lbs. and was suffering from the effects of both the physical and mental torture. I had grown a thick red beard. My uniform hung loosely on me as I stepped off the Air force plane at Clark Air Force base just north of Manila in the Philippines.

My chest swelled with pride as I walked down the steps. My eyes filled with tears as I saluted the commanding general and shook hands. The Air Base was U.S. territory and I was one of those who kneeled down and kissed the ground."

Cindy interrupted: "I remember when you came home. I read about your experience in the newspapers and saw you on television. You are a legitimate war hero. But, what does all this have to do with your break up with Carole?"

"I'm getting to that." Roberts replied. "Please, let me tell it in my own way. If you understand the background, you'll better understand the reason we broke up.

I spent almost two years at Travis Air Force Base in California building up my strength and recovering from wounds that were inflicted during the torture. I ended up with only a few permanent scars. The major problem, however, was psychological. I suffered from what the doctors called post Vietnam traumatic syndrome. It was that problem that kept me there most of the time. When I was released in early 1975, my physical strength had still not fully returned. I tried to polish my basketball skills, but I was in no shape to go back to basketball. It was shortly after I finished law school in 1978 that I married Carole in 1979. The first few years were great, but shortly after Mark was born, I had another reaction to the Vietnam syndrome. Maybe it was the pressure of my law practice. In any event, I had a relapse. The memories returned. I had frequent nightmares, of going down with my plane, and of being beaten. Even though the Air Force had confirmed that I had not hit a school, the picture of the dead children kept coming back. I would see Major Kay's grinning face in my nightmares. At first, Carole tried to help. When I woke up during the middle of the night drenched with sweat Carole would clean me up and comfort me. I became moody and withdrawn. I would go for long walks. I began to feel caged in."

"What does all this have to do with the children?" Cindy asked.

"Well," David replied. "Because of my moods, depression and my obsession with my memories, I paid less attention to the kids and to Carole, too."

"I seemed all right during the day. It was the nights that were horrible. I started to drink to get my mind off the memories that were causing so much pain. Then, I'd come home already high and have a few more before I passed out for the night. That didn't stop the nightmares. I still woke up during the middle of the night. All of this was wearing on both me and the family. Carole became suspicious and thought I was having affairs when I came home late. I wasn't. Even if I had wanted to, I was in no shape, physically or mentally to do it."

"Didn't Carole understand the reason for your problems?" Cindy asked.

"I thought she should have, but, you have to remember that most people were not sympathetic to post-Vietnam traumatic syndrome. People were tired of the Vietnam war. There were protests, and we certainly were not treated as war heros. I can understand, I suppose, that she didn't really understand it. I thought she should have at the time, but looking back on it, I can see why she reacted the way she did." Roberts said.

"But, this was personal with you." Cindy said. "Her husband was hurting through no fault of his own, and the atmosphere among the public should have had no bearing upon her view of things with you."

"You're right, but it doesn't do any good to lay blame at this point." Roberts said.

"In any event, I had started out-patient counseling and by 1989 I was getting much better even though Carole and I had drawn apart. Then, I made a big mistake. I decided to run for the legislature. Maybe, it was a way to regain my self-esteem, or maybe I really wanted to do something more useful. I don't know. However, this meant campaigning every night. I hardly saw the children. Carole and I drew even further apart. She began to accuse me again of having affairs. Sometimes, there was lipstick on my collar. This came from women who were shaking my hand and kissing me on the cheek. Sometimes they missed the cheek and ended up kissing my neck, probably because of my height. It was totally innocent, I swear, but Carole didn't believe me. I asked her to campaign with me, but she refused. I guess she resented my being pulled away from her by voters and campaign people. In any event, it was all downhill from there, and we divorced in 1991. Bobbie was eight and Mark six. Carole told them I'd been having affairs and that it was all my fault. What I thought was a relatively mild divorce became very bitter."

"She poisoned their minds against you. How unfair!" Cindy said.

Roberts continued: "I suppose if Carole really believed I was having affairs, I can't really blame her. She felt rejected and bitter. Not only did she blame me but she told the children that I had ignored them and didn't love them. Call it brainwashing, call it whatever you want, but the kids refused to see me even on court ordered visitation. I tried to enforce my rights through the courts. I even tried to have Carole held in contempt for refusing visitation. She came back with the argument that the children didn't want to see me. Of course, that's because she had turned them against me. I even got the judge to order a Family Relations study. The Family Relations Officer interviewed the children, but they were so convinced that I had broken up the marriage and was rotten that Family Relations concluded that, regardless of the reason, the children would have to be forced to be with me, and that was not good for them. I sent them letters, birthday presents, Christmas presents and never received a reply. I'm sure Carole intercepted the letters. Whenever I would call, Carole would tell me that they were asleep or they were studying or made some other excuse. I wasn't going to go to their school and make a scene. My political activities were in the newspapers so I'm sure the kids knew what I was doing, but Carole's bitterness had been transmitted to the kids, and no matter how hard I tried, it just didn't work."

"But, they're older now." Cindy said. "Isn't it about time that they gave you a break?"

"We're estranged. Let's face it, no matter what I do I can't seem to get through to them. I've even written to them at college so the letters would not be intercepted. The result has been a deafening silence." Roberts said.

"When was the last time you talked to them?" Cindy asked.

"I basically haven't talked with them since the time of the divorce, over ten years ago."

"What a shame!" Cindy said.

"My only contact is that I send Carole support checks for them and finance their way through college. I go to the basketball games to get a look at Bobbie and Mark who sits behind the bench. I don't try to speak to them. I don't want to embarrass them or make a scene. That's why I insist that I not be introduced to the audience. I even sit at the top of the first level of seats as inconspicuously as possible. I don't even get up at half time. A friend gets me some refreshments."

"That's horrible" Cindy remarked. She put her arms around him and wiped the tears from his face.

Roberts looked at her. She could see the pain in his eyes. “The inability to be with my children is the biggest tragedy of my life” he said. “I’d give up being governor if I could have my children back.”

“Don’t worry” Cindy replied. “I’ll try to think of something.”

“Gampel Pavilion just ahead” Ray said.

“Let us off here” Roberts replied, “in front of the Greer field house.”

12

Inspector Cassella was in his office when his secretary buzzed. "Officer Simmons is here with a prisoner" she said. "Show them in" Cassella replied. The door opened, and a uniformed prison guard from the Hartford Correctional Center came in accompanied by a short, slightly built man wearing an orange prison jumpsuit. His hands were handcuffed in front of him. He appeared to be in his mid fifties. He had thinning brown hair. His nose looked as if it had taken a beating several times. It had been broken and repaired at least twice. His face was florid as if he were no stranger to alcohol. He had a small stubble on his chin, and his eyes were a little watery. He was still shivering from the cold weather. It had snowed heavily the night before and the temperature was just over 20 degrees. It was the second week in January. Even his hands were red from the cold.

Simmons put his hand on the prisoner's shoulder. "Inspector, this is Robert Forrester. He's being held on a $20,000 bond for the sale of marijuana."

Cassella got up from his chair, but didn't offer to shake hands. "Officer Simmons, would you wait outside? Thank you for bringing him, but I'd like to talk to the prisoner alone."

"O.K." said Simmons. "What about the handcuffs?"

"Leave them on for now." Cassella said. "Thank you officer."

Cassella believed that having a defendant in handcuffs and prison uniform lowered the prisoner's self esteem and made it clear who was in charge. People like this were more easily pressured into telling what they knew. "Scumbags" Cassella had described them, "but sometimes we need them to make a case." The prosecutors would tell juries that the State's Attorney's office took the witnesses as they found them; couldn't select or choose who was to be a witness to a crime.

Forrester's self esteem was already low, he thought. *It shouldn't take much to find out what he knows*. Cassella buzzed his secretary and told her he did not want to be disturbed and "I don't want anyone seated near my door, including Officer Simmons."

Cassella pointed to the chair closest to his desk. Forrester sat down.

Cassella took out a small notebook, placed it on the table and glanced at his notes. He said, "Well, Mr. Robert Forrester, you're in a lot of trouble. You have a terrible record."

He picked up three pages stapled together. You've had larceny convictions, drug convictions, a Robbery 2, a Burglary 3, two convictions for DWI. You've had at least 3 felonies. Right now you're charged with sale of marijuana, which, as you know, is also a felony. The Hartford Police have you cold on this one. You sold the stuff to an undercover cop. In light of your record you can get at least 7 years for the sale, and we can convict you of being a persistent serious felony offender which carries another 23 years; so you're facing 30 years." He looked at his notes again. "You do odd jobs, live in a room on Wethersfield Avenue.

You're an alcoholic which is the reason you can't hold a job; no family; you're divorced, you never see your kids. You've never supported them. Not a very pretty picture, Robert. Your life's a mess, and it's going to get worse. Maximum John certainly isn't going to give you a break at the time of sentencing."

Cassella was referring to Judge John Ambrosini, whose nickname came from Federal Judge John Sirica. "Maximum John is known for giving very stiff sentences." Cassella explained to Forrester.

Forrester was already perspiring. Cassella walked over to Forrester who shifted in his chair.

"You're a loser, Robert" he said roughly.

Cassella lit a cigar and blew the smoke into Forrester's face.

"You're a scumbag, Robert. You should be locked up for the rest of your life. And that's exactly where you're going if you don't tell me the truth. Do you hear me, Robert?" Cassella shouted as he leaned down a few inches from Forrester's face.

Forrester shrank back, he started to shake. "Yes, sir" he mumbled.

"What's the matter? You don't like my cigar?" Cassella took it out and put the lit end close to Forrester's right eye. "You afraid I'm going to burn your eye out, Robert?"

Forrester looked at him. He pulled further back.

"There's no escape, Robert. You think losing an eye is tough? When you go to prison for the rest of your life, your eyes will be the least of your worries. You won't be in Hartford. For a long stretch you'll probably go to Somers. There'll be some big, tough guys in your cellblock who are just waiting for someone like you. Is that what you want. Robert?"

Tears were streaming down Forrester's face. He shook his head.

"That's what's going to happen to you, Robert." Cassella put his lips near Forrester's left ear. He lowered his voice but it was still intense. "They'll treat you like a piece of garbage, which is what you are. You'd better hope you have a heart attack. That's the only way you'll get out of it."

Cassella pulled back. "You hear me?" he shouted as he thrust the cigar into Forrester's face.

Forrester was terrified. His hands were shaking. He couldn't stop, and he was drenched in sweat. He pushed against the back of his chair hoping that it would somehow protect him.

Cassella returned to his chair, leaned back and then suddenly leaned forward. "What do you have to say to all that, Robert?"

Forrester trembled. "I don't want to go to prison for a long time" he cried.

"Well", Cassella replied. "You're facing at least 30 years in the slammer. What do you want to do about it?"

"I'd, I'd like to help you" Forrester said. "You know, cooperate; a deal.

"Deal?" Cassella raised his voice. "Who said anything about a deal? If you tell me the truth, we, the state's attorney and me, we'd start to believe that you're trying to turn your life around and you probably won't commit a crime again. We might also think that you should get started on your new life as soon as possible. But." he emphasized. "Let's not talk about deals. Understood, Robert?"

"Yes, sir" Forrester replied.

Cassella handed him a sheet of paper. "Read that, Robert" he said as he leaned back in his chair with his hands clasped behind his head.

Forrester studied the words on the paper. Cassella lit another cigar.

"O.K. Robert, what do you want to tell me?" Cassella asked after Forrester had finished reading.

"Well, your honor" Forrester stopped, a little flustered. "I'm sorry, I mean, sir. On Christmas Eve, this last Christmas Eve, last month, I was partying at a bar in the south end of Hartford; you know, Little Italy. I think it was called Angelo's Place." Forrester looked at the paper. "When they closed up, I went to my friend's apartment next door, and had a few more drinks. I left about 4:30 Christmas morning. My stomach was upset, and my mind was a little fuzzy. Instead of going to my place, I drove up Wethersfield Avenue. I turned right onto Charter Oak Avenue trying to circle around to get back to my apartment on Wethersfield Avenue, but I got lost. The next thing I knew I was near the Charter Oak Bridge. I realized I was going the wrong way, so I made a U-turn; but I was so tired, I parked by the side of the road, right in front of some real nice condominiums, to rest for a few minutes. I must have fallen asleep because the next thing I heard was the church bells ringing, playing Christmas music. It was about 5 after 7. I looked at the clock in the car."

Cassella interrupted. "Did you see anything?"

Forrester looked down at the paper again. "Yea, I saw this big fellow with red hair go into the door nearest the driveway at the end; where the turnaround circle was."

"Then, what did you do?"

"I still had some coffee left. It was cold, but I figured I needed something to wake me up. I had some peanut butter crackers. They were almost frozen. I ate them anyway. I was really hungry."

"Then what?"

"I was just finishing the coffee and crackers. It was about 7:20, and I was about to leave. I saw this same man come out of the condominium. He slammed the door behind him and ran down toward the river."

"Would you recognize him if you saw him again?" Cassella asked.

"Oh, sure, I wasn't that far away. Besides I know I've seen him before."

Cassella took a photo of Roberts out of his desk drawer. "Is this him?" he asked.

"That's him" Forrester said. "He wasn't wearing no suit like he is there, but that's him. I'm positive."

"Do you know who he is?"

"Yeah, now I remember where I seen him. That's Governor Roberts. Hey, I ain't gonna get into no trouble, am I, identifying the governor and all?" Forrester asked.

"No, Robert, you won't." Cassella smiled. As a matter of fact I'm proud of you for coming forward to do your duty as a citizen. In view of this change in attitude, I think we can reduce the charge against you to simple possession of less than 4 ounces of marijuana. That's a misdemeanor so you won't be charged as a persistent felony offender."

"What will I get?" Forrester asked.

"The maximum sentence is one year. We can suspend that after 6 months. You have to do some jail time. Otherwise it'll look as if we're giving you special treatment. But, you can spend it in the Hartford jail on Weston Street; and you'll get credit for time served."

"Is that O.K. with you?"

"I'll do it" Forrester said.

"You're going to have to give a statement now, and then sign it, and, of course, you'll have to testify in court as to what you saw. And one more thing, you're not going to tell anyone about this discussion. If anybody asks you about a deal, you deny it, even in court. Just say that you're telling this because it's the truth. It is the truth isn't it, Robert? There is no deal, right?"

Forrester smiled a knowing smile and nodded his head. "Right" he said, "but when do I get the six months?"

"After you testify. You'll probably be out in a few months with credit for time served until you testify."

Forrester appeared a little nervous. "Uh, I hope you won't be mad at me, sir, but shouldn't I hear this from the state's attorney who's got my case?"

Cassella got up and leaned across the desk, pointing his cigar at Forrester. "What's the matter, Robert, don't you trust me? If you want to forget all this, that's O.K. too."

“No, no” Forrester mumbled.

“Good” Cassella said. “You let me worry about the state’s attorney. You just study the statement so you’ll remember every word of it.”

“Now, just a few more things, Robert. The defense attorney is going to try to trap you, make you look untrustworthy. Do you understand that, Robert?”

“Ah, no sir. What’s untrustworthy?”

“It means you’re a liar, Robert. They’re going to make you out to be a liar. Now do you understand?”

“Yes, sir, but they can’t do that. I ain’t no liar.”

Cassella rolled his eyes. *That’s exactly what I’m telling him to do*, he thought. He leaned forward again. “They’re going to ask you about your criminal record. Make sure you answer yes to any crime you’ve committed.”

“Any crime, sir?”

“Not the ones nobody knows about, you stupid shit. They’re only going to mention the ones you were convicted of. Don’t volunteer anything.

They’ll have your record. They’ll try to trip you up. Here study this record although I’m sure you’ll remember most of them. Whatever you do, don’t deny any convictions that you know of. If you do, they’ll be catching you in a lie. If you’re not sure, just say you can’t remember. Got that, Robert?”

“Yes, sir.”

"O.K. what if they ask you where you got the car you were driving?" Cassella asked. "What are you going to say?"

Robert didn't say anything. He clenched his teeth, but remained silent. "I don't know. I don't own no car."

"You borrowed it from a friend. Do you have any friends, Robert? I mean ones who were not in jail?"

"Yeah, Jimmy DePace, Billy Joy. They could have been with me that night."

"Do they own a car?"

"Jimmy does, Billy I don't know. Never seen him with one."

"What kind of car?"

"I think it's a Ford, an old one, maybe a '94."

"Alright, you borrowed Jimmy's '94 Ford Taurus. I'll have that written down for you. Remember it." Cassella leaned over to Forrester. "And remember, Robert, we never had any conversations about any of this, right?"

"Right." Forrester replied.

"One more thing, Robert. If they ask you why you took a ride in the car, just say 'I wanted to get some fresh air.' Understood, Robert?"

"Yes, sir."

"I'll go over this with you again before trial, but not a word of this to anyone."

"Yes, sir. Thank you sir."

"No, thank you, Robert, for having such a good memory and doing your duty as a citizen" Cassella said. He buzzed his secretary. "Jean, would you come in here to take a statement, please."

13

It was 8:45 the next morning when Deputy State's Attorney Arlene Powell, Cassella and Detectives Shaw and Hopkins arrived at the Hartford courthouse on Lafayette Street which housed G.A. (Geographical Area) 14, the Part B criminal jurisdiction.

Powell took everyone in through the private entrance to the State's Attorney's office. They were scheduled to meet with Judge Arthur Kennedy at 9 a.m. Kennedy had told Powell to get there early before he got tied up with conferences concerning the day's court business.

They entered Kennedy's chambers which were located on the second floor. They were small and spartan like. The courthouse was located on Lafayette Street, a long block south of the State Capitol.

"Good morning, your honor" Powell said. "We appreciate your seeing us on such short notice."

"Hello, Arlene," Kennedy replied. "It's good to see you again."

Powell introduced Cassella, Shaw and Hopkins. They all sat down at Kennedy's invitation. Superior Court Judge Thomas Kennedy was 48 years old, a native of Hartford and a classmate of Powell's at UConn Law School. Upon graduation, they had worked together in the Democratic party, had been very close in those years prior to reaching their present positions. Although their different status kept them apart more, they still remained good friends.

Kennedy was known as a no nonsense judge who was not afraid to hand out heavy sentences. He was 5'10" tall, solidly built with a leathery face and a close cropped crewcut left over from his days as a Captain in the U.S. Marines. He was always impeccably dressed. He retained his military bearing and projected himself in a crisp, efficient manner. He acted as if he feared nothing and no one. "Perfect for this warrant application" Powell thought.

Kennedy's only vice seemed to be the perpetual cigar that he chomped on when off the bench. He took one out of his mouth and placed it on the ashtray still lit.

"Now, what's this arrest warrant all about, Arlene?" Kennedy inquired. "You said on the phone that it's very important."

Powell handed over the warrant. "Take a look at the name on the top."

"David Roberts; you mean like in Governor David Roberts?" Kennedy asked. "And for murder in the first degree?"

"Exactly" said Powell.

Kennedy looked skeptically at Powell. "Well, I suppose they don't call me fearless Tom for nothing" he said; "but you better have solid probable cause on this one."

"We've got more than that" Powell said. "We've got a solid case for conviction."

"Let me take a look." Kennedy read through the affidavit which had been signed by Cassella who, as Chief Inspector, was a police officer. It was approved by Powell.

Kennedy studied it silently going back over it. “You certainly have the elements; motive, opportunity, placing him at the scene, actually in the condo at the time of the murder. Will this fellow, Forrester, hold up?”

“Yes, he will” Powell commented. “But even without him Roberts was still in the area, the letter from the Governor of Massachusetts places him in the condo very late Christmas Eve or early Christmas morning.”

“And, he apparently lied about it.” Kennedy said. “He may also have incriminated himself to the victim’s sister. It’s circumstantial, but I think you have a good case. People have been convicted of murder on less than this. You certainly have probable cause.”

“I’ll sign it” he said. “I really don’t have much choice. The probable cause is there.”

“There’ll be enough repercussions on this to blow the lid off the capitol dome.” he said. “But, you’ve gotta do what you’ve gotta do!” Kennedy stated as he started to sign his authorization on the arrest warrant.

Powell and Cassella exchanged satisfied looks.

“Bond?” Kennedy asked.

“I know he’s the Governor, but this is a murder case.” Powell said. “How about $1 million?”

“I’ll give you $500,000. There has to be a relatively high bond in view of the charge; but I doubt if he’ll take off. He has too much to lose by not fighting this charge. This will probably keep him overnight, but after all, he’s still the Governor and has to run the state. He should be able to get a bondsman to take him by tomorrow." Kennedy said. "Here it is, good luck. You may need it."

Judge Kennedy got up and shook hands with everyone.

"Thank you, Judge. We really appreciate this" Powell said.

"One thing," Kennedy said as they moved toward the door. "Don't sic the media on me. Talking to them is your job, not mine."

14

Powell, Cassella, Shaw and Hopkins returned to Smith's office. Cassella driving the S.A.'s black Ford Crown Victoria with the whip antenna on the rear.

"Pat, close the door." Smith said. He had summoned his secretary into his private office. As the others watched, he barked out orders: "Call the Governor's office and get me an appointment with him for 3:30 today. Tell him it's of the utmost importance. Don't take any crap from his staff. We know he'll be there, we checked his schedule yesterday. If they ask what its about, tell them it is highly confidential. The State's Attorney says he has to talk to the Governor about it alone. He doesn't trust the telephone. If they try to make it before 2:00 p.m., tell them I have serious court business this morning and a luncheon speaking engagement that I can't break. Tell them the matter came up this morning, and I must meet with him before the end of the day."

"Well, this is going to be a big day." Smith said while Pat went into the outer office to make the call.

"Now, remember, this isn't the end of the investigation." he said. "We've got to come up with more. Talk to the people at the capitol who knew of his relationship with Anne Tremaine, review the crime scene reports; and, Tony, make sure Robert Forrester is kept isolated. I don't want him spilling his guts to anyone."

Pat stuck her head in the door: "The earliest he can see you is at 4 o'clock. Should I take it?"

"Yes," Smith replied. "That'll be just right for the 6 o'clock news."

A few minutes later Pat came back in to tell them that the 4:00 p.m. appointment was confirmed at the Governor's office.

"Two more things, Pat. Call all of the major media, you know the ones. Tell them I'm having a news conference at 3:45 in front of the entrance to the capitol. Tell them that I have a major announcement to make on the Tremaine case. They'll probably think I'm going to announce my candidacy, anyway; but they can't afford not to come if they think it's a breakthrough on the Tremaine murder. Don't tell them anything more than that. You don't say anything else. Just tell them to be there. And, I won't take any calls from anyone before then, not even the Governor. It's 11:15 now, start making the calls at 3:15. I don't want the fact of the news conference to be on the air too early."

"Oh, and in the meantime, make 50 copies of this arrest warrant. The media will want copies. Thank you, Pat. Let me know the reaction from the media. Remember, all of this should be played close to the vest as much as possible until 3:45."

Pat walked out the door with the warrant. Smith turned to Cassella, "Tony, call the Hartford Police Chief. Call him about 3:30. Tell him we're about to make an arrest on the Tremaine case, that it's someone who is very well known but don't tell him who. We expect to be able to bring the suspect to police headquarters by 4:30 and to place extra officers on board to help control the media."

15

It had been a sunny day and a little warmer. Some were talking about a January thaw; but by 3:45 it was starting to cloud over, and it was getting a little cooler. Mobile units from channels 3, 30 and 61 were already at the south entrance to the State Capitol Building. The channel 8 van was driving up as Smith, Powell, Cassella, Shaw and Hopkins walked up the front sidewalk. Smith's office in the criminal court building was only a block away. There was a grey concrete overhang in front of the Capitol building supported by columns. It was an area for cars to drive through. Smith stood in front of the outer columns so there would be enough light for the cameras. More print and radio reporters had arrived. Smith waited a few minutes until he was sure all of the major papers, the wire services and the major radio and TV outlets were there.

Promptly at 5 minutes to 4 he began to speak: "Ladies and gentlemen of the media, welcome. Please turn off all video cameras and voice recorders. You'll see why in a moment." He waited until the cameras and microphones were withdrawn. Then he smiled. "I told you I'd let you know when we had a breakthrough in the Tremaine murder case. Well, this is more than a breakthrough. It's a bombshell. The real news will come inside, so I suggest you get your equipment ready and follow Deputy State's Attorney Powell into the building. Stay behind her, be quiet and remain outside the office until Inspector Cassella gives you the signal to come in. I'm not going to take any questions at this time so don't even try."

He turned on his heel flanked by his officers and Powell and strode onto the first floor of the State Capitol. He headed directly up the stairs, turned left and reached the door to the Executive Chambers. He told Cassella, Shaw and Hopkins to stay out of sight and come in when the Governor appeared; and to keep the media back in the meantime. Smith turned to Powell. "Arlene you come with me. I want you to take my place at the right time. I'll pull back. If I'm actually part of the arrest, it will look too political.

Smith and Powell walked into the office and spoke to the receptionist. "I'm State's Attorney Frank Smith. This is my Deputy, Arlene Powell. I have an appointment with Governor Roberts at 4 o'clock."

"Oh, yes, Mr. Smith. Won't you have a seat?" The woman smiled. "I'll let the Governor know you're here." Ann Leahy, a petite young woman with dark hair had been with Roberts campaign and had signed on to his staff when he took office. She put the phone down and said to Smith "The Governor will be right out." Smith breathed a sigh of relief; he had hoped he wouldn't have to do this in the Governor's private office.

A few minutes later, Governor Roberts walked out of his office toward the opening in the railing that separated his staff from the reception area. He stuck out his hand "Hello, Frank." he said. Smith walked up to him, shook hands with him and introduced Powell who had the arrest warrant in her left hand. At the same time, he motioned with his left hand for Cassella, Shaw and Hopkins to follow. Smith waited a moment for them to enter. Smith pulled back leaving Powell alone. The press was right behind. As soon as the camera lights went on, Powell said in a loud voice "David Roberts, as Deputy State's Attorney of Hartford County, I hereby place you under arrest pursuant to a warrant of the court for the murder of Anne Tremaine."

There was a sudden silence from the staff. The typewriters stopped. No one answered the phones. Ann Leahy had her hand to her mouth with a look of utter disbelief. Roberts stood motionless, in what appeared to be a state of shock. His face grew white. He looked bewildered. Then his face got red, and he angrily exclaimed "What, are you crazy? If this is a joke, it's not very funny!"

"It's no joke," Powell said. "Detective Hopkins, cuff him. Shaw, read him his rights."

Cameras were clicking and rolling. The bright lights stayed on. Microphones were thrust between Roberts and Powell, Hopkins moved behind the Governor with handcuffs at the ready. He pulled Robert's left hand back and applied the handcuffs. He was reaching for the right hand when suddenly Bill Donovan, the Governor's chief of staff and an attorney appeared next to Roberts and shouted "Wait a minute! You can't do this! Let me see the warrant."

Powell handed it to him. Donovan started to read it. Roberts said "This is ridiculous. I haven't killed anyone."

By this time, Hopkins had cuffed the other hand, and he and Cassella were each holding an arm. Smith had disappeared. Shaw had pulled out his card with the Miranda warning on it, and started to read it aloud when Donovan interrupted him "The warrant seems to be in order. It's signed by Judge Kennedy but for God's sake, man. He's the governor of this state. You can't arrest him like a common criminal."

"No one is above the law, Mr. Donovan. You should know that. This is the routine procedure when we make an arrest, including the handcuffs," Powell retorted.

Shaw started again, but Donovan interrupted "But, can't you at least tell us where you're taking him?"

"The Hartford Police Department for booking. Now I've had enough. If you persist in this, Mr. Donovan, I'll have you arrested for interfering with an officer."

"She's right, Bill" Roberts intervened. "No one is above the law. Let him do his job. We'll straighten all this out later. Meanwhile, call Brian Kelly and tell him to meet us at Hartford police headquarters."

Powell held up her hand and turned toward the press "Keep it down, people. I want him to hear his rights. Go ahead, Detective Shaw."

Shaw started again as a hush fell over the crowd. Microphones were put in front of him "You have the right to remain silent - anything you say can and will be used against you in a court of law. You have the right to have an attorney represent you........"

"I'm innocent" Roberts declared. "I haven't killed anyone." he repeated.

“That’s for a jury to decide” Powell said. “Let’s go.” She and Cassella started to push their way through the crowd toward the door with Hopkins and Shaw now holding Robert’s arms as they followed.

“Isn’t it true you once had an affair with Anne Tremaine?” one reporter asked. “No comment,” Roberts replied. He stood up straight, his eyes looking straight ahead.

“What about your wife, is she going to support you?” asked another.

“Who’s going to run the state while you’re in jail?”

Roberts looked around and replied “It’s too early to say anything. You know as much about this as I do.”

As they went through the doorway, Roberts’ bodyguard, State Trooper Ray Wilson and another Trooper moved toward him. Roberts spotted them “It’s O.K., Ray. Don’t interfere. Let the procedure take its course.”

Roberts was hustled down the stairs, the media in front and back, the cameras rolling; reporters still shouting questions. It was all a jumble to Roberts. They reached the outside door and then Smith’s car. Hopkins pushed the Governor’s head down slightly as Roberts slid into the back seat, Hopkins and Shaw on either side of him. Powell got into the front passenger seat and Cassella was driving. As the doors closed, and the car started to pull away, reporters took out their cellular phones and radio and TV newsmen began their live reports.

16

At 4:25 p.m., the television screens of channels 3, 8, 30 and 61 went blank and the words "Special Bulletin" appeared. Channel 30's report was typical. "We interrupt this program to bring you a special bulletin. Governor David Roberts, just a few minutes ago, was arrested for the murder of Anne Tremaine, reputed to be the Governor's ex-lover. For a live report, we go now to Nancy Scott at the State Capitol for this late breaking and shocking story."

"Thank you, Bob. This was the scene at a little after 4:00 this afternoon in the Governor's office as Deputy State's Attorney Arlene Powell placed Governor David Roberts under arrest for the murder of Anne Tremaine."

The videotape of the scene in Roberts' office then came onto the screen, words and all.

"The Governor was taken away in a car driven by Inspector Tony Cassella of the State's Attorney's office. In the car were Attorney Powell, Detective Brian Shaw and Detective Mark Hopkins of the Hartford P.D., and, of course, Governor Roberts. Roberts was taken to the Hartford P.D. to be booked and processed. Judge Thomas Kennedy in Hartford Superior Court signed the arrest warrant earlier today and set a bond of $500,000 on the warrant. Sources say it is unlikely the

Governor will be able to post that bond right away, so the Governor of the State of Connecticut is expected to spend at least one night in jail. As you heard, Roberts insisted he is innocent of the charge, and he had his chief of staff, William Donovan, contact famous criminal defense attorney Brian Kelly."

"With me now is the Governor's press secretary, Bob Sweeney. Mr. Sweeney, what can you tell us about this startling development?"

"This arrest is outrageous. It was sprung on the Governor suddenly with no warning although the media had been notified to be here, and were on hand to see and report the spectacle. It's a travesty of justice."

"What about the allegations in the arrest warrant? Don't they appear compelling?"

"I haven't had a chance to study them, but I'm sure they will be proven false. Dave Roberts is an honest, straightforward individual who, in a million years, could not commit murder."

"What about Attorney Kelly?"

"Bill Donovan contacted Mr. Kelly. It took a little while to catch up to him. He should be on his way to Hartford Police Headquarters as we speak."

"Thank you, Mr. Sweeney. This is Nancy Scott reporting live from the State Capitol. Now, back to you in the studio."

"Thank you, Nancy," anchorman Bob Bennet said. He looked at the camera: "We'll stay on top of this dramatic story as it unfolds. We'll have more on the early news coming up shortly. Now back to our regular programming."

6:30 p.m.

"This is the CBS evening news, Bob Schieffer reporting. An amazing and shocking arrest took place late this afternoon. At the State Capitol in Hartford, Connecticut, the Hartford County Deputy District Attorney arrested Connecticut Governor David Roberts for the murder of attorney-lobbyist Anne Tremaine. Miss Tremaine was found murdered the day after Christmas last month in her Hartford, Connecticut condominium overlooking the Connecticut river. She was apparently strangled to death and is reputed to be a former lover of the Connecticut Governor. In what appears to be an historic first, a sitting Governor in the United States has been charged with murder."

"For an up to date report on this still developing story, we go now to our CBS affiliate in Hartford, WFSB, and reporter, Michael Poliner."

"Thank you, Bob, this is Michael Poliner reporting live from the Connecticut State Capitol. Last month, Anne Tremaine, a Capitol lobbyist, was found murdered in her luxury condominium located just south of here on the west side of the Connecticut river. A former Miss Connecticut, the very pretty blue-eyed blonde is reported to be a former lover of Governor Roberts in the early nineties before Roberts married Cindy Stevens, now the Democratic president pro tem of the state senate. Despite this relationship with Miss Tremaine, Roberts' arrest today stunned everyone, including it seems, Governor Roberts himself. Here's the scene earlier at the Governor's office at the Capitol."

The complete videotape of the arrest and Roberts being taken away in handcuffs was shown again up to and including Cassella driving out of the State Capitol grounds.

The scene then shifted again to Poliner, microphone in hand, standing in front of the Capitol building.

"As you saw, the arrest was made by Deputy State's Attorney Arlene Powell who is the chief assistant to State's Attorney Frank Smith. Smith and Roberts have been at odds over such issues as search warrants and how to cure the drug problem. Smith is considered a possible opponent to Roberts in the next election; but, that would seem to be the least of Roberts' problems at this point."

"Governor Roberts is presently being held in a cell at the Hartford Police Department under a $500,000 bond set by Judge Thomas Kennedy when he signed the arrest warrant. He is expected to remain there overnight pending arraignment in Hartford criminal court tomorrow morning. Now, back to you, Bob."

"Thank you, Mike. That's Mike Poliner of WFSB reporting live from the Connecticut State Capitol where, in case you've just joined us, Governor David Roberts was arrested for murder, the first sitting Governor in an American state to be arrested for such a crime. Many questions, however, remain unanswered:

First and foremost, did he do it? Roberts has insisted he is innocent.

Does he have to step down as Governor while all this is going on?

Who will take over for him? CBS news has learned that Lieutenant Governor Edwin Lincoln is on vacation on a remote island in the South Pacific. This would mean that if anyone were to succeed Roberts, at least temporarily, it would be his wife, Cindy Roberts, who, as president pro tem of the state senate, is next in line of succession.

How is Roberts standing up under all of this? Reports are that he is taking this calmly and quietly. You might remember that Roberts was an All American basketball star at the University of Pennsylvania. He then joined the Air Force and was shot down over Vietnam. He survived for nearly 2 years in the infamous Hanoi Hilton prison camp. He has also survived and done well in the political arena. His only comment as he was brought into the Hartford jail was, "It's nicer than the Hanoi Hilton. If I could stand it there, I can stand it here."

This arrest, however, may well be his biggest challenge yet. He will probably need the same stamina, courage and determination he used in meeting and overcoming his previous challenges to successfully overcome this one.

We will keep you informed of future developments as they occur. We'll have more CBS evening news after this."

17

Roberts was sitting in his cell alone, his tie, belt and shoes having been taken from him. He was leaning against the wall with his knees hunched up in front of him.

My God, he thought. *I never thought I'd be in a prison again.* He closed his eyes and his mind went back to when he was captured in July, 1971.

The day had started out routinely. It was early morning at Tan Su Nut Air Force base, in South Vietnam. Air Force Lieutenant David Roberts was strapped into his seat in the front cockpit of his F-4C Phantom Jet, a fighter bomber used heavily in the Vietnam War. It was a two engine plane that could reach a top speed of Mach 2 (1430 mph). Today it carried eighteen 750 pound bombs and a variety of air to air and air to surface missiles as well as electronic counter measures (ECM) to detect and block the Soviet built SAM (Surface to air) missiles. Roberts reached the head of the runway. The bomb racks had been connected and the missiles plugged in. "Ready to go?" he asked his Radar Intercept Officer (RIO), Lieutenant Sam Rosen, who was in the rear seat. Rosen was responsible for the use of the radar and the air to air weapons system. "Affirmative" said Rosen. The early morning sun was bright as Roberts moved the throttles all the way forward. The F-4 hurtled down the runway. Airborne at 200 knots, Roberts pulled up the flaps and landing gear. He ignited the afterburners and the Phantom responded like a powerful animal freed from its bonds. It quickly reached 800 knots. Roberts rotated the aircraft and climbed to 15,000 feet. Back on the ground was the next Phantom in the flight ready to take off.

As the rest of the flight caught up to Roberts and went into formation, he headed north. Looking down, the forests seemed peaceful and quiet. *It's not going to last*, Roberts thought. Their mission was to destroy the Gia Lam railroad yards, the Yen Vien railroad switching yards just north of Hanoi and the rail line running northwesterly to Kunming, China which was being used to carry supplies to North Vietnam. As they reached the outskirts of Hanoi, black puffs of smoke appeared before them. This was the flak from the anti-aircraft guns.

"Climb to 20 angels" Roberts directed the flight "and watch out for the SAM's."

Roberts started his bomb run over Yen Vien. He could feel concussions from the shells exploding around him. Roberts released his 750 lb. bombs and then pulled his plane back into the sky trying to get away from the flak and the SAMs. He turned and headed back toward the western end of the rail yard to smash the rail line running to China. As he started on his final bombing run, he saw the SAMs that darted toward his flight. *There were dozens of them* he thought. *It's like a fireworks factory blowing up.*

Roberts dropped lower over the rail line. The missiles were fired rapidly one after the other. At a speed of 500 knots the missiles were spread apart and destroyed the tracks in separate places over a five to ten mile distance.

"Let's go home" Roberts said as he pulled his aircraft up in a left turn to head south. Suddenly the Phantom was bracketed above and below by the exploding SAMs. Shrapnel set the left wing on fire and shattered the cockpit glass. Cold air rushed through the hole, decompressing the cabin pressure. The rudders and stabilizer didn't respond. Roberts pulled the canopy release switch. The canopy fell away from the aircraft. As he ordered Rosen to eject, Roberts pulled his eject lever. He shot straight up into the sky.

Roberts watched a SAM rocket past him as he drifted down in his parachute. He could see a fireball falling to earth off in the distance, the remainder of his Phantom jet. There was a hole in his flight suit, and he could see that his left arm was bleeding. He steered his parachute away from a river toward an open field. As the ground started coming toward him, he didn't see anyone and thought that he might just make it. He was quickly disillusioned as a burst of bullets came from the ground almost hitting him.

He touched down, took off his chute and his helmet and was reaching for his gun when he was suddenly attacked by a large group of North Vietnamese soldiers and civilians. They surrounded him, and immediately took his gun, his watch and his boots. They stripped him down to his shorts and made him run what seemed like miles through a gauntlet of people who attacked him with bamboo poles. Then, two soldiers grabbed him by the arms and threw him into the back of a truck. The soldiers climbed on board and tied him to the side of the truck so he was standing up. As they reached Hanoi, people threw stones at him. Some even managed to hit him with bamboo poles. He was actually relieved to arrive at the Hao Lo Prison in Hanoi; the one the prisoners called the "Hanoi Hilton."

Roberts marched into a dirt covered yard called the "entry compound." The soldiers held his arms tightly. Roberts kept pointing to the wound on his left arm. The soldiers said nothing and threw him into a dark cell. The cell had a dirt floor, a small canvas cot for a bed with one blanket and a pillow. The toilet consisted of a bucket. The only light came from between the metal bars of the cell door. A few minutes later, a soldier with a red cross arm band and a North Vietnamese officer entered the cell. Roberts was on the bed. The officer, who spoke perfect English, introduced himself. "I am Major Duc Can Kay" he said. 'You are in Hao Lo Prison in downtown Hanoi. This is where we keep the criminals. We do not recognize the Geneva Convention. War has not been declared. You are nothing more than an imperialist air pirate, a criminal who must be punished. You have been charged with murder. One of your bombs scored a direct hit on a school with many children in it."

"Were you ordered to destroy that school?"

Roberts stood at attention. "My name is Lieutenant David Roberts, United States Air Force, serial #A02247111."

Major Kay motioned to a soldier outside, who entered, took his rifle butt and smashed it against Roberts' face twice. His nose started to bleed, two teeth fell out of his mouth, and his forehead was bleeding. The soldier then smashed the rifle butt into Roberts' midriff knocking the wind out of him and causing him to fall back onto the cot. The other soldier threw large pieces of cotton, bandages, tape and a bottle of iodine onto the cot. "Take care of yourself" Major Kay said with a grin as they walked out.

Eventually, Roberts was able to clean himself up and put on a thin shirt and pants, and slippers lying on the cot.

For a little more than a year Roberts remained alone in that cell. The highlights of his day were the two meals that usually consisted of watery soup and a slice of bread or a bowl of rice. Some days it was only one meal. He lost 65 lbs. during his captivity. The low points were being taken to the "Fitness" room to be beaten with rubber hoses and strips. Sometimes his hands and feet were tied in a sitting position and one of the soldiers would push his head and arms forward forcing him to bend so far that he suffered extreme pain in his back and legs. No telltale scars resulted.

It was almost a relief for Roberts and his fellow prisoner to be tied against the side of a truck clad only in their shorts and driven slowly through crowds lining the streets of Hanoi. Signs had been hung from their necks. Some said "capitalist hired guns," some said "imperialist air pirates," some simply said "criminal". Roberts' sign said "children killer." The crowds were whipped into a frenzy, shouting at the prisoners in Vietnamese hurling sticks, cans and bottles at them. Actually, the signs protected part of their upper body.

Then there was the cold. During the harshest days of winter. Roberts was given another thin blanket but that did not prevent the cold from seeping through the blanket and thin clothing he was wearing. Still, Roberts continued to resist giving a confession or giving away any useful information.

Major Kay insisted that he give a confession to bombing the school under orders from his commanding general. Roberts protested that he had not bombed a school. Major Kay showed him pictures of dead children lying on the rubble of a bombed out building. Roberts continued to deny it believing the photos to be fake; yet, in his mind he had a nagging feeling that maybe he had destroyed a school. This added a sense of guilt which made him feel even worse.

The beating hurt, and the times when he was forced to bend forward in a sitting position were sheer agony. He used his own form of mind control to withstand all of this. He envisioned leaving his body. He could see his body being beaten as he drifted upwards. The next thing he knew, he was lying on the beach at the Connecticut shore with his girlfriend Carole Chapin. She was putting suntan lotion on his back. Then they were in the surf together. He willed himself to believe that the rubber hoses were huge waves that struck his back and legs. He visualized Carole lying next to him embracing and kissing him. This flashback did not always work, but when it did, it was sufficient for him to gain relief from the frequent torture.

At the end of the day the prisoner's exhaustion from the beatings usually enabled them to drop right off to sleep.

The guards, to weaken the prisoners further, would clang bamboo sticks along their bars at least once an hour.

Roberts could hear the clanging. This time it didn't stop. He heard "David, wake up." He opened his eyes and there was Brian Kelly outside his cell holding a closed umbrella inserted between the bars of his cell door. "David, are you all right? You seemed in a trance, and you're perspiring."

"I'm all right" Roberts said as he turned and put his feet on the floor. "I guess I just had a nightmare."

18

A police officer opened the cell door to permit Kelly to enter.

"Brian, thanks for coming on such short notice." Roberts said as the two shook hands. "Let me say right off the bat that I didn't kill Annie, I haven't seen her since the first week in December. I was very fond of her. I need you to represent me on this. Will you do it?" he asked.

Kelly replied "Of course, I will, Dave. I know you couldn't do something like this; and besides, what are friends for?" he said as he smiled at him and put his right arm around Roberts' shoulders. Roberts let out a sigh of relief.

They sat down on the small bunk. Kelly turned to Roberts "It's not going to be so easy, Dave. Based upon the arrest warrant, they seem to have a pretty good case against you. I'll admit it's circumstantial, but convictions have been won on less than what they have here."

"I have a copy of the warrant here; as a matter of fact two copies. I got them from one of the reporters outside." He handed one to Roberts who skimmed it quickly. "It does look bad if these things are true, but they're not" Roberts insisted.

"We'll go over that later" Kelly replied.

"Right now, I want to get you out of here. The Governor of Connecticut should not be sitting in jail overnight."

Brian Kelly was considered one of the better and probably the best criminal defense attorney in the state. He had never lost a murder case, and he had tried at least twenty-five of them in his twenty years of private practice. Several of them had been high profile cases which was what gave him his reputation. He won an acquittal in the "Seaside Strangler" case which gained him national notoriety. The real serial killer who had terrorized Connecticut shoreline communities was eventually caught and convicted. Kelly also won a new trial for a wealthy, Hartford insurance company CEO who had been convicted of killing his wife. The case had been highly publicized, and Kelly gained an acquittal at the retrial which occurred several years after the first one. Kelly, too, had been a federal prosecutor before going into private practice. Kelly was tall and slim with a thick head of blonde hair. He had brown eyes and a light complexion. A native of Boston, he had gone to Boston College Law School. He lives in Glastonbury with his wife and four children. He served one term in the State House of Representatives at the same time as Roberts. After one term Kelly realized that he didn't really like politics or being a legislator. He had devoted his professional life to what he called the "real world of human conflict." He was a huge success as a trial lawyer. He had an infectious smile, he was handsome and used his Irish charm to help convince jury after jury of his client's innocence. He was thorough and meticulous in jury selection, and once remarked "I've never met a jury I didn't like." He had a strong knowledge of the law and used his courtroom skills to great advantage. He was considered one of the top criminal defense attorneys in the state and had won several high profile cases. That's the major reason why Roberts had selected him over Ben Brown. He and Roberts had maintained their friendship since the legislature. Kelly had even overcome his dislike of politics and had worked hard in Roberts' campaigns, mostly in fund raising. His usual warm smile was missing now. His face was grim. In fact, he even had a small scowl as he looked at Roberts.

"I agree with you that they're playing hardball. They and their buddy, Kennedy, have refused to arraign you until tomorrow. I'm going to call Pat Amenta and see what I can do." Judge Patricia Amenta was the presiding judge for criminal matters in the Hartford Judicial District.

"Call Phil Jordan, too." Roberts said. He lives in Simsbury; I'm sure he's in the book. Amenta will recognize him as an expert on constitutional law. I want her to be convinced that I can't be forced out of office."

"O.K." replied Kelly. "Let me see what I can do. Hang in there, Dave. Hopefully, I'll see you later tonight." He tapped on the cell door to call the guard.

Upstairs he joined Roberts' Chief of Staff, Bill Donovan. The two huddled together for a few minutes and then went into the chief's office to use the telephone. Ten minutes later, Kelly and Donovan were on their way to the parking lot surrounded by members of the media. "Attorney Kelly, are you going to represent him?" asked the Hartford Courant.

"Yes," Kelly replied.

"Did he do it?" came a shout from the crowd.

"Of course not." Kelly said with a flash of anger. "Dave Roberts is an innocent man wrongly accused. I've known him for a long time. He is honest, responsible, intelligent and a man of compassion. He is not capable of killing anyone."

"Not even in a moment of passion?" asked the New York Times.

"No," Kelly retorted. "There was no relationship between Dave and Miss Tremaine other than just friends."

They had reached his car, a red Mercedes. Kelly was not afraid to spend the money he earned.

"What about the affair he had?" asked WTIC radio.

"I won't even dignify that with an answer. That's all I have to say for now." Kelly slid behind the wheel and closed the door. The crowd parted as he drove away.

19

"All rise!" the marshal intoned. "The Superior Court for the Judicial District of Hartford, G.A. 14 in Hartford is now open and in session in this place. All persons having cause or action to be here, give their attention according to law. The Honorable Patricia Amenta presiding."

Everyone in the packed courtroom stood up as Judge Amenta in her black robe came through the door behind the judge's bench and sat down in the large light blue high backed judge's chair common to all Connecticut courtrooms.

"You may be seated" said the marshal. There was a rustle of noise as everyone sat down. This was courtroom one, the arraignment court where defendants were first presented, where guilty pleas, sentencings, motions and other related matters were heard. It was not a jury trial courtroom. It was a large courtroom which tonight accommodated many members of the state and national media most of whom had been keeping a vigil outside. Ordinary citizens filled up the remainder of the courtroom drawn there by the drama of the event that was about to unfold and by the announcement on local radio and television stations that this hearing would commence at 9:00 p.m.

"Your honor, I protest the holding of this special session to accommodate Governor Roberts. No one is above the law, and he should wait until tomorrow like everyone else arrested today." Arlene Powell had stood up and was addressing the judge. To her left was Brian Kelly and then two marshals between whom was Governor Roberts still in handcuffs.

"Be quiet, Attorney Powell," Judge Amenta said. "You'll speak when I tell you to."

Pat Amenta was a short, dark haired woman with wire rimmed glasses perched on the lower part of her nose. She was in her late forties, had a scarf around her neck under her robe and spoke in a firm voice. No one had a problem hearing her. She was known as a judge who maintained control over her courtroom at all times.

"Marshal, remove the handcuffs from the defendant" she ordered. The handcuffs were removed.

"This is the matter of State of Connecticut versus Governor David Roberts, docket number 14-76434167. Will counsel please identify themselves for the record." she said.

"Deputy State's Attorney Arlene Powell representing the State of Connecticut."

"Attorney Brian Kelly representing the defendant, Governor David Roberts, who is present and standing immediately to my left."

"Thank you" Amenta said. "Ladies and Gentlemen. I have convened this extraordinary evening session because of the identity of the defendant. While it is true, Attorney Powell, that no one is above the law, including the Governor of this state or even the President of the United States, the public interest must also be served. This is a very unusual situation and the people of this state have a right to know, at the earliest possible moment, whether the chief executive officer of the state will remain in jail or be available to conduct the business of the state. This is a procedural hearing, not a hearing on the question of guilt or innocence. Further, to advance this hearing by 13 hours hardly places the defendant above the law, and in any event, the timing must accede to the public interest I've just described."

"Now, before we proceed, let me call your attention to the fact that by my order, all cameras and recording devices have been barred from this hearing. The media is here, apparently in force" (the judge smiled for the first time). She continued "and are, of course free to observe and take notes. However, because of the seriousness of this matter and in order to preserve the dignity and proper decorum of the courtroom and this proceeding, I have banned live and recorded coverage of this hearing by the media. The ends of justice will not be served by turning this session into the spectacle that could result from such coverage. Now, Madam State's Attorney . . . ."

"Your Honor, may I be heard?" A man walked to the front of the courtroom, "I'm Attorney Rob Wilson representing Channel 3, protesting your exclusion of cameras and recorders based upon the First Amendment rights . . . ."

"You may not be heard, counsel. You have no standing at this time, and my decision on this hearing is final. Please step back."

"Now, as I started to say, Madam State's Attorney, do you wish to be heard on the issue of bail?"

"Yes, your honor," Powell replied. "The state requests that the defendant be held without bail."

A gasp was heard from the audience.

"Please be quiet in this courtroom" Judge Amenta said as she gave a stern look toward the crowd. "Please continue, Ms. Powell."

"Thank you, your honor," Powell remarked. "Mr. Roberts is charged with a vicious and horrible crime. There is no more serious crime in this state except for multiple homicides. His actions show him to be a danger to the community and because of the strong likelihood of incarceration for the crime, the risk of flight by this defendant is very high. The state requests, no, even demands, that Mister Roberts be held without bail."

"Attorney Powell, no one demands anything in this courtroom. Further, you may refer to the defendant as the defendant or Governor Roberts, not Mister Roberts. He is still the Governor of this state, and his position is not to be demeaned by stripping him of his title at this point." Judge Amenta said. "Mr. Kelly?"

"Yes, your honor. I agree this is a serious charge; but that's all it is at this point, a charge. The case against Governor Roberts is all circumstantial. I am well aware that people can be and have been convicted on circumstantial evidence; but as I look at the arrest warrant, there is no eyewitness to the crime. This is not a DNA case. The likelihood of conviction and, therefore, incarceration is not strong with such a circumstantial case."

"Further, I've known Governor Roberts for many years. I know him not to be a person of violence. Everyone who knows him, and that is a lot of people, know that he's not a violent person. He has no history of violence, he obviously has no criminal record; so to paint him as a danger to the community is ludicrous."

"As for risk of flight, he is a person with several solid roots in this area. He was born and grew up here. He has lived in this state all of his life except when he was serving his country in Vietnam. He's been a successful governor, and will continue to be. He values his reputation and strongly desires to stay here and clear his name. My God. He's the Governor of this state, duly elected by the people of this state. It is unthinkable that he would flee the jurisdiction."

"Finally, let me say that because he is the Governor, special consideration should be given, not to him, but to the people of Connecticut. They elected him, and they're entitled, particularly in view of the presumption of innocence which is afforded to him by the Constitution, to have him continue to be their Governor. To incarcerate him prior to trial would be to remove him as the Governor of this state without due process. It is a step that the court should not take."

"Attorney Kelly, does your client intend to resign or withdraw temporarily from his duties pending the outcome of this matter?" Judge Amenta inquired.

"Absolutely not." Kelly replied. "I've discussed that with him. He insists that he is innocent of this crime, and he intends to continue to serve the people who elected him."

"Can he be forced to resign?" the Judge asked.

"No, your honor. In anticipation of that question, present here in court is Professor Phillip Jordan of the University of Connecticut

Law School, who as you know is both an attorney and a professor of constitutional law. As your honor well knows, he has a national reputation as an expert in constitutional law."

"Professor Jordan, would you please step forward and enlighten the court on this subject" Judge Amenta asked.

"Certainly your honor." Professor Jordan, in his late fifties and sporting a white beard and strands of white hair on his head, walked toward the bench and stood to the left of Roberts.

"Attorney Kelly is correct. There is nothing in the Constitution, in the statutes or in case law that requires the Governor of the state to step down under these circumstances. I've researched this thoroughly right up to this evening. Perhaps, your honor will recall 1980 when Governor Ella Grasso was terminally ill. Despite her illness, she remained Governor and resigned only shortly before her death; and she didn't have to do that. The law has not changed since then."

"Thank you, Professor Jordan. Mr. Kelly, can your client make any bond?"

"Not any substantial bond, your honor. Certainly not the $500,000 on the warrant. Governor Roberts would have to come up with $50,000 he doesn't have. He is not a wealthy man, your honor. He's been a public servant most of his life, he has children for whom he has to provide; and as your honor well knows, there are not many public servants who have been able to set aside much in the way of savings."

"All right. Attorney Powell, do you wish to be heard further?"

"Yes, your honor. A lot of Attorney Kelly's remarks were political in nature. Governor Roberts' popularity, which, I might add, may not be very high right now, or his duties as Governor or the qualities that Mr. Kelly alleges he has should not be a consideration; nor should Professor Jordan's unsubstantiated remarks. Again, Governor Roberts is not above the law!"

"Your honor, Governor Roberts committed a vicious crime, he is a danger to the community, and, for all the reasons I've stated, he poses a substantial risk of flight. I don't believe he should be released and, with all due respect to the court, it will be on your head if he kills again or if he flees the state."

"Thank you for your concern for the court's exposure, Attorney Powell," Judge Amenta said with a note of sarcasm.

"However, I'm willing to take that chance. These are extraordinary conditions and require unusual consideration."

"Both counsel have touched on the two main concerns of the court in determining bail. First, whether the defendant is a danger to the community. In addition to the reasons described by Attorney Kelly, I should also consider that the victim was someone whom the defendant knew well and with whom he apparently had a prior relationship. This would indicate, even if the defendant were to be found guilty, a sole or unique target of the crime. It would not be a random crime; there is no claim he is a serial or multiple killer. Also, Governor Roberts does not have any history of violence or criminal conduct. Accordingly, I do not find that he is a danger to the community."

"As for risk of flight, I find it hard to believe the Governor of the state, with roots in the community and a potential political future here, would flee the state prior to trial. After conviction, if there is one, is another matter; and finally, precisely because he is the elected Governor of this state, I do not believe I should in effect remove him from the office the people elected him to fill and the duties which they expect him to fulfill. This consideration has to weigh heavily in my decision. Further, a small bond would be meaningless, and I'm convinced that he does not have the resources for a substantial bond."

"Accordingly, I hereby release the defendant on a written promise to appear. Madame Clerk, please have the appropriate paperwork completed here. Upon signing same, Governor Roberts is to be released here, no longer to be held in custody and is not to be returned to the lockup."

"Anything else, Counsel?"

"Yes, your honor" said Powell. "May this case be transferred to Part A?"

"Motion granted. This matter is transferred to the Part A criminal docket with a continuance date of Thursday of next week, January 12th. Adjourn court, Marshal."

Judge Amenta left the bench as everyone stood up. The marshal adjourned court. Roberts signed the promise to appear. He shook hands with Kelly and Jordan, thanked Jordan for coming and embraced his wife, Cindy, who had been seated in the first row.

The reporters gathered around him, but Roberts said "Not here, outside." He took his wife's hand, and accompanied by Kelly and his chief of staff, he walked out of the courtroom, down the corridor, down the stairs and out onto the sidewalk where the TV lights were almost blinding.

"Governor, any reaction?" one of the media asked.

Roberts looked at the crowd and into the cameras "I appreciate the court's consideration. Cindy and I are going to go home, and tomorrow we'll get on with the business of the State."

"As for any other comment, I refer you to my attorney and my good friend, Brian Kelly. In view of the eloquence he just displayed, at this point, he can probably say it better than I can." Roberts said as the famous Roberts' grin spread across his face.

Kelly looked into the cameras. "This charge is nothing more than a political vendetta launched by the State's Attorney's office. They would have liked nothing better than to have Dave Roberts remain in jail for the prejudicial effect it would have on potential jurors. The way the investigation and the arrest were handled, particularly the spectacle at the Governor's office this afternoon with the State inviting the media to be there, and Attorney Powell's performance tonight were all designed to hurt the Governor's reputation and put him further on the defensive."

"Well, it won't work. Governor Roberts is innocent, and we intend to prove it. That's all I have to say at this time."

Roberts and his wife, Kelly and Donovan pushed their way to their cars and left with the cameras still going. It was 10:00 p.m. and still time for the late news.

20

“Why are you so hard on Governor Roberts?” Janet Smith asked her husband after they and their two children had taken seats around the dinner table, and Frank had said grace. “In your prayers, you always ask God to forgive, but you don’t seem to feel that way about David Roberts” she added.

“I’ve never disliked the man personally, at least up until now” Frank replied “I used to think of him as a pretty nice guy. He showed a lot of courage in Vietnam, he was pretty good on the basketball court and he’s very bright. It’s his policies I don’t like, especially on crime, and his moral values are disgusting.

He divorced his first wife, he had an affair with Anne Tremaine and who knows how many others. His recent affair with the Tremaine woman was while he was married to Cindy, his second wife. Let’s face it. He cheated on his wife. He committed adultery; and worst of all, he killed her. It’s reprehensible to commit murder and have an extramarital affair. It’s against our law, and, more importantly, it’s against God’s law. If there’s anyone who should uphold the law, who should have high moral values, it’s the governor of this state. He’s supposed to set an example for others, especially young people. What message does it send to our children when the governor commits murder and has extramarital affairs?" Smith said. "Roberts has the morals of an alley cat."

Andrew spoke up. "What are affairs, daddy?" he asked.

Smith didn't know what to say. Janet intervened to save him. "They're very close friendships" she said.

"Like me and Billy Thomas?" Andrew asked. "Are we having an affair?"

Frank almost choked on his water. "I sincerely hope not. Affairs are close friendships between a man and a woman" he explained.

"But I don't like girls," Andrew replied.

"That's because you're not ready yet" Frank responded. "When you get older, that'll change" he said with a grin on his face.

Brian, Andrew's older brother, raised his hand and looked at his father. "Are affairs like what the men and women do on TV, like on the afternoon shows?" he asked.

Janet blushed, and in a slightly raised voice, she said, "You've been forbidden to watch those shows." she looked at her two children. "You're supposed to be doing your homework after school. Besides, you don't get home until 5 o'clock. They don't let you watch TV at school, do they?" she asked.

"No," Brian said. "We have sports or study hall in the afternoon."

Brian and Andrew attended a private school. The Smiths did not support school integration, and did not want their children to attend the public schools which they considered inferior.

"But, there are vacations, and there's not too much to do when it's raining out" Brian continued.

"Well, you are still forbidden to watch TV in the afternoon unless it's a sports program. Do you understand that?" Janet asked in a firm voice.

They both nodded. "Yes", they replied.

"Now that you've finished with your dinner, you're excused. After you put your dishes in the sink, you may both go up to your rooms" Janet said.

"And be sure you don't watch any of those nighttime soaps either" Frank called after them.

When they had gone upstairs, Frank looked at Janet and laughed. "That was sure embarrassing" he said. "Sometimes, I think we should throw out all the TV sets and listen to the radio."

"Even then you'd have to monitor them to make sure they don't listen to the rap music that calls for killing policemen and breaking the law" Janet replied. "Or the talk shows that go into people's intimate problems" she added.

"People wonder why I talk so much about family values and losing our moral compass" Frank said. "It's an uphill battle but we've got to continue to fight for our principles. As for Roberts, you know how I feel about divorce. I may be a little old fashioned, but I believe in the marriage vows. Marriage is forever until death do us part" he said. He looked at his wife and thought *she is not the young, pretty girl from the south end of Hartford I married eleven years ago. She's certainly no Anne Tremaine.* he mused. *But, I guess no one is. No woman could be that beautiful or that sensuous. I close my eyes and picture her when I'm making love to Janet.*

"Frank, did you hear me? Do you want more coffee?" Janet asked.

Startled, Frank focused on his wife. "No thanks." he said. He felt guilty. *Janet cares for me and the kids, and I do love her.* he thought.

"Janet, I realize there are problems in marriages, that love isn't always forever," Frank continued with a sigh, "but once you marry, you stay married. It's the breakup of the family that's been the cause of most of society's problems."

"What about your friend Jim Spaulding. Isn't he considered somewhat of a ladies man despite his longstanding marriage?" Janet asked.

"Those are only rumors, and Jim has denied them to me; but he's certainly right on the issues. He's constantly preaching family values and a return to the moral principles that made this country great. He's the one who, at my urging I might add, introduced the constitutional amendment that would allow the good faith exception to a defective search. It didn't take much urging. He's shoulder to shoulder with me to find ways to combat crime more effectively."

"Roberts, on the other hand, has opposed the amendment and he's threatened to do it again. He wants to pass social legislation to get at what he calls 'the root causes of crime.' I don't have a real problem with that, but until these programs work, we still need the tools to do an effective job against crime now. But we won't have to worry about him anymore. What he did was horrible, but if it results in his having to leave office, it could be a blessing in disguise."

"Besides," he added, "I belong over there, not him" Smith pointed to the back of the house. The Smiths lived in a large eight room colonial in the wealthier section of Hartford's west side. The back of their house faced west toward the Executive Mansion on Prospect Avenue which was right behind him.

"I hope you can do it, Frank. You'll make an excellent governor" Janet said.

"Yes," he replied. "And we won't have to move our furniture very far."

"Are you sure Roberts is going to be convicted?" Janet asked.

"No question about it" Smith replied. "he killed her, and the evidence will prove it. There's no way he can weasel out of this one. The letter and the glasses with his fingerprints on them will bury him."

Frank yawned and started to get up. "We have a busy weekend. I'm taking the boys swimming tomorrow at the University of Hartford indoor pool in the morning. In the afternoon, we'll go ice skating. I don't know how much skating I'll do, but at least I'll start off with them. Tomorrow night, you and I are going to that fund raiser for the archdiocese. Sunday morning is church, and I was planning to take all of us to the UConn-Syracuse game at the Civic Center Sunday afternoon. Don't tell the kids, though. I want the basketball game to be a surprise for them" he said.

21

A light snow was falling two days later. It was 9 o'clock Saturday morning, and the small group had gathered in the library of the Governor's Mansion on Prospect Avenue. Seated around a crackling fire were Roberts, Brian Kelly, Chief of Staff Donovan, Cindy and Becky Brown who would be the lead defense investigator for the case.

"Becky, thanks for joining our team and coming here this morning." Roberts said as he put down his coffee cup.

"I want to mention a few things before we start talking about the trial. First, I am not going to resign or even step aside temporarily. I know there are some editorials and politicians who have already called upon me to do just that. Well, I'm not going to do it."

"I don't want to leave this state in the hands of our distinguished Lieutenant Governor who is presently sunning himself in the South Seas and hasn't even gotten in touch with me since the arrest."

"He's out of touch in more ways than that" Donovan remarked. This produced a chorus of laughter.

"That may be true, Bill" Roberts said, "but that's to stay in this room. We can't even hint that he's incompetent. Otherwise, people will wonder why we picked him as a running mate."

"O.K., but I've always wondered about that." Donovan replied. "I know, I know, we needed his delegates, and, of course, he masked his lack of ability very well with a smooth, glib line of talk."

Roberts continued "Also, it's better if I demonstrate confidence in my innocence. I can do that better if I look at the trial as a mere glitch in my life in which a verdict of not guilty is a sure thing. That's why I can give full attention to my duties as Governor." He looked at Kelly "Don't worry, Brian, I'll be available whenever and wherever you need me. Cindy and Bill can keep me fully informed of what I need to know."

Roberts paused "Secondly, I want this trial to take place as soon as possible. The longer this drags on, the worse it will be for my reputation and the reputation of the State of Connecticut. Also, most people seem to be shocked at my arrest and don't believe I could have done it. The longer this goes on, the more likely it is that people may start to question their original feelings. It's in everyone's best interest to get this behind us quickly. I want to start this trial in two weeks."

"Two weeks!" Kelly exclaimed. "Now, just a minute. We all know you're innocent, but on the surface at least, the state has a strong case against you. If we're going to win, we need some time to investigate."

"Two weeks to start jury selection. That'll probably take at least a week; so we have three weeks to investigate; also, we can put the pressure on the prosecution to go with what they have. There's been enough publicity on this so anyone who can come forward with information to help us will do it in the next two weeks. Besides, in Becky, we have the best there is; and that goes for you, too, Brian."

"I appreciate the compliment" Kelly replied. "But, that brings me to another point. Do you want me to bring in a special defense team?"

"No, I don't want to turn this into any more of a spectacle than it's already become. Hiring anyone else makes it look as if we're unsure of my innocence. Besides, we can't afford them. We don't need DNA experts. I think we can be reasonably confident in the state crime lab. I don't trust the prosecution or some of the local police, but I do trust our Medical Examiner to be both competent and impartial."

Kelly shrugged "All right, it's your call, but will you keep an open mind on this?"

"Of course, I trust your judgment. I'm not exactly a stranger to the criminal justice system, but I'll admit that knowing I'm innocent, I may be too optimistic; and I may not see the overall picture as well as you."

"If you want a speedy trial, then you're going to have to waive the probable cause hearing." Kelly said.

Connecticut has not had the grand jury system for many years; a system that requires a defendant to be indicted for murder by a grand jury after the members hear the prosecution's evidence. Most criminal charges are by an arrest warrant and on information in which the prosecutor brings the charges. There is an exception in the case of murder. Since there is no longer a grand jury to decide whether there's enough evidence to bring a defendant to trial as in the federal system, Connecticut has replaced the grand jury with, in the case of murder, a hearing held before a judge, who after hearing some of the prosecution's evidence, decides whether that amounts to probable cause that the defendant committed the murder and that a trial should take place.

Roberts nodded his head, "You're right. A probable cause hearing will take too long, and it will give the state a chance to rehearse its evidence presentation. Besides we know what their so called evidence is. Nothing can be gained from a probable cause hearing."

'O.K." Kelly said. "Let's discuss the evidence. How did your fingerprints get on the glasses and how did the letter from Governor Malone received in your office the day before Christmas get into her bathroom if the last time you were there was the first week in December? These are crucial questions, Dave, and we have to have answers."

"I don't have an explanation, Brian. I wasn't there then and even when Ray and I stopped in on December 3rd, we used coffee cups, not glasses."

"Did you have a glass of water while you were there?"

"No, just the coffee. If we did have water, Ray's fingerprints would be on one of the glasses, and mine wouldn't be on both of them. I don't know how the glasses got there with the fingerprints. I never gave her any glasses."

"Are you suggesting that someone framed you?"

"I don't know; but I know I haven't been there since that time in early December."

"We have our work cut out for us" Kelly said. He turned to the Chief of Staff, "Bill, I want you to question the members of your staff as to the letter and the glasses. Did they see anyone near them? Find out who was invited, who may have dropped in. The letter and the glasses are no secret ever since the media got a hold of the arrest affidavit."

"Becky, go over to the condo area. Question everyone who lives there or who might have been there. Their witness says he saw Dave go in and out of the condo. See if anyone else saw that. I doubt it, because Dave wasn't there. Check out this witness and his car. Find out if anyone saw him or the car."

"Cindy, you've been pretty quiet. Any thoughts on this?"

"Not really, Brian. I agree with everything that's been decided." She took her husband's hand and squeezed it. "I love David. I trust him completely. If he says he didn't do it, then he didn't do it. He is not capable of murder. Also, I believe we should all express confidence in David's innocence, and confidence in our Lieutenant Governor as well."

"Good." Kelly said. "And, Dave, don't talk to the media anymore in regard to the case other than to proclaim your innocence. Blame me. Tell them to talk to me."

Roberts nodded, shook hands with Kelly and said "Thank you, Brian." He put his arm around Kelly as they walked toward the front door. "I have every confidence in you, Brian. I know you can win this thing."

As Kelly got into his car, he thought: *He's got more confidence in me than I do. This is going to be a tough fight. The sky was gray, and it looked as if it might snow again. The gray sky matches my mood.* Kelly thought as he pulled out of the driveway and headed south on Prospect Avenue.

22

Becky leaned on the rail of the Nantucket as the ferry from Woods Hole, Massachusetts on Cape Cod made its way through choppy waters toward Martha's Vineyard. The 100 square mile island was located 4 miles off the southeastern coast of Massachusetts. It was a popular resort area during the summer months making it very difficult to obtain an automobile reservation on the ferry; but this was January and Becky had left Hartford early that morning, driven her Bronco up the Mass Pike, down I-495, over the Bourne Bridge and into Woods Hole, the home of the steamship authority. As the three tier steamship plowed through the waters of Vineyard Sound, Becky considered what brought her there.

After the meeting broke up, she had gone to lunch with Brian Kelly, and that afternoon she had gone to the area of Anne Tremaine's condominium. She spent Saturday afternoon and again Sunday afternoon interviewing the victim's neighbors. No one had seen anything early Christmas morning. Those who hadn't slept late were busy exchanging gifts with their children around their Christmas trees. Some people weren't home on Saturday but were there on Sunday. Only two condos were not occupied on Saturday and Sunday, their owners apparently away for the weekend. It wasn't until late Sunday afternoon that Becky finally got a break. A middle aged couple told her that their neighbor,

Margaret Halleck, had been out walking her dog Christmas morning. Mrs. Halleck had told them that she saw a black car drive up to Anne Tremaine's condo, a man get out and go inside and then drive away 20 minutes later. She told them that she had given this information to the police, but never heard from them again. Mrs. Halleck is a widow in her early 70's, who lived alone. The reason she wasn't home this weekend was that she was visiting her son and daughter-in-law who owned the Sea Breeze Inn on Martha's Vineyard.

The wind got stronger on this bleak looking day with gray skies. Becky pulled her overcoat tighter and her dark blue seaman's knit cap down over her forehead. She shivered a little as the ship passed West Chop and headed into Vineyard Haven. She had called Mrs. Halleck who told her the same story she had just heard. She had agreed to Becky's coming up to talk with her. Becky decided to drive rather than fly because of the uncertain flying weather during the winter.

Becky drove her Bronco off the dock at Vineyard Haven, turned left and headed across the island toward Edgartown where the Sea Breeze Inn was located. As she stopped at the light in Vineyard Haven, the Tisbury Inn was on her right, and she looked down Main Street which was almost deserted. *What a difference* she thought. *During the summer it's filled with people and traffic. You could walk down Main Street and meet all sorts of celebrities. Art Buchwald got his hair cut there; once she had run into Mike Wallace at Leslie's Drugstore, and the actress, Patricia Neal walking out of the deli across the street. Walter Cronkite had a place "up island" as did Carly Simon. Jackie Kennedy had owned land nearby. More than 60,000 tourists come each summer. The permanent residents who call themselves "Vineyarders" number about 10,000. There is somewhat of a love-hate relationship between them and the tourists. The Vineyarders like their privacy and the quiet atmosphere of the winter, but seem to be willing to put up with the tourists because of the business they bring to the island. Some older residents trace their ancestry back to the inhabitants of the 17th century. It was the explorer Bartholomew Gosnold who named the island for his daughter Martha and the grapevines he found when he visited there in 1602.*

Becky drove onto one of the small side streets near Edgartown Harbor and parked in front of a two story white clapboard building with black trim. She got out of the car and looked down the street. She could see the dock where the "On Time I" and "On Time II" ferry boats took people and cars to the island of Chappaquidick. She turned and looked at the Sea Breeze Inn. A sign with the year 1760 A.D. was to the left of the front door. Soon she was sitting in an overstuffed chair in the living room. A fire was blazing in the fireplace at the far end of the room. Mrs. Halleck sat at the end of a sofa to the front and left of Becky, with her son Charles Halleck. Becky had met Charlie's wife Kay, who was busy in the kitchen preparing dinner.

"I'm sorry you had to come all this way to meet with me" Mrs. Halleck said. "But I come up here every year at this time so I can spend time with Charlie, Kay and my grandchildren. It's nice and quiet here, and January seems to be the warmest time of the year during the winter up here. We rarely have guests at this time of the year."

"I appreciate your seeing me on such short notice," Becky replied, "but this is important to us." She took a sip of the scotch Charlie had given her. "This is not a dry town like Vineyard Haven" he had said when he offered her the drink she had wanted ever since being exposed to the wind and cold on the ship coming over. She was finally able to relax.

"It's too bad about the Governor." Mrs. Halleck remarked. "He seems like such a nice man; and his wife is so pretty."

"I agree with you." Becky said. "He's innocent and hopefully with your help, we can show that."

Kay Halleck was at the entrance to the living room. "Dinner is ready" she said with a warm smile.

After dinner, they were back in the living room. Dinner had been a delicious New England Clam Chowder, a Yankee pot roast with mashed potatoes, corn and hot baked rolls. Becky had told Kay that it was delicious, and it was; a traditional New England dinner with all the trimmings topped off by a warm apple cobbler. Becky was ready to fall asleep.

Kay was putting the children to bed. Becky turned on the recorder Mrs. Halleck had agreed to, and began.

"Mrs. Halleck, tell us what you saw Christmas morning last year." Becky said.

"Well," Mrs. Halleck began "As you know, my condominium is in the same group as Anne Tremaine's. I'm on her right side closer to the road. She was a very nice young woman; you know; so pretty and so friendly, and she certainly did have a lot of male visitors. Poor girl, what a tragedy." she said.

"What did you see?" Becky asked trying to prod her along.

"It was about quarter to seven. Horatio had to go. I could tell. That's Horatio, my English Setter.

I put on some clothes, picked up my pooper-scooper, and took Horatio downstairs. I walked him toward the road. I keep a tight leash on him. He likes to run off on his own. We walked around to the back, down toward the end of the last condo, and turned the corner. That's when I heard it."

"Heard what?"

"I heard a car screech to a stop in front of Anne's condo. It was just about 7:00 because the church bells began to ring. By this time, I was close enough to see the driveway and Anne's condo. A man got out of the car and went into her condo."

"Could you see who it was?"

"Not too well." He had his hat down low on his forehead.

"Was it this man?" Becky asked as she passed over a photograph of Roberts.

"Oh, heavens, no. That's Governor Roberts. I'd know him anywhere, especially with his red hair, even with a hat on. No, the man I saw was shorter and sort of bent over."

"How about this man?" She showed her a picture of Inspector Cassella.

"Well, I don't really know. He was short like him, but I couldn't see his face. His hat was low down on his head, and he had a scarf around his neck. It covered most of his face. Maybe he was hiding his face. It was very windy and cold so he might have been just protecting himself against the wind. I'm pretty sure his hair was dark, at least what I saw of it; but, I know this man. This is the detective who asked me questions two days later. The day after they found out poor Annie was dead. He said his name was Inspector something. I didn't catch his last name. He also showed me a badge. Inspector, I remember thinking, that's a funny first name." Becky held her breath for a moment.

"What happened next?" Becky asked.

"Well, by that time, Horatio had peed, so I took him back upstairs. About 20 minutes later, I heard a door slam. I looked out the window. The same man came out, got into his car and drove away."

"Did you tell the man with the beard about this when he interviewed you?"

"I sure did. I told him what I just told you; or most of it, anyway; but he only showed me a picture of the Governor. I told him that the man I saw was not the Governor."

"Did he ask you anything else?"

"Well, yes. He asked me to describe the car. I told him it was black, and it had four doors. I told him I didn't know what kind of car it was, but it was the same kind of car that I saw him driving away from there the day after Christmas; you know, I saw it on the evening news."

Becky's heart leaped. "What did he say to you?"

"He had a funny look on his face. He told me not to talk to anyone about what I saw; even about his being there, until he got back to me. Especially, don't talk to the press he told me. It might, now what was the word he used, it might jeopardize the investigation."

"Did he ever contact you again?"

"No, I told reporters I didn't want to talk to them; but the Governor was arrested, I figured the investigation was over. Then, you came along, and I didn't see any harm talking to you."

Becky turned off the recorder.

"No, there's no harm but I'd still avoid the press if I were you; and please, for now, don't tell anyone that you talked with me."

"Thank you very much, Mrs. Halleck." Becky was elated. Her adrenalin was running. *I'm wide awake* she thought. *I'll never get to sleep now.*

She turned to Charlie "I'd sure like another scotch" she said. "As a matter of fact, make it a double if you don't mind."

23

"Line one of the regular docket:

State of Connecticut vs. Governor David Roberts" the clerk announced: "Charge, murder in the 1st degree."

"You don't have to repeat the charge. It's listed on the docket, Mr. Clerk." Judge Patricia Amenta was on the bench for a status call on the pending Part A Criminal Docket.

She had taken the bench moments before in the center courtroom on the 3rd floor of the Criminal Courts Building at 101 Lafayette Street, Hartford which was located a block south of the State Capitol. The courtroom was crowded with reporters, lawyers and their clients. TV, radio and recording devices had again been banned from the courtroom. Some radio and TV people were in the lobby of the 3rd floor and several were down at the front entrance to the building hoping to do interviews with the Governor, the prosecutor and defense attorney. They had already taken location shots of the red brick criminal courts building, and looking north showing the Capitol with its gold dome shining brightly in the winter sun. On the right you could also see a statute of the Marquis De Lafayette on horseback facing the Capitol, in honor of the French military leader who was so helpful to the colonists in the Revolutionary War. They were going to use those for backdrop shots in case they were unable to place people they interviewed at the right spot.

“We’re taking this matter up first so we can reduce the size of the crowd, and so the Governor can get back to work. Will counsel please identify themselves for the record.”

“Attorney Brian Kelly representing the defendant, Governor David Roberts, who is in court standing to my left.”

“Deputy State’s Attorney Arlene Powell, representing the State of Connecticut.” A 12 year veteran of the State’s Attorney’s office under both Steve Hogan and Frank Smith, Arlene Powell had moved up to be Chief Deputy in charge of trials upon Smith’s ascension to the S.A.’s post. An attractive woman, she was 5’6” with a thin build, light brown hair and hazel eyes. She was a graduate of Boston University and the University of Connecticut Law School. At 38, she had specialized in murder trials in the last 5 years and had not lost a murder trial in the 11 cases she had tried in that period of time. Attorney Powell was considered a tough, no nonsense prosecutor, well versed in the law and trial tactics. Her integrity was beyond question, and outside the courtroom her demeanor was warm, friendly and unassuming. She and her husband, Fred Powell, an executive at Aetna Life & Casualty in Hartford, lived in Simsbury, a Hartford suburb, with their 2 children.

“Oh, what happened to the State’s Attorney?” asked Judge Amenta. “He seems to be very vocal in this matter.”

“I’ve been assigned to try this case, your honor. It is Mr. Smith’s judgment that this would be more appropriate.”

“This gets him somewhat off the hook on the political vendetta charge” whispered Peter Reeves of the Hartford Courant. “You’re right” replied Randolph “Randy” Kearn of the New York Times. “If there’s a conviction, he can look like the leader in the fight for justice while remaining above the fray and not getting his hands dirty in a nasty trial. If Roberts is acquitted, he, of course, did not try the case and the blame is focused on Powell." They turned back to the proceedings.

"Attorney Kelly, what is your position on a hearing on probable cause?"

"My client, Governor Roberts agrees to waive his right to a probable cause hearing. We don't expect to get much more information from a probable cause hearing, than what's in the arrest affidavit and through discovery. My client insists upon his innocence and wants a jury to decide after a full airing of all the facts in this case; and besides, considering his position of Governor, he wants to remove this cloud from him and the State of Connecticut as soon as possible and a probable cause hearing will only delay the trial."

"All right, then, I'm going to canvass Governor Roberts with the standard questions to place on the record that he understands this; Governor Roberts, do you understand that by waiving your right to a probable cause hearing, you can never ask for one again?"

"Yes, your honor."

"Do you also understand . . . ." Judge Amenta continued her questioning.

Many years ago, Connecticut had the grand jury system, as the federal courts still do, in which the prosecution would present its evidence to a group of grand jurors selected without participation by the defense attorney. The grand jury would then present "a true bill" of indictment against the defendant if the grand jury believed, based solely on the state's evidence, without the defendant or his attorney even being present, that there was sufficient evidence to bring the accused to trial. If there were insufficient evidence, the grand jury would refuse to return a true bill and the charges would be dropped. The prosecution had total control over the proceedings, which caused some defense attorneys to comment that a district attorney could indict a ham sandwich if he chose to do so.

This system was replaced many years ago by prosecutors filing an information with the charges based upon an arrest by the police at or about the time the crime was being committed or by an arrest based upon an affidavit in which a judge has determined there is probable cause to arrest the accused as in the Roberts' case. Even if there is an on site arrest without a warrant, a judge must find probable cause from the police report that is presented to the judge at the time the accused is first presented in court. However, in the case of a charge of murder, the defendant is entitled to a probable cause hearing before a judge, not a jury, to make a further finding as to probable cause. In such a hearing, the prosecutor has to present sufficient evidence to back up claims in the warrant affidavit or police report to convince the judge there is probable cause. In such a hearing, witnesses are subject to cross-examination by the defense and in the judge's discretion may offer witnesses to dispute the prosecutor's case, although it is rarely done.

There are advantages and disadvantages for the defense to request a probable cause hearing. The advantage is an opportunity to see and test the evidence and state's witnesses before trial. The disadvantages are delay in reaching the actual trial, and in the event a trial is a long time away and a key prosecution witness becomes unavailable to testify at trial, his testimony at a probable cause hearing where he is subject to cross-examination becomes immortalized in the probable cause hearing transcript which can be introduced as evidence in the trial itself. If the witness is unavailable for trial, there would normally be no testimony. If he testified earlier at the probable cause hearing, his testimony would be preserved and introduced even though he was not present.

Judge Amenta had finished her questions. "Based upon the responses to the questions I propounded to the defendant, the court finds that the defendant has freely, voluntarily and understandingly, with the assistance of competent counsel, waived his right to a hearing in probable cause. Accordingly, the case may proceed to trial."

"Now as to the trial dates. I agree with Attorney Kelly, the longer the delay, the longer a cloud remains over the Governor and over the State. Whichever way this trial turns out, the people of the State have a right to a decision and have a right to a Governor without a cloud, whether it be the defendant or someone else. Jury selection will being next Tuesday, January 20th at 10:00 a.m. in Courtroom A, our largest trial courtroom. I've assigned Judge Alan Bronner to try this case. A jury panel will be brought in Tuesday. Further all discovery must be completed and turned over to the other side by 2:00 p.m. Monday, January 19th, in particular, all exculpatory material. I will hear you at 3:00 p.m. Monday in this courtroom if either side feels there has been inadequate compliance. Any objection to this order, Mr. Kelly?"

"Yes, your honor. We would like jury selection to begin at 2:00 p.m. on Tuesday. Governor Roberts is scheduled to deliver his State of the State message to the General Assembly at 10:00 a.m. on Tuesday. Other than that the defense has no objection."

"Can he deliver his message after 5:00 p.m. on Tuesday, in an evening session?"

"May I confer with my client?"

"Certainly."

Kelly and Roberts talked for a few minutes.

"Your honor, my client believes he can arrange that. After all, it's his message, and he doesn't see a problem with the House and Senate leadership."

"All right, we'll plan to start at 10:00 a.m. If you have an insurmountable problem, get back to me with the Assistant State's Attorney."

Judge Amenta turned to Powell "Do you wish to be heard, Attorney Powell?"

"Yes, your honor; not as to the 2:00 p.m. vs. 10:00 a.m. issue. The state objects to proceeding to trial so quickly. The state has to go first, as you know, and we need more time to marshal our evidence. It's a highly unusual procedure and it seems to me the state's case could be prejudiced by such an early starting date."

"Well, it seems to me" said the Judge "that based upon the arrest warrant affidavit, you have your scientific evidence and your witness. Also, jury selection will probably take 2 weeks. If you know what your evidence is, you shouldn't need more time to prepare questions for jury selection; and this schedule gives you more than 2 weeks to actually prepare for trial. If that means working nights and weekends so be it. The defense is essentially under the same time constraints. They may have more time to investigate but they're starting from scratch. You did most, if not all, of your investigation before applying for an arrest warrant."

"And as I've said, this is an unusual case, and for the reason I've already given the people have a right to a jury decision on this matter as soon as possible. Your objection is overruled! My original ruling stands. Next Tuesday is D-Day." Judge Amenta concluded.

"Now on another subject; as presiding Judge, I hereby issue the following orders:

1. Cameras, microphones and recording devices are barred from the courtroom commencing with jury selection.
2. I do not intend to have the jury sequestered. I don't think this has been done since 1922 in Connecticut or before, and I see no reason to change that now.
3. The following people are prohibited from saying anything to the media, except hello, goodbye or no comment:
    A. All members of the defense staff, including those employed by the defendant and defendant's attorney. The defendant himself. You may declare your innocence when speaking to a pubic gallery or even the media; but not more than a simple statement that you're innocent.
    B. All members of the prosecution staff, including investigators and those assisting from labs or other agencies and contractors

of the prosecution. In addition, members of the Hartford and State Police departments.

C. No one is to talk to or communicate with any jurors, alternates, prospective jurors and alternates or excused jurors and alternates; and this includes the members of the media not talking to them."

"I think that's as far as I can go at this time. I'll probably get objections from the media, anyway; but I don't want the jurors sequestered and at the same time I don't want them unnecessarily influenced by what goes on outside the courtroom. Judge Bronner can admonish the jurors at the proper time. Oh! And one other thing, there are to be no leaks from either side. If there are, I will hold such side responsible and impose sanctions."

"Is there anything else at this time?"

"No, your honor."

"No, your honor."

"All right. Before we take up the next case, the court will take a short recess." Judge Amenta left the bench as the Marshal said "All rise, the Superior Court is now in short recess."

Kelly and Roberts accompanied by the Governor's bodyguard went down the back elevator to the underground parking lot. As they drove out, a media crowd had gathered. They started shouting questions. Roberts kept the window shut and mouthed the words "No comment." He also waved. As they drove away, Kelly said "Did you see those signs?"

"No."

"Well, they were in the back. People were carrying signs saying "Murderer," "Resign," "Impeach the Governor," things like that. At the bottom of the sign was "Citizens against Crime." Kelly said.

Roberts replied "'Citizens against Crime' is a volunteer group supposedly started by Senator Jim Spaulding. It's a support group for Spaulding's views on fighting crime, and Spaulding hopes to use it to his political advantage when he runs for office."

Kelly laughed "But he wouldn't use them in this situation, would he? Anymore than he'd use this case to promote his political ambitions. Our tough on crime Senator isn't political is he?" Kelly asked sarcastically.

"Right!" Roberts replied in the same tone of voice.

"Ray, let's go into the Capitol on the north side of the building, so we can avoid all this."

But the media and protesters were smarter than that. They had people at both entrances.

"Oh, well," Roberts said. "I guess we can say 'no comment' north or south!"

24

Becky breathed a sigh of relief as she pulled her blue Bronco into the snow filled 4 wheel drive way of her home in Litchfield. Litchfield, Connecticut is in the northwest hills and a 4 wheel dive is very handy in the winter. Litchfield is in approximately the center of Litchfield County and is the seat of the Judicial District that covers Litchfield County. Civil cases and all of the serious criminal cases are tried in the Litchfield Courthouse. Litchfield is a town of about 8,000 people. With a few other towns, it is a part of the 66th General Assembly District represented by Becky's husband Benjamin Brown. Representative Brown is serving his eighth straight year in the Connecticut Legislature. He is an attorney in private practice with an office in Litchfield. Litchfield is an historic Connecticut town having been incorporated in 1719, a full 57 years before the writing of the Declaration of Independence. Becky's house was also historic, a dark red colonial with a black on white sign on the front specifying the year it was built, 1762. When she and Ben began their research of the house's history, they were excited because it was rumored that George Washington had slept there. Further research indicated that it was Benedict Arnold. They abandoned the research.

The Litchfield hills are very scenic and rustic, and the area north and west of Litchfield contains homes owned by such well know people as

Henry Kissinger, former New York Senator and D.C circuit court of appeals judge James Buckley, Meryl Streep, Susan St. James, Dustin Hoffman and Law and Order's Sam Watterston. If you want to get away from the big city, Litchfield County is the place to go.

Becky opened the door to the kitchen and put the grocery bag she was carrying on the kitchen table. "Well, I guess we can eat again." she said as she walked into the living room. Ben was kneeling in front of the fireplace moving burning logs around with a poker. "Hi, dear" he said to Becky as his lanky frame started to unfold in the process of getting to his feet. He leaned down and put his arms around Becky and kissed her on the lips. "I've missed you" he said. Becky is shorter than Ben, 5'5", petite but with a strong body toughened by years of physical training with the state police. Ben's favorite song is "I dream of Becky with the light brown hair!"

"You're so warm" Becky said as she leaned against him. I'm still shivering from the cold outside." Ben started to stroke her back. Becky was wearing a simple black skirt and a black sweater with a single strand of pearls around her neck.

"We could go upstairs right now and get very warm very quickly" Ben said with a mischievous smile. He paused and then pointed to the liquor cabinet. "I have something right here that will take the chill out right now, before we have dinner." He walked over to the cabinet and poured the martinis into two glasses, added an olive to each, and handed one to Becky and said "Martini, straight up, stirred, not shaken, as James Bond would say."

Becky smiled as they sat down on the couch. "I could use James Bond right now" she said. "I've got a really tough case this time."

Ben looked at her, took a sip of his martini and then said "Start from the beginning."

"As you know" Becky replied, "Brian Kelly has retained me to help him defend Dave Roberts. The state seems to have a strong case. They found two glasses with the gubernatorial seal on them at Anne Tremaine's condo with both his and her fingerprints on them. Even worse, they found a letter to Roberts from Governor Malone stamped in on December 24th, the day before the murder, with Roberts' fingerprints, located on the floor of the bathroom. Roberts not only proclaims his innocence, but he even told the police that he hadn't been to the victim's condo since the first week in December. That was before he knew of the letter. Also, as most people around the capitol know, Roberts and the victim had a torrid affair about ten years ago. This was about two years after his divorce while he was still single. One theory is that she wanted to get back together with him, and he didn't. Nevertheless, she persisted, became a nuisance, and when he tried to talk to her, he flew into a rage and strangled her. The other theory is that he succumbed to her advances, had a brief affair, and when he broke it off, she threatened to go public with it. That would be a motive for killing her."

"What do you think?" Ben asked.

"I think both theories are hogwash. There's no evidence of an affair, and you don't kill someone for being a nuisance. David Roberts is always in control of himself and he's very bright, streetwise as well as intellectually. He wouldn't do such a thing. Besides, I believe him when he says he didn't do it."

"If he didn't do it," Ben asked, "then who did?"

Becky shrugged her shoulders. "Whoever killed Anne Tremaine obviously framed Roberts. All I have to do is find the person who had the motive and the opportunity to kill Miss Tremaine."

"That's a lot harder than it looks" Becky said. "I have to know who's been close to her. She is a very successful lobbyist. I thought you, someone who really knows his way around the Capitol, might have some thoughts on it."

"Well, let me tell you what I know about Anne Tremaine" Ben said. "It might give you some ideas."

"First, she's a beauty. . . I'm sorry, she was a beautiful woman, a very beautiful woman. Years ago, she was Miss Connecticut. She was also very hot, very sexy. She would come on with most of the men she was trying to persuade on behalf of her client. She was also very smart. She was a lawyer, she had a bubbling and friendly personality and she was very successful. She probably would have been a great candidate for public office.

She seemed to be at the Capitol every day the legislature was in session. She spoke at many public hearings, either for, or against bills that were being considered depending upon the client; but she was much more effective behind the scenes, in one on one situations. I enjoyed talking to her. Sometimes I went with her, sometimes I didn't. I let her know early on that her beauty and her body movements did not persuade me either way."

"Well," Becky commented. "I'm glad to hear that! How did you accomplish this herculean feat?" There was a twinkle in Becky's eyes.

Ben laughed. "It was easy. Every time she tried to come on to me, I started talking about you; how much in love we were; that even though we had been married a long time, we still found each other as sexy as we did when we got married. That we did it every night. Things like that. It didn't take her long to get the message."

"Every night!" Becky exclaimed. "You've got to be kidding."

Ben leaned over close to her ear. In a soft voice he said "We should go to bed early tonight. You wouldn't want to make a liar out of me, would you?"

"Of course not." Becky smiled. "You're on" she said.

"But this still doesn't give me any suspects" she continued. "Tell me about her relationships with others."

"I think you'd have to look at who supported her most on legislation" Ben replied. "She wasn't above having affairs with legislators whose help she needed. The problem was, as I understand it, that she would break off the affair once she got what she wanted. She used people. She probably had a few unhappy or even angry ex-lovers" he added; "But I don't know whether any of them would be angry enough to kill her; but, of course, you never know. A wise man once said men can get into a lot of trouble if they think with any part of their anatomy besides their head. I think that's the cleaned up version; and I may be wrong about the wise man. The source may have been one of those talk show hostesses. You know, the ones that give advice on matters of the heart; or matters of any other part of the body" he said with a big grin.

Becky laughed. "I always knew that lawyers were frustrated psychologists" she said. "But, let's get specific. Give me names that I can use."

Ben turned serious. "These are based upon rumors I've heard and things I observed. With that caveat, my first suspect would be Jim Spaulding. You know him. He was chief of police in Torrington when you were assigned to the Western District here in Litchfield. You must have worked with him on some criminal investigations. After his retirement, he was elected to the State senate from this area. He's presently co-chairman of the Public Safety Committee."

"I remember him" Becky replied. "We did work together several times. He also had a roving eye. We used to call him the man who never met a woman he didn't want to touch. He came on to me, but I always brushed him off. His extra-curricular activities are surprising considering he's supposed to be a happily married man with three children."

Ben laughed. "Some say they're the worst kind."

"He goes even further" Becky replied. "He's a strong law and order man, he constantly talks about the need for family values, the moral decline in our country, why we must return to religion. He's the last person I would think would be playing around, or maybe I should say should be playing around."

"The other point on Jim," Ben remarked, is that I once commented to Anne that she had done very well with the Public Safety Committee.

She grinned at me and said something like Jim Spaulding and I have a special relationship! I thought at the time she was joking; but in retrospect she may have been serious."

"Who else?" Becky asked.

"The only other person who comes to mind is Tom Price. He's a former state representative from the shoreline area, Old Saybrook, I think. He was chairman of the General Law Committee, and a lot of Anne's bills were treated favorably in that committee while he was chairman" Ben stated.

"You said former state rep" Becky said. "Why isn't he still there?"

"Tom had an alcohol problem. He was convicted of assault 2nd with a motor vehicle; that's driving drunk and seriously injuring someone. He was in a head on collision that permanently injured two people. This was last summer. He served 30 days. He had already been renominated and he refused to drop out. But as you might imagine, his drunk driving and jail time didn't set well with the voters. He lost big time. Anne dropped him once he was no longer in office; but that didn't stop Tom. He was obsessed with her. He repeatedly tried to contact Anne. She refused to talk to him, so he started to call her at all hours, follow her, send her flowers, that type of thing. He even followed her around the Capitol. When she brushed him off, he'd hang around outside the Hall of the House telling his troubles to anyone who'd listen. Whether he was hurt because she used him or really in love with her or both, he couldn't stop trying to get back together with her. She finally threatened to have him arrested for harassment and stalking. This would have become public.

It would have totally ruined his reputation and probably his marriage. As far as I know, he stopped trying to reach her. But you never know. Both Spaulding and Price are married with children. If Anne threatened to tell their wives about her affairs with these two romeos, I can see why they'd be very nervous. They each had a motive to kill her."

"That's all I can think of now" he continued. "Let me give it some more thought later."

Becky had been taking voluminous notes. She looked up. "Okay. This, at least, gives me a start. I'm going to start dinner, the solid food variety" she said. "Would you let Alice know that we'll be sitting down in 45 minutes. Adam should be home by now. He's been out skiing. Tell him, too, as soon as he gets home."

Becky and Ben had two children, Adam, nineteen, who was a freshman at UConn. He was still home on a between semesters break. Alice, seventeen, was a junior at Litchfield High School.

An hour later all four were seated at the dinner table. Alice had asked her mother about her being retained by Governor Roberts. Becky was summarizing what she was doing. They were all fascinated by her work as a private detective.

"Do you think you'll be able to solve this?" Alice asked.

"I'm cautiously optimistic" Becky replied. "Most importantly, I really believe Roberts is innocent. Your father has given me some leads to pursue. The problem is that the letter and the glasses, although put there by the real killer, right now is strong evidence for the state; and, of course, there's not much time before the trial starts."

Ben turned to Adam. “What’s new with you Adam?”

“I can’t solve Mom’s problem” he replied. “But I have come across a way to solve the federal deficit.” Adam was majoring in economics.

“It’s really very simple” he continued. “I wish I could say it was original with me, but it’s not. I heard it on a talk show” he said.

“We’re all ears” Alice commented. “I’m ready to write it down, and then fax it to the President” she grinned.

“You won’t need much paper” Adam replied. “The government prints our dollar bills. The proposal is to print them on one side and sell advertising on the other side. We’d probably be able to bring in enough revenue to pay off the deficit in a few years.”

There was a stunned silence from the others.

Ben cleared his throat. “Don’t you think that cheapens the United States?” he asked. “The next thing you’ll want to do is put billboards on the Lincoln Memorial, the Capitol, in every national park and on every federal building in the United States; and why stop there. I’m sure coca-cola would pay a high price for a billboard on U.S. Embassies” he said.

“No, no” Adam protested. “That’s different. These memorials are like places of honor, of national pride. Currency, on the other hand, is not peculiarly American. It’s used primarily in commerce. There’s certainly nothing patriotic about exchanging money” he added. “And isn’t it worth it in light of all the bad predictions if we don’t do something quickly about the deficit.”

"Not bad, not bad" Becky said. "This may sound strange, but I think you have an easier way of solving the deficit problem than I do of solving the murder of Anne Tremaine."

Alice spoke up. "Are we still going to Florida during winter vacation?"

"That depends," Becky replied, "on how long this case is going to take. I certainly can't leave until Dave Roberts is cleared. I've not only been hired to work for him, but he and his wife are close personal friends of ours."

"But what about the swimming you usually do while we're in the warm weather?" Alice asked. "I thought you liked to swim in the salt water." Becky had been an outstanding swimmer in college and had almost qualified for the Olympics. She had kept at it while with the state police and planned to try out for the next Olympics.

Becky sighed. "It'll just have to wait. I can continue to practice at the Jewish Community Center in West Hartford; and, of course, you can continue to join me. Now," Becky smiled, "let's finish dinner."

25

Superior Court Judge Alan M. Bronner was making his opening remarks to the 35 members of the jury panel who had been brought in for jury selection.

". . . . . . . .So, think of the gulags and the concentration camps, the ethnic cleansing and the sham proceedings that pass for trials, think of all those proceedings and all of the suffering that has been endured by men, women and children at the hands of tyrants and brutes who were not answerable to average men and women just like you in a jury box.

Think of it, and understand that even though we have had over 200 years of sacred jury service by the citizens of the United States, that as you consider your service today, you have a contribution to make because human liberty is an edifice that is constantly to be built.

So may I ask you to fashion your small brick in that edifice and, by your honorable and decent service here. . . . ."

"In a few minutes, I will introduce you to the parties and their lawyers, and you will hear the names of the witnesses they intend to call to see if any of you know them in such a manner that you might have a conflict of interest. Then, we will proceed to the process of voir dire, French for 'To speak the truth.' Connecticut is very unusual in the way we conduct voir dire. Here, by our rules, we allow individual voir dire;

that means that each of you will come out individually and alone and take the witness stand and be questioned by each lawyer. There is generally no time limit although we ask the lawyers not to repeat the questions asked by their opponent. The lawyers will try not to ask questions that are too personal, and there are no right or wrong answers. It's their way of evaluating you, getting a handle on you so to speak to determine in their mind whether they believe you would be a suitable juror in this case. I will restrict them on not getting into principles of law because it's my job, not theirs, to explain them to you, and I will have the final say on what questions may be asked of you. They each have several peremptory challenges, meaning either side can excuse you from this jury without giving a reason. Please don't take it personally. It's just that for whatever reason, one side or the other does not want you as a juror. They may feel that your background might subconsciously make you partial to the other side, your opinion on crime or the criminal justice system might make you too sympathetic to the other side, or it may simply be that one side rejects you because the other side has accepted. Of course, each side has to use their challenges carefully since they are limited. There's an old saying that might apply here, 'The devil you know is sometimes better than the devil you don't know.'

Now, Connecticut is one of only 2 states in the nation that allows such individual questioning by the lawyers. This right is contained in Article I of the Connecticut Constitution. In federal court and in most states the judge asks the questions submitted by the lawyers but approved by the judge. There is a dispute over the value of this system. Those who don't like it believe that it delays the proceedings. Those who favor it believe it is the best way to ensure selection of a fair and impartial jury. Most defense lawyers swear by it and its favored by most prosecutors. Then you have the view of the late Edward Bennett Williams who grew up in Hartford and went on to become one of the best criminal defense lawyers in the country. His practice was in Washington, D.C. and he represented some very high profile defendants including Jimmy Hoffa. He was quoted as saying that he could step out of the Baltimore Courthouse and select the first 12 people he saw and get as good a jury as through the voir dire process. Whether that's an accurate quote or not, I don't know, but in any event, I respectfully disagree. Voir dire is valuable as you will soon see.

Now let me introduce you to the attorneys who will each disclose their associates and the witnesses they expect to call so you can determine whether you might have a conflict of interest. We'll start with the prosecution. Deputy State's Attorney Arlene Powell, you may address the jury panel."

After the introductions, Judge Bronner excused those jurors who had conflicts of interest, medical problems, or unbreakable important commitments. Ten panelists were excused, the remaining twenty-five were escorted back to the jury assembly room with a caution from the judge not to take episodes of Matlock, L.A. Law or Perry Mason too seriously.

"All right, marshal, bring in the first panel member, Irene McDonald." A medium height brunette, 49 years old, light complexion, with a nervous smile was escorted to the witness chair and sworn in by the clerk. The attorneys each had a copy of the prospective juror's questionnaire which gave their basic background and information and their experience or lack of it with the court system.

Judge Bronner turned to Mrs. McDonald and said "There are only three requirements: First, you must relax. This is a painless process, I assure you. I'm not a dentist, but I can still make that promise." Mrs. McDonald smiled back at him.

"Secondly, you have to speak up so everyone can hear you. Be sure you speak into the microphone."

"Finally, you must answer audibly, whatever it is you want to say. As I've said there are no right or wrong answers. The court stenographer cannot pick up a nod. You have to answer each question audibly even if you nod, too."

Mrs. McDonald let out an appreciative laugh, and there was a chuckle from the spectators. It was the judge's way of helping her to relax.

"Oh, and one final point. This case, as I'm sure you know, has received a lot of publicity; so there's a larger crowd than usual; but don't let that bother you. There are no cameras, microphones or recorders in the audience; probably no one is going to publish what they say, and whether you are selected; and remember, much of the audience is more nervous than you are." He smiled at her again. She smiled again, coughed nervously but nodded her head up and down and said "O.K."

"We'll start the questioning with Deputy State's Attorney Powell." Judge Bronner said.

Arlene Powell rose and approached the witness chair. "Thank you, your honor. Mrs. McDonald, I'm Arlene Powell, a member of the State's Attorney's office and I represent the State. I'm going to ask you some questions. I'll try not to get too personal. If you don't understand any of the questions, please say so. If you would prefer not to answer a particular question, please let me know; or if you have any other problems, let me know that too. Basically what I want to do is just get to know you." She smiled. "Is that all right with you?"

"Yes, fine."

"I see that you're married and have two children. How old are they?"

Powell went through Mrs. McDonald's background and experience, asked her what she knew about the court system, whether she had any reason to be biased against prosecutors and then asked:

"Mrs. McDonald, did you vote for Governor Roberts in the last election?"

Mrs. McDonald looked startled, and before she could say anything, Attorney Kelly was on his feet "Objection, your honor. The question is both improper and irrelevant." There was a stir in the audience.

"Do you claim it, Ms. Powell?" asked Judge Bronner.

"Yes, your honor."

"All right. Mrs. McDonald, would you excuse us for a few minutes? The lawyers and I have to take up a legal point which you really shouldn't hear. It'll just take a few minutes. Marshal, would you escort the panelist back to the jury assembly room? Mrs. McDonald, please don't discuss the questions with the other panel members."

As soon as the door closed behind her, Judge Bronner turned to Kelly and said "Mr. Kelly, what is your objection?"

"Well, your honor, whether the juror voted for Governor Roberts or not is irrelevant. Whether she believes he's been a good Governor or not has nothing to do with whether she would be a fair and impartial juror. Secondly, it's improper. We still have secrecy of the ballot, and, therefore, it might even be unconstitutional; and where does it end, is the next step to ask whether she agrees with him on certain issues?"

Judge Bronner looked down at both attorneys, "Before I hear from you Attorney Powell, I want you both to know that many years ago, in the 60's, I was attorney for the plaintiffs who claimed that the mandatory party lever on the voting machines was unconstitutional; that, among other things, it destroyed the secrecy of the ballot because a voting machine tender could hear the clicks of the pointers being moved up and down and would then know that the voter had split his or her ticket. The machine tender was usually a member of the local party's Town Committee. That person would then know if a voter very active in the party had strayed from voting for all of that party's candidates. That vote was no longer secret. However, a three judge panel in Federal Court in Hartford told us there was no constitutional right to secrecy of the ballot as strange as that may seem. So, I cannot consider your objection, Mr. Kelly as to the issue of denying secrecy of the ballot.

Ms. Powell, would you care to speak on the other parts of his objection?"

"Yes, your honor. I think the question is relevant. If a juror voted for Governor Roberts, then that would indicate that she approves of him and that could influence her decision in this case in his favor. The state, and the defense have a right to know what bias she may have."

"Attorney Powell. The fact that she voted for or against him in the last election does not necessarily indicate whether she would do so now. Secondly, does that mean you're going to challenge for cause every juror who voted for him, and then Mr. Kelly will challenge for cause every juror who voted for his opponent? If I go along with that, then the only jurors we could accept are those who didn't vote at all and isn't that juror suspect for failing to exercise his or her civic duty to vote; unless, of course, he or she had a sudden heart attack on the way to the polls. Isn't that a little extreme?"

"Of course, it is your honor; but, I'm not suggesting a challenge for cause. I'm talking about having that information about the juror to determine whether or not to exercise a peremptory challenge."

"It seems to me you would use up your peremptory challenges very quickly, and thus, it would speed up the jury selection process which would be good. However, using that as a factor and using up those challenges too quickly would harm our ability to obtain a fair and impartial jury. It seems to me it would do more harm than good. It is irrelevant. The objection is sustained."

"But, your honor, this question. . . . ."

Bronner interrupted her, "I've already ruled, Attorney Powell. Counsel, you should both be aware of the way I'm going to conduct this trial.

Under our rules, you may argue an objection only if the court requests or permits it. I can rule immediately without argument. I generally do allow it; but, one bite of the apple is enough. When I do allow argument, you will each have one opportunity to speak and only one. If you can't make a cogent argument the first time and if I can't understand it on the first go around generally, then we're all in trouble.

When Mrs. McDonald returns, the court will ask her a question that I believe will cover the situation. As to the next juror, you may ask a similar question. Marshal, please bring the panelist back in."

Mrs. McDonald was back on the witness stand. Judge Bronner turned toward her. "As we all know, the defendant is a public figure. He's the Governor of this state. Now, you either voted for him or his opponent or not at all. I don't want to know what you did. What I want to know is however you voted or not, whether you believe he has been a good Governor or not, whether you agree or disagree with him on various issues, can you set all that aside in considering your decision in this case; in other words, can you consider solely the evidence presented in this courtroom in making your decision as to a verdict in this case, and put aside any other feelings you may have? If you can or cannot, say so. No one will criticize you for either answer. We just want you to answer honestly."

"Yes, I can, your honor."

"Thank you, Mrs. McDonald. Attorney Powell, you may proceed."

After that, the jury selection process moved ahead quickly.

Courtroom observers who had seen Judge Bronner in action over the years believed he was ideal for this case. He had a warm, friendly and sometimes humorous personality. He remained calm, never seemed to succumb to pressure and was always in complete control of the courtroom. At age 62, he was a 15 year veteran of the trial bench. High profile cases did not seem to phase him. He was a graduate of the University of Connecticut and its School of Law. He was married and had two grown children. He was 6'1", heavy set with thick black hair brushed back with some strands of white. He was of medium complexion, wore light brown glasses and smoked a pipe when not on the bench. He usually dressed conservatively. He was considered a scholar of the law and frequently recalled testimony more accurately than the attorneys. He was decisive, often ruling from the bench. He tended to move the proceedings along as quickly as possible. "Exactly what is needed in this case," opined several attorneys who had appeared before him several times.

26

Becky was seated at a table in the Fish Tales restaurant on Main Street in Old Saybrook, a quaint and historic town on the Connecticut shore located four towns west of New London. It was the middle of winter so this shoreline community was relatively quiet without the huge vacation crowd that swelled the population during the summer. Becky was following up on one of the leads her husband, Ben, had given her. She had called Attorney Tom Price, the former representative who had been blown off by Anne Tremaine. The rumor Ben had mentioned had grown into reality. Price had been arrested for harassing and stalking Anne Tremaine in early December.

Price had accepted her invitation to lunch, and Becky had arrived a half hour early to make sure she could get a table in a corner in the back of the restaurant. She felt like a member of the mob sitting with her back to the corner. She wasn't protecting herself from being shot; she just wanted to be able to see Price when he came in.

Becky was just starting on her second fuzzy navel when a tall heavy-set man in a large overcoat approached her table. "Becky?" he asked.

"Yes" she replied as she stood up and extended her right hand which then almost disappeared in Price's strong handshake. "I'm Tom Price" he said. Price looked like an alcoholic he was reputed to be. His beer belly hung over his belt, he was florid-faced, and his shirt collar was too tight around the neck. He was perspiring even though it was only 20 degrees outside; but he was friendly. He sat down and with a warm smile he said "This must be pretty important to bring you all the way down here on such a cold day," he paused, and motioned to the waitress "and speaking of cold, I need something to warm me up in a hurry. A scotch on the rocks" he said to the waitress. "Chivas Regal, please; and, what the hell, make it a double" he grinned.

"Don't worry" he looked at Becky. "I may be an alcoholic, but I can hold that. How about you? Would you like another?" he pointed to her drink.

"No thanks, this is already my second."

"So" Price said, "you're investigating the death of Anne Tremaine, and you were hired by the Governor to get him off. Right?"

Becky flushed and started to say something, but Price kept speaking. "Roberts isn't a bad guy. I got along well with him even though we're on opposite sides of the political fence. The only thing we have in common, really, is that we're both castoffs of Anne Tremaine" he laughed.

"There is a difference" Becky said. "Governor Roberts' affair with her was many years ago, and yours was as recently as last year. Also, he's a happily married man" she said.

"And I'm not" he replied. "Connie and I have had our problems. We're still married, but not happily at this point. Having an affair with another woman, being arrested for pursuing her, and being an alcoholic has put a strain on our marriage, I must admit" he said.

Becky stared at him.

"All right" he said, "that's probably an understatement" he added with a sheepish look on his face. "As a state legislator, I was pretty well known, and still am; and this is a small town. Connie's embarrassed by all this; and I understand that. It is my fault. But we're still trying to make it work. We have three wonderful children, and now that I'm no longer in the legislature, I'm spending more time at home trying to make it up to her." Price let out a long sigh.

They had ordered their lunch. By this time he was nibbling on french fries having finished a hamburger club sandwich. Becky was relieved when he ordered a black coffee. She wanted him to stay with her on this. She was still eating her bluefish. He had warned her. "This may have been caught near here, but probably last summer. It's been frozen since then. It's certainly not fresh."

Nonetheless, Becky found it delicious. "Besides," she told him "when I'm at the shore, winter or not, I'd feel guilty not ordering fish."

"Look" Price said as the waitress finished clearing away their plates, "Let's cut to the chase."

"Yes, I had an affair with Anne Tremaine. It started during the '91 legislative session. It was a very close and meaningful relationship, at least on my part. That's why I stayed overnight so often during the legislative session. I told Connie I was too tired to drive home, that I was staying at a hotel or a colleague's home in the area. I did drive, but it was only to Anne's condo in West Hartford. Not every night though. I knew she was seeing other members of the legislature."

"Did that bother you?" Becky asked.

"Of course it did, I was jealous, but I knew if I became possessive, she'd cut me off. I was in love with her. At least I thought I was, and I didn't want to lose her."

"In love or obsessed?" Becky prodded.

"In retrospect, I was probably obsessed, maybe like a teenager with the first girl friend he went to bed with; but, no it was more than that. Becky, you have no idea how beautiful she was. She was warm, full of fun and incredibly thoughtful and understanding. I suppose you could say I was addicted to her. Having sex with her was pure ecstacy. I couldn't get her out of my mind."

"I knew she was using me. I was chairman of the General Law Committee, and I helped get some of her bills through; and underneath it all, I knew she was sleeping with other legislators. That's why she was so successful as a lobbyist. I knew it, I was jealous, but I couldn't stop. She was so, so . . . . alluring. That's the best word I can think of. It's almost as if she cast a spell over me. When I was with her, I couldn't think of anything else. It was like heaven."

"Who else was sleeping with her?" Becky asked.

"I don't really know" Price replied. "She wouldn't talk about it. She tried to keep it a secret, and she pretty much succeeded. There were a lot of rumors, but the only one I'm pretty sure of is Jim Spaulding. He's a senator from Litchfield County, and one night I saw his car parked near her condo. It was after midnight."

"What broke it up?" Becky asked.

"I guess the real cause was my drinking. Last summer I was in an accident and I was arrested for drunk driving here in Old Saybrook. It was all over the papers and on radio and TV. I pleaded guilty and served thirty days. Also, I had spent so much time with or thinking about Annie, I brushed off my constituents. I didn't show up for speeches or meetings, and I hardly campaigned. It wasn't a very pretty picture, and the voters let me know it on election day. I really screwed things up."

"Then, what happened?" Becky asked.

"As soon as I lost the election, Annie blew me off. She discarded me like a piece of garbage. She wouldn't talk to me, she hung up on me, she didn't reply to my letters. When I tried to see her, she slammed the door in my face. When I persisted, she threatened to call the police. You see, once I was no longer a state representative, I was no use to her; so, she dropped me." Price said with a mournful look on his face.

"Just like that?" Becky said.

"Just like that" Price replied. "But, I couldn't take no for an answer. If someone had asked me what I didn't understand about the word no, I would probably have said I don't believe it. You see, I was still obsessed with her. I kept trying. I left messages on her answering machine. I wrote her letters. I followed her, usually by car. If she was having dinner with someone I'd maneuver to get a table near her. I even put roses at her door and on the windshield of her car. I was like a puppy dog seeking my master's favor. I just couldn't believe it was over."

"What finally ended it or did it end?" Becky asked.

"Oh, it ended all right: abruptly, when I was arrested for harassment and stalking her. I pleaded guilty and was given a suspended sentence. I'm on probation, and if I were to go near her, I'd have to serve time in jail. Of course, that all ended when she died. It's ironic though. I was the author of the stalking bill when I was in the legislature. How do you like that?" he asked with a weak grin.

"Were you bitter?" Becky asked.

"Yes, at first, but it got less and less, especially after she died."

"I know what you're thinking" Price continued. "I had a perfect motive for killing her. A lover spurned, a lover so obsessed with her that he continued to harass and stalk her; and then I killed her because if I couldn't have her, no one else could."

"It works for me" Becky replied.

"Well, I hate to disappoint you, to burst your bubble, but I didn't kill her. I have a perfect alibi to prove it" Price said.

Becky looked surprised.

"On Christmas Eve, early Christmas Eve, I was in another accident. I was arrested for drunk driving again, and was held overnight at the state police barracks in Westbrook. Connie came to get me around noon time Christmas day. We had lunch at a diner on U.S. 1 which was the only place open on Christmas day. We ran into people we knew, and didn't leave there until 2 o'clock in the afternoon. I'm facing another DWI charge, and I'll probably go to jail again. My law practice isn't doing too well, but Connie is standing by me. That's what love is really about, isn't it?" Price said.

"You're right about that" Becky replied. "You probably don't deserve it, so she must really be in love with you to take you back. I'm not sure I would."

"Thanks!" he said. Becky started to get up. He held up his hand. "Wait a minute. So, this isn't a completely wasted trip for you, I'll try to help you out with some leads. I don't think Roberts did it either."

Becky sat down.

Price continued "I'd take a close look at Jim Spaulding. He had a reputation as a ladies man; but he was always talking about family values, ethics and morality. On the floor of the senate he used to talk about his family a lot. He used them as an example of the perfect family; how wonderful they are. He was holier than thou, a real conceited S.O.B. What a fraud. Maybe Annie was blackmailing him."

"You should also check out Annie's list of clients at the Secretary of State's Office. You'll find that one of them was Citizens Against Casinos. There was a bill in the legislature to permit a casino in Stratford, in the Lordship area just east of Bridgeport. The location is near Long Island Sound. They want to use hover craft to bring people in from Long Island and New York City. They're planning on an Amtrak special into the casino property from New York and Boston; and the Bridgeport airport is nearby in Stratford. There's a lot of money involved in this. The land is owned by Jack Thompson who's a general contractor with heavy equipment. He's also a friend of the Lieutenant Governor. Rumor has it that the casino would be owned by people from Atlantic City who are tied in with organized crime. Roberts is opposed to the casino, actually any more casinos anywhere in the state, and Annie represented a group of citizens from the Stratford area who are against this proposed casino. What better way to get rid of the main opposition than killing Annie and blaming it on the Governor. If Roberts is convicted, the Lieutenant Governor, Thompson's friend, would become governor" Price said.

"But, why would Annie be against the casino?" Becky asked. "There's not much money in it for her from a group like Citizens Against Casinos. It seems to me she'd rather be working for the people who are behind the casino. That's where the money is."

"You're forgetting one thing" Price replied. "CAC, short for Citizens Against Casinos, is just a group of average citizens, but there may be others behind them. Don't forget the Indians. Foxwoods and Mohegan Sun don't want any more competition. Foxwoods is already the biggest casino in the United States, and the Mohegans are starting to catch up. They're in the southeast part of the state, but they still draw from the greater Metropolitan New York area. They don't want that business cut off at Stratford which is much closer to New York. Besides, they have all the money Annie would ever want. And they're nicer to deal with. The Indians are not into crime or violence. I hear that once you go to work for the mob, they own you" Price added.

"Of course, I can't prove there was a contract out on Annie. A lot of this is rumor at this point. I'm sure you can check it out, and don't forget to talk to your buddies in the State Police about my arrest on Christmas Eve" Price said.

“I will” said Becky as she stood up and dropped thirty five dollars on the table. “This is on me” she said.

“Thank you” said Price. “Anytime you want another fish dinner, call me” he said. “If you make it during the summer, I should be out of jail and the fish will be fresh.”

“Will a fish story go with it?” Becky asked with a grin.

“Of course not” he said. “I never tell fish stories” he chuckled.

“Hang in there” Becky said as they shook hands again.

As she walked to her jeep, Becky pulled her scarf up to protect her face from the cold wind blowing in from the Sound. Even with her nose covered she could smell the salt water. She smiled, but she couldn’t totally shake the uneasy feeling that somehow she’d been had.

27

Later that night, Becky and Ben sat in their living room each holding a glass of Drambue. The fire in the fireplace had lessened considerably while Becky was describing her meeting with Tom Price. Ben had listened intently as Becky talked, interrupting only twice to ask questions.

When she was finished, Ben pretty much confirmed what Price had told her. "I've heard most of the same rumors, and what he said about the competing casino interests makes a lot of sense. As far as I know, there are no casinos in the New York area, and Stratford would be perfect for those New Yorkers who don't want to travel as far as Atlantic City. There are plenty of lobbyists around the Capitol promoting the bill that would allow a casino in Stratford. Ben leaned over and put his arm around Becky in what might be called a protective hug. "Honey, you'd better be careful on this one. If you're on the other side of the mob, this could be very dangerous. If it was a hit man who killed Anne Tremaine, they won't hesitate to get rid of you. Are you sure you want to do this?" Ben asked.

"I've thought about it, Ben. I can take care of myself. I didn't spend all that time as a state police officer for nothing. Besides, I committed myself to Brian and to the Governor. This is no ordinary case, and

I'd feel guilty if I backed out now. I've got a lot of people counting on me."

"How about taking someone with you, someone who knows how to handle a gun?" Ben asked.

"I work better alone, at least at this stage. I'm less conspicuous by myself, and besides what about all those sharpshooting medals I won? Have you forgotten about them?" she asked with a smile.

"No, of course not, but please take a pistol with you. You've reached the danger stage on this one; you shouldn't go around unarmed any longer." Ben replied.

"O.K. Now let's go to bed. It's late, the fire is just about out, and I need some warmth. I'll go upstairs while you put out the fire. The sheets will be cold, so hurry up." She smiled as she kissed him lightly on the lips.

28

The next morning was sunny and a little warmer as Becky drove up to the Stratford Town Hall on Main Street. She was wearing blue slacks, boots, a heavy sweater and a waist length white jacket. A small caliber pistol was in a holster taped to her right leg just above the ankle which was concealed by the boot. She also carried a 45 magnum affixed to the inside of her slacks at the rear and top just under the small of her back. It was covered by the loose fitting winter sweater she was wearing.

A few minutes later she was in the vault of the Town Clerk's Office where land records, maps and other documents were kept. Her jacket was hanging on the coatrack. Before her was a book opened to the recorded copy of the option to buy the land on which the casino was to be built. She had found it with the assistance of the Town Clerk, Joe Popple. She had told him she was "with the Governor's office," and he had been very helpful. People were constantly coming to the counter in the outer room, but she noted only two people, apparently lawyers, in the vault with her. They appeared to be doing title searches.

Becky noticed that the option agreement was between Thompson, the owner and Casino, Inc. of New York City. The Town Clerk had provided her with a map of the area. She was studying it when the Clerk returned accompanied by a tall, smiling man wearing a parka.

"Mrs. Brown, I'd like you to meet Councilman Jack Barnes" Popple said. "I've told him who you are." Becky and Barnes shook hands. "Call me Jack" he said.

"Jack has been on the Town Council a long time" Popple said, "and he's very familiar with the casino project. Jack agreed to take you on a tour of the site, if you'd like to go. It might help you to understand the situation a little better."

"That's wonderful," Becky replied with a smile. "I'd love to go" she said as she looked at Barnes.

"How about right now?" Barnes asked.

"Fine, let's go" she said "and thank you Mr. Popple."

"While you're gone, I'll get you a copy of the map" he said.

Barnes escorted Becky out the front door to his car, a green Mercury Sable. As he pulled away from the curb, he said: "As you know, it's located in the Lordship area of town. I thought we'd go up onto the turnpike, I-95, and get off at the Lordship exit just as if we were coming from out of town."

"Sounds good to me." Becky replied.

Barnes drove up onto the highway headed west and then got off at the Lordship exit and headed south toward Long Island Sound. They reached the Great Meadows, a huge vacant piece of land on the right hand side. "That's where it'll be built" Barnes said as he pulled over and stopped. As Becky got out of the car, she could see the sun sparkling off the water in Long Island Sound. The wind was picking up causing the high grass to sway in the breeze.

"The Bridgeport airport is just on the other side," Barnes said as he pointed to the opposite side of the Great Meadows. "They're planning to have a Penn-Central spur coming onto the property. Hovercraft will bring people to the shore on Lordship Beach. The people will come from Long Island and New York City," Barnes continued as they walked along the road toward the beach area.

"How do the neighbors feel about it?" Becky asked.

"Most of them favor it" Barnes replied. "In 1973, they were all opposed. A group of developers from Stamford and Norwalk tried to put a horse race track in here. The residents fought it. A local doctor headed up a group called CAT, Citizens Against the Track. Sound familiar?" He chuckled. "The Planning and Zoning Commission called for a referendum. It was like a political campaign. The developers lost by a wide margin and that ended that" he said.

Becky gave him a skeptical look. "What makes you think it'll go through this time?"

"That was 33 years ago" Barnes replied. "Times have changed. The economy is in worse shape than it was then. The defense industries like Sikorsky Aircraft, Norden and Allied Signal have all downsized. People need jobs, the town needs tax revenue. This project will be a big boost to the local economy; and maybe the town can make a deal for a cut of the gambling revenue just like Governor Weicker arranged to have the State get a percentage of the slot machines at Foxwoods."

"The State needs the revenue, too" Barnes continued. "I think we'll eventually be all right with the zoning and the State. The developers have lobbyists in Hartford. They know how to hit the right buttons here and there, and they have plenty of money behind them" he said.

"You mean mob money?" Becky said.

They were walking back to the car. Barnes stopped and held up his hand. "Not that I know of." His face was flushed "As far as I know, Casino, Inc. is a legitimate business. Besides, the state police will do a background check before they get a license."

As they reached the car, Becky thought: *It wouldn't be the first time the front men for the mob passed a background check.*

The two had been talking so intently that they hadn't noticed a repair truck parked on the grass at the corner where Lordship Boulevard turned west to run alongside the beach; nor did they notice the man inside with a long range camera who had been photographing them.

29

The members of the State Senate and House of Representatives were packed into the hall of the House in joint session. Television cameras were in the rear looking down at the Speaker's podium to which a more than usual number of microphones had been attached. Media interest was very high for this year's State of the State address of Governor Roberts. Connecticut State Police Troopers were patrolling the corridors. Security was high. More police were outside the building keeping protestors from Citizens Against Crime away from the actual entrance to the Capitol building and away from those entering the building who had come to hear the speech; the media, members of the legislature, state officials and spectators.

Inside, on the speaker's dais were Speaker of the House Barry Spivak of Farmington, the minister who would deliver the invocation, Lt. Governor Edwin Lincoln, who had quickly returned from vacation, and the president of the state senate, Cindy Roberts. The clock over the dais showed 7:00 p.m. as the speaker rapped his gavel.

"The House will be in order! Ladies and gentlemen, please take your seats. The crowd quieted down. Those who couldn't find seats sat on the steps on either side of the huge hall, carpeted in dark blue with seals of the State of Connecticut interspersed throughout.

"Mr. Speaker. Mr. Speaker" called out a tall middle aged man with white hair standing by his chair on the aisle about a third of the way up the stairs to the left of the speaker. The majority leader, Republican Bob Evans from Glastonbury was seeking recognition. The House was controlled by the Republicans, the Senate by the Democrats.

"The Chair recognizes the majority leader, Representative Evans from the 31st district."

"Mr. Speaker, I move that the House go into joint session with the Senate to hear an address by His Excellency, the Governor of Connecticut."

"Second!" said the representative from the 57th District, Ned Nicoli of Ellington.

"The motion having been made to go into joint session and seconded is now before us for a vote. All those in favor say aye."

"Aye" came from all of the representatives.

"All those opposed say "nay." The ayes have it; the motion is adopted." The Speaker banged his gavel twice.

He continued, "The senate having previously voted to go into joint session, and its members now being present, the Chair declares the Connecticut General Assembly to be in joint session." Again, he rapped his gavel.

"Please rise while the Reverend Walter Wheeler of the Congregational Church of West Hartford, Chaplain of the House, delivers the invocation."

Reverend Wheeler strode to the podium as everyone stood. "Let us pray. Almighty God, give these dedicated public servants, assembled in joint session, the wisdom and the strength to carry out their duties for the benefit of the citizens of this great State. Give them the courage to meet the great challenges that face them in the next five and a half months. May thy will be done. Amen."

As everyone sat down, Speaker Spivak resumed the podium:

"Ladies and gentlemen, it is my pleasure to present to you the President of the State Senate, the Honorable Cynthia Roberts of Hartford."

The members broke out in applause, many of them standing and cheering. Cindy Roberts' popularity crossed party lines.

Cindy waved to the crowd as the television lights reflected on her face. "Thank you. Thank you. Please be seated" she said. The crowd took their seats and quieted down.

"And thank you, Mr. Speaker, for giving me the opportunity to introduce the Governor, an honor that is usually yours."

"Ladies and gentlemen, I requested this opportunity to speak at this time because of the unusual circumstances in which our Governor, my husband, David Roberts finds himself; a sitting Governor who is accused of a serious crime. I have not said anything publicly regarding this charge up to now. David is restricted from saying almost everything about this case by order of the Court. I don't believe I have such a restriction, and I'm going to tell you what I think and what my heart tells me.

David and I have been married for a little more than a year, now; but we were close for a long time before that. Although we try to avoid political and legislative conversation, we do share our innermost personal thoughts with each other, holding nothing back. We are deeply in love, and I'll be the first to admit I'm not unbiased; but I can tell you, I know this man! I know his integrity, I know his compassion, I know his temperament and his character, and most of all I know his spirit, his deepest thoughts and emotions, and what is within his heart; and I can tell you he is not capable of harming anyone, under any circumstances; he values human life, and when he tells me he is innocent, I know he is telling the truth. David does not lie; he does not strike out physically or emotionally in anger or frustration or for any other reason; so I ask you not only to give him the presumption of innocence to which he is entitled, but I ask you to believe in his innocence. I do, with all my heart and strength. In this trying time, I ask for your help for him, for me and for the people of this state who sincerely need his leadership. He is my husband, he is my lover, he is my best friend; and he is an innocent man.

Ladies and gentlemen. I present him to you now; the Governor of Connecticut, David Roberts!"

Cindy wiped a tear from her eye as the crowd erupted in a standing ovation. She turned to the door on her right as two state troopers led the way into the television lights. Behind them came Governor Roberts waving and smiling his big infectious grin. He strode to the dais, embraced Cindy, and then they both turned waving to the crowd. It was a bipartisan audience, but it looked as if he had just accepted the nomination of his party at a political convention.

When the applause abated, he said "Thank you Madame President. You are wonderful; and if I haven't told you in the last hour, I love you!"

Again, the crowd applauded as he pulled Cindy forward and kissed her. She returned his kiss, waved again and sat down next to the speaker.

"And thank you, ladies and gentlemen, for your warm welcome. I'm sure most of your applause was for Cindy, but nevertheless, I would still like you to be on the present jury panel."

A smaller and more scattered applause began, and Roberts quickly spread his hands and lowered them to quiet the clapping just as it was beginning.

"This is serious business," he said "and I don't mean to make light of it, but this trial is a trying time for me and for the people of Connecticut who certainly are neither accustomed to nor pleased at having their Governor on trial for murder. So forgive me if I take a little pleasure in your applause whether for Cindy or for me and no matter for what reason because, believe me, I can use a little uplifting of the spirit at this time."

The crowd had again gone into a hushed silence. The audience was listening intently.

"I have been ordered by Judge Bronner not to say anything publicly about the trial except that I may insist upon my innocence. Well, I do that now, to you, and to the people of this state. I am innocent! And

I will be found innocent! The cloud over my head individually and as Governor will soon be gone. Now, let me get on to the business of the State of Connecticut, which is the real purpose of my speaking to you tonight." He continued quickly to stop the commencement of more applause as he held out his hands again in a way designed to forestall any further applause.

"Other than what has just been mentioned, this is not a trying time for Connecticut. The state of the state is good.

Our economic revival is moving ahead at a good pace. We have built upon the initiatives of my two predecessors, Governor Rowland and Governor Weicker; but more needs to be done in this and other areas. The problem of illegal drugs has not gone away . . . . ."

Roberts outlined his proposal to add 1 percent to the sales tax for drug education, and proposed spending substantial monies to beef up law enforcement agencies. He went on to portray a state that was succeeding but that needed to do more. His remarks which lasted 30 minutes, were well received. He was interrupted by applause 11 times as he spoke to specific issues and received a warm ovation as he concluded and he and Cindy left the chamber. Not surprisingly, during his speech, more applause came from the Republican than the Democratic side of the aisle. As they walked out the south entrance of the Capitol, they were besieged by the media. Janet Jones of Channel 8, New Haven, stepped forward toward Cindy, "Senator Roberts, didn't your remarks, although well intentioned, amount to prose version of the song 'Stand by your Man'?"

"Of course not," Cindy said a little sharply. "Even if David were not my husband, I would believe in his innocence because I know him and I know he is not capable of harming anyone."

"How about if he were just your lover?" someone shouted from the back of the crowd.

Cindy bristled. "I won't dignify that question with a response" she said.

"But you don't know who did do it, do you?" Jones persisted.

"No, but that doesn't change anything. If I knew the real killer or if the State's Attorney would do his job and find the real killer, this whole mess would be resolved" she said. "But not knowing who did it hardly means David did it."

"Governor Roberts" asked Tom Doyle of NBC News 30, "wouldn't you say that the applause in the beginning that was for you, not for your wife, was really an expression of hope in your innocence as Governor rather than an expression of belief in your innocence?"

"I don't know, Tom. I can't look into the people's minds. I'll leave that for you to judge if you can."

They had reached the door of the Lincoln. Cindy was already inside. Roberts turned with his back to the car entrance and faced the crowd. He held up his right hand, "Ladies and gentlemen, all I can say is that I am innocent, and when the trial is over, you will believe it, too. Thank you and goodnight." He got into the backseat, the door was closed and the car started to pull out. As it did, Allison Perry of Channel 3 turned to the camera.

"Well, there you have it. In an extraordinary and unprecedented occurrence, the Governor addressed the state legislature and the people of his state through television, and proclaimed his innocence on a charge of murder; and, also, unprecedented, the members of the General Assembly, when his wife, the president of the senate, introduced him and proclaimed his innocence, gave him a standing ovation. What it means is anybody's guess. However, it did seem to buoy his spirits. Allison Perry reporting live form the State Capitol in Hartford. Now, back to you in the studio."

As the car drove west on Capitol Avenue, David and Cindy looked at each other and said simultaneously, "You were wonderful." They laughed. "Shows we're still on the same wave length," David said with a grin.

"We're also an example of domestic tranquility," Cindy said as she leaned against him.

"And an example of political union" he said as he put his arm around her and kissed her.

She remarked, "Neither of us will be re-elected if we can't find better lines than those."

30

Becky was jolted forward in her seat as the Metro North train started to pick up speed for the 90 minute trip to New York City. She had parked her jeep in the nearby parking garage and then boarded the 10:30 a.m. train from New Haven. There was a light rain falling presenting an especially gloomy scene as the train moved out of the New Haven railroad yard. Becky's view somewhat matched her mood. The train picked up speed and she could both feel and hear the constant clickety-clack as the wheels passed over the tracks. The steady clickety-clack, clickety-clack put Becky into a thoughtful mood as she gazed out the window. *I really haven't accomplished that much* she thought. She reviewed the events of the last few weeks. Obtaining the statement from Mrs. Halleck on the Vineyard would be helpful. When she told Brian Kelly about it, he suggested that they take a look at Tony Cassella. "It's clear that Cassella has deliberately withheld what Mrs. Halleck told him. He may be part of the frame-up of Dave Roberts. He hates Roberts, and he's certainly not above taking a bribe. He also has a lot of connections on both sides of the law. I would certainly include him as a suspect. Check his bank records, his phone bills, do an FBI check on him. You might even consider putting a tail on him. But whatever you do, be careful. If Cassella suspects you're checking him out, he could become very dangerous.

They don't call him 'Tough Tony' for nothing" Kelly had said. Becky had called upon certain resources to obtain the bank and telephone records. She had hired another private investigator, Jeff Daniels, to lift a fingerprint from something Casella had touched, and through a friend in the state police she would have an up to date FBI check made. She also instructed Daniels to follow Cassella for a few days, day and night. "Watch yourself" she warned him. "He can spot a tail in an instant when you least expect it, and he can bring the police in anytime he wants to" Becky said.

The train had stopped at the Stratford railroad station, which brought Becky back to the present and why she was on the train. She was going into the city to have lunch with Chad Burnham of the New York Daily news. Burnham was a columnist for the news who was considered an expert on organized crime. The veteran reporter had also written several best sellers on the inner workings of the Five Families. His revelations had made headlines, but still the Mob continued to flourish. Becky had contacts with the organized crime division of the state police and a reporter for the Hartford Courant who knew Burnham. Through them, she had obtained an introduction and Burnham had agreed to meet with her.

By now they were traveling along the Gold Coast, lower Fairfield County which was considered the wealthiest area of the country and no doubt contributed to Connecticut consistently having the highest per capita income of the nation. The coastal towns of Fairfield, Westport, Darien, Stamford and Greenwich are backed inland by Easton, Weston,

Wilton and New Canaan. *Will the Mob invade the Gold Coast?* Becky wondered as the train crossed into New York State.

Becky hailed a cab outside Grand Central and arrived at Charlie O's Restaurant just west of Madison Square Garden where she was to meet Chad Burnham. It was the middle of the luncheon rush hour, but Burnham had reserved a table for two in the back corner of the dining room. He said he would be wearing a white carnation and a bow tie. Some said he was eccentric in his dress. He preferred the word "distinctive" which in a weak moment he confessed that it was "to distinguish himself from the hundreds of hacks who sit on their duffs and have the imagination of an owl." He was tall and good looking with a shock of dark hair Becky noticed as she introduced herself and reached forward to shake his hand.

"I hope you don't mind that I've already started" he said as he took a sip from his martini.

"No, of course not," she replied. "I'll have what you're having."

His face broke out into a grin. "Wise choice" he said. "Curry up to your source. That's an old newspaper trick" he added. "But don't forget, it's my tongue you have to loosen if you're going to get me to talk; so if you're not used to it, I wouldn't have too many martinis."

Becky laughed. "I know my limit; and besides, from what I hear, you're not as tough as you try to look" she said.

"Very perceptive" Burnham replied. "The image of the last of the oddball, hard drinking reporters is partially true, but mostly it's an act. I'm always hoping I'll be selected to play such a role in a hit movie."

Becky ordered liver and onions which was supposed to be a specialty of the house. Burnham ordered a corned beef sandwich on rye. “I’d have cabbage with it” he said “but I’m saving that for St. Patrick’s Day.”

Becky then launched into a detailed account of the murder of Anne Tremaine, her investigation and how she had come to the conclusion that organized crime was behind the development of the Stratford Casino. Burnham listened attentively without interruption except to order another martini. They had almost completed their meals by the time Becky finished talking.

“So, what is it you want to know?” Burnham asked. “Who’s behind Casino, Inc.?”

“Exactly,” Becky replied.

“I have no doubt it’s the Mafia” Burnham said.

Becky’s heart began to beat faster.

“But let’s call it what it is” Burnham continued. “You’ve used the terms organized crime and the Mob; but you seem to have been avoiding the use of the word Mafia” he said.

Becky started to say something, but Burnham held up his hand. “The Mafia does exist. With all due respect to the late J. Edgar Hoover whose opinion was both inaccurate and now certainly untimely, the Mafia is alive and well and was active in Hoover’s day even though he denied it. Whether you call it organized crime or the Mob, it is still the Mafia. I’m almost positive it’s the Mafia that is behind this proposed casino, financially, laundering of money, the overall control and planning and anything else that's needed, whether its muscle, bribery, or whatever."

Burnham leaned closer and lowered his voice. "The Mafia may well be responsible for the hit on Anne Tremaine. The way she was strangled is not a Mafia type killing. Usually, it's done with a firearm, normally with a silencer, or it could be running a car off the road or the use of a bomb in the car. However, if they're trying to get rid of Roberts, too, they don't want to make it look like a hit. They make it look like a crime of passion. Trying to frame Roberts would get their buddy, the Lieutenant Governor, into the governor's chair. If that's what they're trying to do, so far they've been pretty successful at it" Burnham added. "Can I prove it? No, at least not right now" he said.

"But, what about Casino, Inc.?" Becky asked.

"That's very hard to penetrate" Burnham replied. "These guys are masters at hiding behind dummy corporations at so many levels that it would take a genius in accounting and corporate law to work through the labyrinth they've set up, assuming you can get access to all of their records, which I doubt. It's a maze that's almost impossible to follow. They've done it this way for precisely that reason, to make their fronts look legal and their involvement untraceable" Burnham said. "They're masters at it."

Becky looked discouraged. "What can I do?"

"Forget trying to trace the source of the money. Even when the Feds are successful, it usually takes them at least two years before they can get information. You don't have that kind of time; and besides, even if you could prove the Mafia connection, that still doesn't prove it was a Mafia ordered hit on Anne Tremaine" Burnham continued.

They were both drinking coffee. Burnham looked at Becky with a smile. "That sad look you have is devastating, so before I see the tear drops fall out of those pretty eyes into your coffee, I'm going to promise to help you out." The smile returned to Becky's face.

"As you can see" Burnham said "I don't believe in all that gender sensitivity business. It may be politically incorrect to say a woman has pretty eyes, but I like to tell the truth." Burnham leaned back and chuck-led.

Then, he turned serious and looked Becky squarely in the eyes. "My success in writing about the Mafia has been based upon research, but mostly the informant type of research, getting to someone on the inside. I still have certain informants. Let me do some digging. Hopefully, I can learn who actually executed the hit and how we can prove it."

By this time, Burnham had paid the check, and was standing with Becky outside the front door.

She started to thank him, but he interrupted. "Not necessary" he said. "You come highly recommended from people in Connecticut to whom I owe favors; and besides, I've always been a sucker for a pretty face." He took her hand, leaned forward and kissed her on the cheek which made a perfect frame for the photograph being taken from across the street.

31

Becky arrived in New Haven at 4:30 that afternoon. She walked to her jeep on the third floor of the parking garage. She noted that it was pretty much deserted at that time. The start of the rush hour from the city hadn't yet arrived. She pressed her button to unlock the jeep. As she opened the door to get into the front seat, she was quickly grabbed from behind by two huge arms in a black cashmere coat. It was like being locked in a vice. She couldn't move her arms. The grip was so tight she thought she would pass out. Another man also in a black coat with his hat low over his face ran up to her and stuffed a ball of cloth into her mouth just as she was about to scream. Becky tried kicking at him. She landed one foot on his shin when suddenly she felt terrific pain on her head just above her right ear. Then, everything went black and unknown to her she slumped forward.

"That ought to keep her quiet" one of the men said. They closed her door and dragged her over to a large black Cadillac. She was put in the backseat. One of the men sat on either side of her. They put up the rear windows which were tinted. "Move it, Joe" one of them said to the driver.

When Becky woke up, her head felt fuzzy and her mouth was dry. She could still feel pain on the top of her head. It wasn't a sharp pain, but it still felt very sore. Her hands were tied in front of her, and she was blindfolded. She could feel the car slowing down as if it were pulling off the highway. She breathed in cigar smoke and started to cough.

"Hey, look who's awake." She heard a deep, raspy voice. "How do you feel. Mrs. Brown?"

The man on her right said: "Let me check the spot." He put two fingers on what had swelled into a bump on her head.

Becky leaned to her left. "Ow! That hurts" she cried. It brought tears to her eyes. She could feel the blindfold become a little wet.

"You're lucky," the voice on her right said. "It's stopped bleeding."

"Who are you? What am I doing here?" Becky asked.

"You'll know soon enough" the voice on her right said. It was higher pitched she noticed, and he didn't have an accent.

Becky started to cough again. "That cigar smoke is awful" she said. "Could I have some water?"

The voice on her left laughed. "Hey, Whadda you think this is, a stretch limo with a bar? This ain't no pleasure trip, you know!" he laughed again.

Becky felt the car go over some bumps. Suddenly fresh air came pouring in from the right side. "There, I opened the window a little bit. That should make you feel better. Now, stop complaining." the voice to her right said.

The air does help she thought. It was cold, and she could smell salt in the air.

"Don't worry Mrs. Brown" the raspy voice said. "Pretty soon you'll have all the water you want."

"Yeah," the other one said. "You'll have so much, you'll be swimming in it." He let out a loud laugh. "Hey, how about that?" he said, obviously pleased with himself.

"You're a riot, Tommy" came the sarcastic reply.

Becky sank back into her seat. She just shuddered. She was frightened. *Don't panic* she reminded herself.

The Cadillac came to a stop. The two men got out taking her with them. Becky's feet felt wobbly. She had worn a dress and heels with a winter coat, scarf and matching French style beret for her lunch with Burnham. They were on a wooden walkway, the men on either side of her, each holding on to an arm. She could smell diesel fuel, and hear the sound of a motor idling.

Suddenly they stopped and lifted her up by her elbows. "Here, take her" one of them said. A pair of strong hands grabbed her around the waist putting her down on a wooden floor. She could feel it swaying underneath her. She knew at once that she was on the deck of a boat. Someone guided her over to a chair. "Sit down and be quiet" he said.

She could hear two men jump onto the deck. The motor revved up, and she could feel the boat starting to move. It quickly picked up speed. She could feel the salt water spray as the boat plowed ahead.

Becky reached up to her blindfold, but her hands were roughly pulled away. "Not yet," a man's voice said.

Becky tried to collect her thoughts. *They're going to throw me overboard* she thought. *I'll freeze to death, but if they wanted to kill me, they could have killed me in the car, and then dumped my body; or* she shuddered. *What's that expression that goes with the Mafia? They'll put me in a cement box.* A chill went up her spine, and it wasn't because of the weather.

"O.K., we're here" she heard a voice say as the boat suddenly slowed down. She felt someone untying the blindfold. At first, she couldn't see. She rubbed her eyes, and then opened them again.

It was already dark out, but she could see the shore off to her right. She looked to her left, and could see the outline of land much further away. She was in a deck chair on a small cabin cruiser. The paint was peeling, the deck was bare. She noticed a green pennant attached to a pole on the bow. The boat had seen better days. She could see a heavy-set man with a dark blue hat and dressed in a P-coat. He was on top of the cabin at the controls of the boat. Two men in black jackets came toward her. One was tall with a mustache. The other was shorter and heavier with a hat pulled down as far as it could go. The taller one did the talking.

"C'mon, Mrs. Brown, this is it!" he said. They pulled her up and walked her toward the bow on the starboard side. They faced her toward the shore, and held her arms so she couldn't move. The boat was idling now, the pilot keeping her headed in a westerly direction parallel to the shore.

"You wanted to see where the casino's going to go?" The taller one pointed straight toward the shore. "That's Lordship" he said. "Happy now?"

Becky looked at a beach area behind which the land rose sharply to the top. "The Hovercraft will dock over there." He pointed to a spot about two hundred feet off shore. The dock will then slope up to the top. We'll even have golf carts for those who don't want to walk."

"Now that you've learned about the casino" he continued, "it's time for you to learn something else. Don't mess with us." He stared at her. "You have to learn to keep your nose out of other people's business." He stated.

Becky pulled back as much as she could from him.

"You're frightened aren't you? Well that's good. You should be." He continued.

"You have two choices, Mrs. Brown. First, you can sit here on the deck while Ralph here takes out his knife and shaves a little skin off your nose. The only problem is that the knife might slip from time to time as the boat rises and falls with the waves. But it will be a permanent reminder to you to keep your nose out of our business." He said.

"The other choice is for us to toss you overboard and let you swim to shore. We're a little under two miles from shore, it's the middle of winter. The water is cold, and so is the air, and you may freeze to death before you reach the shore. Which is it going to be, Mrs. Brown?" He asked.

Becky was already shivering but she replied: "I'd rather swim." she said.

"That's what I thought you'd say." the man replied. "You broads are all alike. You'd rather risk drowning than have your pretty nose messed up."

Suddenly, Mark yelled at him from the wheel house. "Sal, there's a Coast Guard cutter approaching in our direction. It's still about a mile or two away, but I can see its running lights."

"Well," Sal said. "I guess that makes our choice for us. We're going to have to toss you overboard." He grinned.

"You must be a pretty good swimmer being an ex-state cop. We're going to give you a fighting chance though, lady."

He yelled to Mark: "Take her in closer to shore and let me know when we're about a mile off shore."

The boat picked up speed, turned toward shore, and in a few minutes, Mark yelled back: "We're a little under a mile from shore."

"Okay, Mrs. Brown, here's your chance." Sal said as he picked her up, walked to the side of the boat and threw her into the water.

The shock of the water stunned Becky. When she surfaced, she kicked off her shoes and wiggled out of her coat and started to swim toward shore. She could see lights in the distance along the shore.

I have got to swim fast to keep my body as warm as possible and get out of this water as quickly as possible she thought.

The rain had let up, but the waters of the Sound were still choppy. Becky plunged ahead using the standard Australian crawl. She didn't want to develop hypothermia. Swells of the choppy water didn't help. As her face came out of the water, a wave crashed down on her covering her face. *God, that water's cold* she thought. She started to cough. *I must have swallowed some water; my stomach is feeling queasy again.* She coughed up some sea water and started swimming towards the lights. She kept going, lifting her arms forward one at a time and continuing to kick. She could feel herself moving forward. Soon her strokes became slower, she was breathing harder; her arms and legs were really aching.

It's a good thing I kept in shape after I left the state police she thought. *What was it John Mitchell said? When the going gets tough, the tough get going. I prefer Winston Churchill. Never, never, never, ever, give up. Great words. My mind is willing, but the body isn't* she thought, *but I'm not going to let the bastards wear me down.* She clenched her teeth, and, with a renewed burst of energy, she moved forward more quickly. Her arms were beginning to feel like heavy logs. Every time she lifted one, it felt as if she was lifting a heavy weight. Her legs were starting to feel numb. She looked ahead and saw that she was closer to shore, this gave her another burst of energy, and she moved forward again.

The increased activity had tired her even more. She could hardly lift her arms out of the water. Her strokes were shorter. She was barely able to keep her legs straight much less kick them up and down.

I don't want to die. She pictured her husband Ben, and her children, Adam and Alice, sitting on the couch in front of the fireplace, herself among them. *I don't want to leave you.* Her head dropped into the water.

It felt like lead, but she pulled it up startled by the cold water. She was starting to feel numb all over. She just couldn't keep it up. As she began to lose consciousness, she saw a bright light and Ben was talking to her. Her head fell below the water again. This time, it stayed there.

32

"Becky, Becky! It's me, Ben." Becky thought: *I know its you, Ben. Did you die too? Are we in heaven together?*

She dimly saw his face move closer. "Becky, its me, Ben, your husband." She felt a hand on her chin, and then another hand on her wrist. *That's not Ben's hand* she thought. "Who's that?" she asked. "Who's that?" Her eyes slowly opened and she saw a man in a white coat holding her wrist. *Everything is white. I must be in heaven, and Ben's with me. That other man couldn't be God, could he?* she thought.

Her mind was still foggy and her mouth was very dry. The man in the white coat moved closer. *He has white hair and a handsome face* she thought. *Just what I imagined God would be.* She began to feel happy and relaxed. She was in heaven and Ben was with her.

Then God spoke: "Mrs. Brown, you're in Yale-New Haven Hospital. I'm Dr. Friend. You were picked up last night by a cabin cruiser just off the coast of Stratford. You're a mighty lucky woman. They reached you just in time. Another five minutes in the water, and you wouldn't have made it" he said.

Her eyes were open, but her mouth felt like mush. Ben leaned down toward her. "Becky, its me, Ben. Welcome back to the living." he said as he kissed her on the cheek. Adam and Alice came over to her side of the bed. "Hi, Mom," Adam said. They both kissed her. "You gave us a real scare, Mom" Alice said.

Dr. Friend interrupted: "You're suffering mainly from hypothermia, exhaustion and a concussion. That's a nasty bump on the head you've got there." Becky lifted her right hand up and touched a large bandage over the place where she had been struck.

"You lost some blood" Dr. Friend continued, "so we gave you a transfusion. Your son was nice enough to donate a pint of blood." Becky breathed a sigh of relief.

"You had some hypothermia. The hypothermia is much better now." Dr. Friend said, "but rest, medication and warmth has pretty much taken care of that. It's now 10:30 p.m. You've been unconscious since about 10:30 last night, almost 24 hours. We've been feeding you intravenously" he said. "Now, it's time to get you on solid food. With more rest and a build-up of nourishment, you should be able to go home in a few days. You're a mighty lucky woman to have survived."

"There are some visitors here to see you" Ben said.

David and Cindy Roberts walked in followed by Brian Kelly. Ben introduced them to Dr. Friend and the nurse who was in the room.

The Governor walked over to Becky, took her hand and kissed her on the cheek. "How are you feeling?"

"I've been better" Becky smiled weakly.

Cindy moved closer on the other side. "We were absolutely frantic when you were reported missing," she said. "When Ben called us, we rushed down here and have been waiting outside scared to death that you wouldn't make it." She kissed Becky on her other cheek.

"I'm here, too, Becky," Brian Kelly said. "When you commit to something, you really go all out. You're the best." He leaned down to kiss her on the forehead. "Thank God, you made it," he whispered; his eyes moist.

"Thank you all," Becky replied. "I'll tell you what happened, and then you tell me what you've found out. Dr. Friend, could you and Nurse Pritchard (she had noticed the label on the front of her dress) excuse us for a few minutes?"

"O.K." Dr. Friend replied "but make it short. I don't want you to tire yourself anymore than is necessary." They walked out closing the door to the private room.

Becky sat up a little. Ben put a pillow behind her head and gave her a glass of water which she drank eagerly.

"This is the glass of water I was asking for since late yesterday afternoon. I see it doesn't have any salt in it" she smiled.

Becky described the events of yesterday afternoon and evening starting with her luncheon with Chad Burnham. Brian asked a few questions. No one else spoke.

When she finished, Kelly spoke up: "I don't think they were trying to kill you. The boat that picked you up had a green pennant on it, just like the one you described. They were probably following you at a little distance and made sure they picked you up when you went under. I think it was a warning to butt out of their business; a little strong,

I admit, but still no more than a warning. They were trying to scare you" Kelly said.

"Well, they certainly succeeded in doing that" Becky replied.

She continued "I'm not convinced it was just to scare me; but I suppose I wouldn't have made it if they didn't pick me up when they did. They were somehow testing me. I failed the test and would have died if they hadn't picked me up when they did."

"We're assuming it's the Mafia for all the obvious reasons" Roberts interrupted. "Beyond that we don't know much. The boat was probably stolen. We'll know more when they find it. I should say if and when they find it. And don't dismiss Cassella. He has the contacts to have arranged all of this."

Governor Roberts added "Becky, I think you should stop pursuing this lead. It's too dangerous."

"Well, I'll follow other leads" she said, "but I still want to follow up on whatever I hear from Chad Burnham" Becky replied.

Kelly started to talk, but Becky held up her hand. "Brian, I promise I'll tell you whatever I get and get your approval before doing anything with it. Besides, we need the name of the actual killer, not just a suggestion that the Mafia was behind it" she added.

Ben spoke up "I think that's enough, folks. We don't want to tire her any further. So, Becky we'll be . . . ." he stopped. Becky was already sleeping. As they walked out, Brian noticed a state trooper guarding her door.

33

There was a light snow falling as Cindy waited for Bobbie and Mark to arrive. She had called Bobbie and insisted that she and Mark meet for dinner at the Altneveigh Inn near the UConn campus. Cindy was a little tense as she waited in the foyer. It had not been easy to convince Bobbie and Mark to join her. She had met them before when she spoke at a sports award banquet at the end of last season after the women's team had won the NCAA title. Cindy had overcome their resistance by telling Bobbie it was urgent that they meet. Reluctantly, Bobbie had agreed to come.

Cindy was thinking back to her conversations with David. He had told her that her loss of her husband and son was an even bigger tragedy; and he understood how she felt about not having any of her own. But, still he was frustrated. His kids were alive, but he couldn't find any way to even talk to them much less resume a relationship with them.

Just then the front door opened and Bobbie and Mark came in stamping their feet to get the snow off. Mark was taller than Bobbie even though she was the basketball player. Mark had blonde hair with brown eyes and despite his glasses, he looked like an athlete. However, he was not involved in sports. He was a history major and planned to obtain a doctorate and then teach history. Bobbie's 5'8" frame was topped with red hair, similar to David's, with sparkling green eyes and freckles on her face and arms. She was a pre-med student. *Which one will be the politician?* Cindy wondered. *Probably Bobbie*, she thought, *but she'll have to learn to smile even when she doesn't want to, like now*. Cindy's warm greeting was not returned in kind.

They were seated at a corner table that Cindy had requested. Bobbie's back was toward the rest of the restaurant in the hope that people would not recognize her and interrupt their conversation. *This is going to be difficult enough as it is*. Cindy thought.

After some small talk about the weather and the basketball team, Cindy began: "Now, let me get to the reason I asked to meet with you. You father is facing the biggest crisis of his life. Being a POW was very difficult, but being charged with a murder he didn't commit is even tougher. He needs you to get through this."

Bobbie started to speak: "We don't want to hear . . ." Then Cindy put up her hand and cut her off.

"Please hear me out. What I have to say and show you will be a surprise. It may or may not change your mind about your father, but please, listen. It's time you became aware of certain things. What you do afterwards is up to you."

Cindy then went on to describe in detail David's Vietnam experience including the torture he had undergone as a POW. She showed the propaganda photo of his being paraded through the streets of Hanoi, a photo of the Hanoi Hilton and photographs of his arrival at Clark Air Force Base; including his gaunt look and his kissing the ground. She described his nearly two years in the Air Force hospital, and his problems after he got home and what led to the divorce. She told them that David didn't blame Carole because despite his protests, she really believed he was having affairs with other women. Cindy handed them each a thick package of papers. "These are reports from the psychologists, psychiatrists and therapists that were treating him during his relapse. In addition to describing his mental condition at the time, please note the findings that he was impotent at the time he was supposed to be having these affairs. It took forever to get these records from the psychologists and the VA. Some of the psychologists are still available. Note that there is an update saying that although they weren't sure at the time, they are now positive that the antidepressant drugs he took caused him to be impotent. He tried to explain this to Carole at the time, but she just took this as evidence he was worn out by his sexual encounters before he got home or that he no longer found her attractive or both. These copies are all certified, so you should have no problem with their authenticity."

Cindy handed them another set of papers. "These are court records of David's repeated efforts to enforce his rights of visitation. They also include a judge's written memorandum in which he described meeting with you alone in his chambers and his conclusion that, "It may well be that these children have been unfairly influenced by their mother despite my order not to talk disparingly of the father. She denies all of that although her bitterness is still there. However, there's not much I can do about that. Hopefully, when the children get older, they will be able to talk to their father and hear his side of what happened; but for now it's clear that at the moment, the children do not wish to be with their father. Under the circumstances I'm not going to order them to do it."

Cindy told them how much their father loved them. "He has real anguish in his face when he talks about how much he misses you. He was very unhappy that you didn't attend our wedding, but he understood why. Even though you were older, he thought that even if you wanted to come, you wouldn't out of sense of being disloyal to your mother."

She then went on to describe how David had gone to all of the basketball games to be able to at least get a look at them both, that he had stayed away from them out of fear of embarrassing them, and for the same reason he had insisted on not being introduced to the crowd. She told them, in case they didn't know, that David had continued to support them, including paying all their student trips to Europe and their tuition and expenses at college. "In addition," she said, "He sent you more than a hundred letters, cards and gifts and made many attempts to call you, but he heard nothing. Every time he tried to call you, Carole told him you were either sleeping, weren't feeling well or had gone out." *They appeared surprised by this*, she thought.

Bobbie and Mark asked a few questions. *They seemed to have warmed up to me* Cindy thought, *but they must be overwhelmed by all of this*.

"I'm not asking you to do anything now" she said "except, please, take these papers with you, read them and think about what you want to do. If you're willing to meet with your father, you'll see how much he loves you."

"I love my husband dearly; and although I'm doing this for him, I'm also doing it for you. This estrangement between you and your father has been a tragedy. It would be even a worse tragedy if it continued," Cindy said. She asked them to call her if they had any questions. They both had thoughtful looks, and when Cindy left, she still didn't know what their reaction would be.

34

It was just 6:00 p.m. as the Governor's Lincoln turned into the driveway of the Executive Mansion. Governor Roberts was greeted at the front door by Cindy who gave him a hug and a long kiss.

"What's that all about?" Roberts asked. "I'm not complaining, but . . . ."

"I'm a little emotional tonight" Cindy cut in. "I also have a surprise for you" she said as she hung up his coat and hat. "Come into the dining room for a minute."

They pulled out two chairs and faced each other. Cindy then told David, for the first time, about her dinner with Bobbie and Mark at the Altneveigh. David began to perspire. "Have you heard from them?" he asked nervously.

"Yes", Cindy replied. "Bobbie called me this morning. She and Mark read all the material I gave them. They talked it over, and they both want to see you." she said.

"Thank God," David said as he let out a long sigh. "When, when?" He asked. "Where?"

"As a matter of fact, they're both here now. They're in the library," Cindy said.

David's face became warm, his heart started to pound, and as he got up, his legs felt wobbly. He held onto the chair for support.

Cindy got up and put her hands on his wrists. She looked up at him anxiously: "David, are you all right? I don't want you to have a stroke or a heart attack over this. Why don't you sit down and do your relaxation exercises?"

David sat down. Cindy loosened his tie and unbuttoned the top bottom of his shirt. David closed his eyes, clasped his hands together against his stomach, pulled his hands inward and took a huge breath. Air filled his lungs. He held it for ten seconds; and then released his breath and his hands. He did this four more times.

"That's better," he said. He got up, pushed up his tie, took Cindy's hand and started toward the doors of the library. His heart was still pounding and his mouth was dry. As Cindy opened the door, he wet his lips. They walked in together. Bobbie and Mark got up from the couch and started forward. "Dad?" Mark said tentatively. Bobbie, Mark and David rushed forward at the same time. They met in the center of the room. David put his arms around both of them. Tears were streaming down his face. Bobbie put her left arm around David's waist and Mark put his right arm around David's waist. David leaned down and kissed Bobbie and then Mark. "Oh, my God" he said. "It's been so long." Bobbie reached up and kissed him. Mark put his head on his father's upper arm and hugged him.

"We're so sorry, Dad." he said as his tears fell onto his father's jacket.

Bobbie looked at David. She was trying to wipe the tears from her eyes. "We didn't know" she said. "We didn't know."

Mark added: "Mom has seen the medical reports and now believes you," he said, "and admitted she intercepted your letters and phone calls."

"Never mind that now. I love you both so much" David said as they continued to hug each other. "You don't know how long I've waited for this moment." He smiled through his tears. He looked at them. "The ache in my heart that's been there all these years is starting to fade." he said.

"We've got to make up for lost time" Bobbie said.

"Why don't you all sit down on the couch together and get reacquainted" Cindy said.

They looked at her. She was holding two handkerchiefs and was wiping the tears from her cheeks and her eyes. She was smiling through the tears. "We're all a little wobbly" she said. "I'll get us something to drink." As she left she placed a box of tissues on the coffee table.

35

"Marshal, bring in the jury." Judge Bronner had taken the bench promptly at 10:00 a.m., had congratulated the attorneys on their prompt selection of a jury of 12 and 4 alternates. Criminal juries in Connecticut usually consisted of 6 jurors and 2 alternatives except in murders cases when 12 and 4 were selected.

The media was in full attendance, but following Judge Bronner's decision, no cameras or recorders were in the courtroom. The national media was also in attendance with reporters from five major American networks as well as French, British and Canadian television, local stations from New York, Massachusetts and Rhode Island, and correspondents from the New York Times and other New York dailies, The Boston Globe, Philadelphia Inquirer and Washington Post. Both major wire services were outside. Cindy sat in the front row behind her husband, alongside David's two children Bobbie and Mark. Inspector Cassella was at the prosecution table, with the permission of the judge. His seat was pushed back a little. Becky was not in the courtroom. "I don't want them to know I'm on this case" she had explained.

"Welcome, ladies and gentlemen, to the first day of actual trial of the case for which you've been selected, the State of Connecticut vs.

Governor David Roberts. Will counsel please identify themselves for the record?"

Powell stood up. "Arlene Powell, Deputy State's Attorney for the State. Next to me is Assistant State's Attorney Donald Blair who will be sitting second chair on behalf of the State." Blair stood up, looked at the jury and then he and Powell both took their seats.

Kelly rose. "Brian Kelly for the defendant, Governor David Roberts who is here in court beside me. Roberts also stood up. I'd also like to introduce Attorney Barbara Allen of my office who will be second chair for the defense." Allen stood up, faced the jury and sat down.

"Ladies and Gentlemen," Judge Bronner turned toward the jury, "I believe this is the first time you've met Attorneys Blair and Allen. Is there anyone who knows them, knows of any connection with either of them? If you do, please raise your hand." The hands remained down.

"Both Miss Allen and Mr. Blair are single, never married and thus have no spouses. Is there anyone who thinks he or she might know their relatives, or in any way know of any connection with them that might cause you to be unable to sit on this jury?" There was no response.

"All right, madam clerk. Please administer the oath to the jurors and alternates." She proceeded to do so.

"Now, ladies and gentlemen, as you know, during the voir dire process, I tried to restrict the attorneys from asking you questions about principles of law that apply to this case. I said that the explanation of those principles are to be given by the court. That's what I will do now. At the end of the trial, I will give you full instructions on the law and how they apply to the evidence, commonly known as the judge's "charge to the jury." At this time, however, I will give you limited instructions on some of the more important principles, a so-called mini-charge."

Judge Bronner described the burden of proof that was on the prosecution, the presumption of innocence of the defendant, the ramifications of the fifth amendment, the difference between direct and circumstantial evidence, the relative credibility of police officers and other witnesses. He described the format and procedure of the trial; and then returned to the presumption of innocence.

"Now," he said to the jury. "I'm going to give you a little quiz the purpose of which will become clear in a few minutes. You, of course, see the defendant, Governor Roberts, sitting at the defense table. If you had to vote now and had three choices, guilty, not guilty or too soon to tell, how many would vote guilty?" No hands went up. "How about not guilty?" two raised their hands. "And how many would vote too soon to tell?" The remaining 14 raised their hands.

"All right, most of you voted too soon to tell. Well, you're wrong! What happened to the presumption of innocence? No evidence of any kind has been introduced; and as you may recall, I told you that a defendant is presumed innocent unless and until the prosecution presents evidence that proves to all 12 jurors that he is guilty beyond a reasonable doubt." Some of the jurors looked embarrassed, and there had been a few chuckles from the audience. Judge Bronner continued, "I apologize for what seems like a trick question; but it is designed to emphasize to you the real meaning of presumption of innocence.

As to your roles as jurors during the trial, let me say this. I have not sequestered you for this trial which I'm sure makes you happy. However, that carries certain additional burdens with it. Since you will not be sequestered, you will be allowed to leave at the end of the day. This will expose you to your family and friends, radio, television, newspapers and magazines. Their reports may well include evidence that is presented in court for me to rule on admissibility, and in most cases, you will be out of the room when that occurs. If the evidence comes in, there is no harm done; but if I rule it to be inadmissable, you should not be aware of it. The evidence may be ruled inadmissable for a variety of reasons; because it is hearsay or irrelevant, for example. The point is, under our rules, you should not hear evidence that is not admitted into evidence. If you watch the evening news, read the paper or even talk about it with your spouse or significant other you may well hear something you are not supposed to hear; and with all due respect to the media, which sometimes likes to edit or put their own spin on what happened, it may be misleading. You should not be influenced by the pundits who express their own opinions in the media. You should not discuss this case with anyone, including your family, friends and even your fellow jurors at this time. Do not listen to what someone else says about the case. You are to decide this case only upon what you see or hear in this courtroom. So, I instruct you not to read newspapers or magazines or watch television, listen to the radio or pay attention to any groups who are demonstrating or promoting one side or the other. You may well see some of that outside this building. To protect you as much as possible on this, I have instructed Court personnel to have you park in a certain place which will be guarded. You will be escorted to and from your car and demonstrators will be kept away from those areas.

The reason I ask you not to expose yourselves to these things is so you will not inadvertently see or hear something you should not. If, for some reason you are exposed to such information, please ignore it and try to put it out of your mind. I realize all of this will be difficult, but believe me, it is better than being sequestered. In fulfillment of your oaths as jurors, I asked you to decide this case only upon what you see and hear in this courtroom. I urge you to follow these instructions closely to the best of your ability. If anyone attempts to provide you with information or opinion, please let me know and we'll remedy the situation.

It's now a little past 11:30, so we're going to take our midmorning recess at this time. Ladies and gentlemen, I'm going to excuse you now for 15 minutes. When you return, the state will begin to present its evidence. In Connecticut, the attorneys do not make opening statements in a criminal case. Recess Marshal." Judge Bronner got up from the bench and left the courtroom.

36

The prosecution case had started at 11:45 that morning with testimony from the two Hartford Police Officers who had arrived at the condominium after Anne Tremaine's sister had discovered her body and called 911. They described the scene, how they had searched the unit and the area around it to make sure no one was there, then secured the area and talked briefly with her sister.

When court resumed at 2:00 p.m. after the luncheon recess, the Deputy State's Attorney called the medical examiner, Dr. Steven Washington to the stand. Powell took him through his credentials and qualifications as an expert. Through him, she established the cause of death as asphyxia, strangulation, and the time of death, Christmas morning at 7:15 a.m. She then asked him to identify the fingerprints found on the two glasses with the Governor's seal on them. He said they were those of Anne Tremaine and Governor Roberts. She then asked him about the letter from Governor Malone to Governor Roberts dated December 23rd.

"Whose fingerprints did you find on that letter, Dr. Washington?" she asked.

"Governor Malone, his secretary, Lisa Mahoney, Governor Roberts and his secretary, Joanne Ward."

"Now, Dr. Washington, it's true that you're a leading expert on DNA evidence as a forensic scientist, isn't it?"

"Yes."

"Please explain DNA to the jury. I feel compelled to ask this question now since juries seem to expect to hear about it in every murder case."

"DNA stands for the molecule of heredity. It can be taken from blood, semen, hair roots, bone and saliva whether the person is living or dead. That molecule contains each person's unique genetic code. We usually use what is known as the PCR test for quick results."

"Did you find any blood at the crime scene, Dr. Washington?"

"No," Washington said.

"As a matter of fact, you didn't find any DNA evidence at the crime scene that you could use, isn't that true?"

"No," Washington said.

Powell looked a little taken aback. "You mean, no, there was no useful DNA evidence at the crime scene?"

Washington looked at her strangely, "No, that's not what I said. My no was in answer to your question as to whether it was true. I did find DNA evidence at the crime scene. I included it in the Addendum to my report."

Powell looked frustrated, "May the jury be excused for a few minutes, your honor?"

"Of course. Ladies and gentlemen, would you please step into the jury room for a few minutes? Thank you." The jury filed out.

Judge Bronner looked at the attorneys, "What is your point, Attorney Powell?"

"Well, your honor, this is the first time I'm aware of any Addendum to Dr. Washington's report. My copy does not have an addendum; and I'd like a few minutes to look it over to see whether I want to question him on it."

"Wasn't this supposed to be provided to defense counsel under discovery? Attorney Kelly, do you have a copy of the addendum?"

"No, I don't, your honor."

Judge Bronner turned to the witness. "Dr. Washington, would you please hand me your report with the addendum?"

"Certainly, your honor." He reached up and gave it to the judge, who read the one page addendum.

"Interesting," he said. "You should both look at this, counsel. Why don't you read it together. There's apparently only this copy."

Attorney Powell said, "May I approach, your honor?"

"Certainly." She walked up to the bench, took the addendum from Judge Bronner and then sat down next to Kelly. They read it silently. A broad smile broke out on Kelly's face. Powell's face was grim. *I'd better bring this out before Kelly does*, she thought; *and the jury has already heard there's DNA evidence. They'll be expecting it, and if I don't bring it out, they'll think I'm hiding something.*

"I'm ready to continue, your honor." she said. She thought to herself, *I don't know who to shoot, someone in my office or Washington's office.*

The jury re-entered the courtroom and took their places in the jury box. Washington had remained on the witness stand.

"What DNA evidence did you find at the crime scene?" Attorney Powell asked in a slightly lower tone.

"I found saliva on the victim's chest. I tested it against saliva from the victim. I took a sample from the victim's mouth."

"And, what did you find?" she asked dully.

"That it didn't belong to Miss Tremaine."

There was a stir in the courtroom and a few gasps.

"So, I concluded that it belonged to someone else." he said.

"There's no question pending, Dr. Washington." she said. *Why does he have to volunteer that*, she thought.

She scanned the addendum again. There was nothing about a time. She decided to take a chance. "But, you can't say exactly when it dropped onto her chest, can you, Doctor?"

"No, I can't." he replied. She breathed a sigh of relief. *It's a good thing he didn't say it was at the time of the murder. It would have been in his report if he could have pinned down the time. At least the jury will think it could have been there from before the murder*, she thought. She decided to end on a high note. "Dr. Washington, you are positive that governor Robert's fingerprints were on the two glasses and on the letter from Governor Malone stamped into the Governor's office on December 23rd?"

"Yes, I am positive about that."

Kelly thought *I could have objected as a leading question, but it would have only brought more attention to it.*

"Your witness" Powell said to Kelly.

Kelly approached Dr. Washington.

"Doctor, did you test the other glasses in the cabinet for fingerprints?"

"Yes, I did."

"Whose fingerprints did you find on them?"

"Those of the maid . . . . . ."

"Just her, nobody else?"

"That's correct."

Kelly pressed on. "Neither Anne Tremaine's nor Governor Roberts' fingerprints were on those other glasses, were they?"

"No, they weren't, just the maid's."

"Let's talk about the other glass in the cabinet, the one with Miss Tremaine's and Governor Roberts' prints on them. Were the maid's prints on that one, too?"

"No, they weren't."

"And wasn't there a residue of liquor in that glass?"

"Yes, there was. It was scotch."

"Thank you Doctor that was going to be my next question." *Why did he have to bring that out. I would have let it go, most people who know Dave, know he drinks scotch. But I suppose Arlene would have brought it out anyway*, he thought.

"Now, Doctor, were all the other glasses clean except for the maid's prints?"

"Yes."

"Isn't it fair to say then, that you could reasonably conclude from this evidence that the maid had washed all the other glasses and placed them in the cabinet but did not wash or place in the cabinet the one with the Governor's seal on it, the one with Miss Tremaine's prints and the Governor's, but not those of the maid?"

"Objection your honor. Calls for speculation." Powell stood up. Kelly started to talk.

"Never mind, Attorney Kelly. Dr. Washington is an expert witness. Objection overruled. You may answer the question." Judge Bronner said.

"Yes, it is reasonable to conclude that" Washington said.

"Doesn't it seem strange to you Doctor that all of the other glasses were washed and this one," he pointed to Exhibit F, "the glass we're talking about, State's Exhibit F, was put in there dirty, with liquor still in it?"

"Objection."

"Overruled."

"Why would Miss Tremaine or Governor Roberts do such a thing?" Kelly asked.

"I have no idea" Washington responded.

"Could it have been someone else?" he asked.

"I don't see how. That person's fingerprints would show up."

"Unless the person used a glove. Isn't that true?"

"Yes, that's possible."

"Objection, your honor. There is no evidence that someone else put that glass there."

"I didn't say there was. I was only trying to elicit from this witness whether someone could have used gloves to put it there without leaving fingerprints." Kelly said.

"Objection sustained. The jury will disregard the last question and answer."

Kelly smiled. He knew the jury had gotten the message.

"Now, Dr. Washington. You can't tell how that letter from Governor Malone got there, can you?"

"Well, since it was on the floor near the toilet, it may have dropped out of someone's pocket while that person was sitting on the toilet."

"But, you don't know that for a fact do you?"

"No, I don't."

"And you have no idea when Governor Roberts or anyone else for that matter, had the urge and necessity to go to the bathroom?"

"Of course not" Washington replied as laughter swept the courtroom.

"Now, Dr. Washington. Did you try to match the saliva on the victim's chest with everyone who might have been near her at the crime scene?"

"Yes, I took samples of saliva from her sister and from the police officers who had been in the room."

"How about Inspector Cassella and State's Attorney Smith?" Kelly asked.

“They arrived after I had already taken the sample.”

“Did any of the samples of her sister or the officers match that of the victims?”

“No.”

“Why didn’t you test Governor Roberts’ saliva?”

“No one asked me to.”

There was a stirring in the courtroom.

“How about if I asked you?”

“Generally, I do this only for the State, but certainly I would do it if the State didn’t object.”

Attorney Powell stood up. “No objection, your honor.”

Kelly continued. “Will you do it then if I make Governor Roberts available for a sample?”

“Of course.”

“Thank you.”

“Now, Dr. Washington. You said in answer to Attorney Powell’s question that you couldn’t tell the exact time the saliva dropped onto the victim’s chest. Is that right?”

“Yes.”

“Well, let’s try to narrow it down a little. It certainly wasn’t after you took a sample, was it?”

“No, it wasn’t.”

“And it wasn’t after the murder because you checked Anne’s sister and the officers who had been there after the murder and before you took the sample, and no one of them matched. Correct?”

"Yes."

"And, you don't know of anyone who was there after the murder before Anne's sister discovered the body, right?"

"Yes."

"So, as far as you know, the saliva was left there either by the murderer or sometime before. Isn't that correct?"

"Yes."

"All right, let's talk about the time before the murder. Assume she had gone out Christmas Eve, to dinner, dancing or whatever, could she have gotten saliva on her then?"

"Well, no, not if she was dressed. The saliva was found between her breasts and lower than her nipples; so she would have had to be undressed for it to land there; at least from below her breasts upward."

"Could it have landed higher up and dribbled or flowed downward?"

"No, because I found no trace of saliva higher up, and there would have to have been some of it coming from above where I found it. Also, the saliva was a very small puddle as if it had been dropped down from above her onto that spot. Of course, she could have exposed her breasts if she had had sex Christmas Eve or morning before the murder. In other words, the saliva could have been there before the murderer arrived."

Powell smiled for the first time. Kelly did not smile, but pressed on.

"How about if she took a shower after she had sex, wouldn't that have washed off that saliva and left her saliva free just before the murder?"

"Objection, your honor. There is no evidence she took a shower Christmas Eve or morning." Powell was on her feet.

"Objection sustained." Judge Bronner said.

"All right" said Kelly. "Did you find any evidence that she took a shower?" Kelly figured he had nothing to lose; and the prosecution hasn't even established that she had sex with anyone.

"Yes" Washington replied. Kelly chortled inwardly.

"How and when?" he asked.

"My examination of the shower stall revealed pieces of the victim's hair. They were still wet, and there was still a small amount of water on the floor."

"What does that tell you as to time, Doctor?"

"That she took a shower, probably within the last 36 to 48 hours before I examined the shower stall. She could have taken a shower anytime Christmas Eve or morning."

"But she would have had to be naked from the waist up with someone after her shower in order for the saliva to be there, correct?"

"Yes."

"Did you find any traces of semen in her, Doctor?"

"No, but she could have washed it out or used a condom."

"Is it fair to say that in order for saliva to get on her chest where you found it, other than from the murderer, she would have to have her breasts, the area of saliva, exposed to someone else after the last shower she took?"

"Objection."

"Overruled, he can answer."

"Yes."

"What if she was standing up or even sitting up after the saliva got there?"

"The saliva would have dropped down below her breasts, at least some of it; it would not have remained in a puddle."

"Did you find any traces of saliva below the spot you found?"

"No."

"When you saw her for the first time, were her breasts fully exposed and was she lying on her back in a position where the saliva could not flow down below her breasts?"

"Objection, your honor. It's beyond the scope of my direct examination and it's a compound question."

"Attorney Powell, you brought out the saliva on direct. As to its being compound, the witness can say "no" if any part is not true. Objection overruled. The witness may answer the question. Do you remember the question, Doctor?"

"Yes, your honor. The answer is yes. Her breasts, and her abdomen were fully exposed, she was lying on her back, and the saliva could not move down."

"And what does that mean?"

"That the saliva could have only gotten on her chest while she was in the position in which she died. It would have to be the saliva of the person who killed her."

"Thank you doctor."

There was a murmur in the courtroom. Judge Bronner turned to Attorney Powell. "Any redirect?"

"No, your honor."

She could have tried to repair the damage, but Kelly had already preempted most of her questions. He focused on the window of opportunity for the saliva to have been placed there before the murderer got there. He suggested that she could have had sex late the night before or very early Christmas morning and let her lover leave without getting up and sleeping on her back throughout the night or early morning. However, the jury looked a little skeptical throughout the testimony.

Dr. Washington was excused.

Then Kelly said, "I have a motion to be heard, your honor."

"Ladies and gentlemen, it is now 4 o'clock on a Friday afternoon, and I have a legal matter to take up with counsel. So I'm going to give you an early weekend and excuse you at this time; remember my admonitions to you."

The judge repeated his admonitions and then wished them a good weekend. When they were gone, he turned to Attorney Kelly.

"Your honor, I move to strike all of Dr. Washington's testimony because of prosecutorial misconduct in that the prosecution failed to provide the defense with exculpatory evidence, in this case the addendum to Dr. Washington's report, which clearly under the rule of Brady v. Maryland, they were required to produce; and under Rule 746 of the Practice Book your honor can impose sanctions including striking the testimony."

"Your honor," Attorney Powell began. "There was not intent to withhold the addendum. I swear, as an officer of the court that I was not aware of it until Dr. Washington mentioned it this afternoon in this courtroom; so there is no misconduct. Perhaps Dr. Washington never sent it to us. I'm appalled at counsel's accusations, and I ask you to deny his motion. The citizens of this state are entitled to a fair trial, too." she said.

"I'm aware of that, Attorney Powell." Judge Bronner replied. "You don't have to remind me.

"Mr. Kelly, I understand why you want the testimony as to the fingerprints thrown out. As to the addendum, I fail to see how you've been harmed by its late disclosure; and I'm not going to throw the baby out with the bath water especially when I see no evidence that the addendum was intentionally withheld. Attorney Powell, I want you, as an officer of the court, to investigate what went on in your office as to the disappearance of the addendum and report back to me on Monday. If I find that it was intentionally withheld, I will reconsider my ruling or impose sanctions. In the meantime, Attorney Kelly, your motion is denied."

"Have a nice weekend, everyone. Marshal, adjourn court."

While the courtroom was being cleared, Governor Roberts motioned Kelly to the side of the room out of the hearing of everyone else.

"Brian, I don't want you to press that motion or do anything else to have the case dismissed on a technicality. It'll look as if I, as Governor, influenced it, and in most people's mind, I'll probably be guilty. I don't want to have that cloud hanging over me.

"Brian you did a brilliant job with Dr. Washington, especially with no time to prepare; but we still have to deal with the fingerprints and the so-called eyewitness. The only way I'm really going to be exonerated is to find the real killer."

"I know, I know." Kelly replied. "We're working on it. Becky is following some leads. She's going to get a look at Spaulding's office to see if there's anything that will help us.

"How's she going to do that?" Roberts asked.

"You don't want to know. I don't even want to know. I don't ask. You shouldn't ask." Kelly said. "Let's go. We have work to do."

37

That same night, Senator James Spaulding was hosting an early evening cocktail party in his office at the Legislative Office Building. It was his yearly "winter blahs party," from 5:00 to 7:00 p.m.

As a chairman of the Public Safety Committee, Spaulding had an especially large office. Located on the second floor, it had a reception area with desks for two secretaries. At the rear of the reception area, there was a divider on either side of an entrance way. The dividers were wooden 4 feet in height and were topped off by opaque glass for another 2 feet. This gave privacy to a large room off to the right which contained desks in an open area and 3 partitioned off private offices. To the left was a large conference room, with Spaulding's private office the same size and to the left of the conference room. The entire suite of offices was carpeted with light blue commercial carpet except for Spaulding's private office which had dark blue plush carpeting. Except for the conference room and the private office, the walls were all battleship grey as were the desks and chairs.

When Becky Brown arrived at 6:30, the suite was filled with staff members, police chiefs from the towns in Hartford and Litchfield Counties, deputy marshals and several of Spaulding's political supporters as well as lobbyists and other legislators. Spaulding had hired a bartender who gave Becky a diet Sprite. *She wanted to be alert tonight* she thought. As she walked into the large conference room, Spaulding spotted her. “Becky” he called out as he walked up to her and kissed her on the lips. “How’s my favorite state police officer?”

“Fine, Jim” she replied. “It’s good to see you again” She smiled at him. *His eyes are already a little glassy*, she thought.

“You know why you’re my favorite? Because you and I worked well together when I was Chief of Police.”

“And another thing” Spaulding said “you’re gorgeous, you know you’re also the sexiest police officer, past or present, I’ve ever seen.” He smiled as he put his arm around her. Suddenly, he got serious, “What’s this rumor I hear about you working for the Roberts’ defense team. You working for Kelly again?”

“Rumor only, Jim” she said. “I’ve got a full plate right now.” She mentally crossed her fingers hoping he wouldn’t remember what she said.

“Yeah, well, you’ve worked for him before, but I suppose that’s where the money is. These rich, fancy defense lawyers make me sick. They’ll do anything for a buck; and Roberts, that mamby-pamby governor who wants to let all the criminals go free. What a bastard. He and Kelly are two peas in a pod; or maybe they both pee in the same pod.” he laughed.

He turned and grabbed Arlene Powell’s hand and pulled her over. She’d had her back to him talking to someone else. “Arlene, you remember Becky Brown, don’t you?”

"Of course, how are you Becky?"

"Good, Arlene. It's nice to see you again."

Spaulding laughed, "Well I'm sure you're feeling better than Arlene right now. She had a bad day in court today on the Roberts' case."

Arlene looked embarrassed, "Jim" she began.

"I'm only kidding, Arlene. That jerk, Washington, screwed you up by not giving you everything; but, it's only a temporary setback. We've got the goods on that S.O.B. Roberts. He's going to spend the rest of his life up in Somers State Prison." Spaulding almost spit the words out.

"But, let's talk about more pleasant things. What are you drinking, Becky?"

She held up her glass "Sprite," she said. "My stomach is a little queasy right now."

"I've got just the right thing for you, a shot of rye" he said as he pulled her toward the bar.

"No, no" she said "Let's compromise on a Bloody Mary."

"O.K. Bloody Mary it is. Sal, do the honors," he said to the bartender.

"Jim!" A tall man with a striking blonde woman on his arm called to him. "Hey, Bill." Smith waved to him. "I'll be right back, Becky." He walked over to the couple.

I'll bet she thought. *He wants to meet the blonde; he'll never change. Happily married man, hah! They should add with a roving eye and hands* she mused.

Becky sipped her Bloody Mary and wandered around talking to people she had known from her days with the state police. By 7:15, the crowd was getting thinner. She was standing next to the door to Spaulding's large private office when he approached her again, "Becky, come on in here. There's something important I want to talk to you about, in private." They walked into his office. He closed the door. They stood near the bookcase.

"Becky, how would you like to come to work for me? Be my chief of staff. I'm thinking of running for governor next year, and you could be a big help."

"Jim, I'm flattered; but, I don't have any political experience."

"Listen, we'd make a great team, you and me" he said as he moved closer. Her back was against the bookcase and his right hand was against the shelf above her left shoulder. He leaned in and kissed her on the lips. She put her hand on his chest to keep him from embracing her, but she kissed back. *Ugh*, she thought. *He smells of liquor and tobacco. My stomach really is queasy, now*.

They broke apart and she looked at him. "You know, Jim," she smiled. "This is what they call sexual harassment in the workplace."

"That's only if you were already working for me; and, of course, only if you're not willing." he said. "Becky, I've been attracted to you for a long time. You and I could have a lot of fun together."

She moved over to the window. The blinds were partially open, and it was dark outside. She turned toward him as he approached her again.

"What about your wife? You're the great advocate of family values. How can you mix an affair with me and your loyalty to your wife?"

"There's an exception to every rule, as you know," he said. "Besides, the family values speech is for public consumption, not for the real world."

This time he put his arms around her as he kissed her. *My God*, she thought, *What I have to do to protect my client.* He then started kissing her neck. She was able to see his desk and noticed wires coming out from the bottom right hand drawer. Her heart leaped.

"How about dinner tonight?" Spaulding said, "and then we'll see."

"I can't, Jim. I'm meeting my husband for dinner at 8 o'clock; but, let's talk some more. It is an attractive offer."

There was a knock on the door. "Jim," someone called. "I've got to talk to you about something."

"I'd better go to the bathroom. All right to use your private one over here?" Becky said.

"Of course," Spaulding said. "That would be very appropriate under the circumstances. I'll call you Monday."

"I'll be right there" he called. Becky went into the bathroom and closed the door. Spaulding walked out of the door to his office and closed it behind him.

Becky flushed the toilet, then went out and turned off the light in Spaulding's office. She returned to the bathroom, closed the door and waited. She could still hear voices outside. She could also hear car doors slamming. She looked out the window and could see only two cars left.

"Let's make sure everyone's gone" she heard Spaulding say.

Becky had her coat on her arm as if she were ready to leave when Spaulding had persuaded her to go into his private office. She quickly put it on and shoved her small purse into one of the pockets. She stood on the toilet seat, climbed onto the sink and grabbed the ledge of the wall above. Her coat was wrapped tightly around her. She boosted herself up so her feet were on the ledge on the wall to her left. She held onto the other ledge with her hands. *It's a good thing I did 500 chin ups a week while I was with the state police and kept it up* she thought.

She heard the outer door open and the light came on. "Anybody in here?" Spaulding asked. He then partially opened the door to the bathroom, but didn't turn on the light. Light did come in from the office. She held her breath and froze. Spaulding shut the door, walked out of the office door, turning off the light and closing the door behind him.

"No one left" he said to his secretary, Linda, with whom he was rumored to be having an affair. "We can leave these lights on for the cleaning crew," he said. "Let's go."

Becky dropped down from her perch and looked out the window. She saw Spaulding and Linda get into his car and drive away. He turned right onto Capitol Avenue and headed west. She had left her car on Trinity Street on the other side of the Capitol. They wouldn't see it as they drove in the other direction. The parking area was now empty.

Becky walked into the office and locked the door by pushing in the button on the doorknob. She turned the lights on. *The cleaner wouldn't find that unusual with the rest of the lights in the suite on*, she thought.

She took out her purse and placed it on Spaulding's desk. She took out a pair of latex gloves and put them on. She got down on her knees to look below the bottom right drawer. *There go my stockings* she thought. She could see wires coming out from the bottom going over to the telephone jack against the wall. The drawer was locked, but she picked it quickly and it opened to reveal a telephone answering machine that was on. She followed the wire leading to the top of the desk. It was hooked into a separate phone. *Must be his private number*, she thought. She flipped the play switch. "Jim," this is Jean Caron of the Courant. Washington really jammed your people in court today. He had an addendum to his report that said there was saliva on Anne's chest that didn't match hers. Kelly made the most of it. I was looking for a comment. I'll catch you at home." Then a male voice came on "January 30th, 4:45 p.m."

Becky sat back. *That doesn't do me any good.*

She pulled the drawer all the way out. There was a pile of tapes in the back. She looked through them. They were all marked by the month. She picked up the one marked December, 2005, took off the tape on the machine and replaced it with the new one. She put the machine on play and started to listen. There were messages from early December. She fast forwarded to December 23rd. Nothing of significance. December 24th. She decided to listen to the entire day. Four calls, the last one at 4:45 p.m. Then, she hit the jackpot.

"Jim, this is Annie. Pick up the phone if you're there, please. I can't see you tonight or ever again. I want you to know that, and I want you to know why."

There was a click and Spaulding's voice came on, "what the hell do you mean you can't see me anymore?"

"I'm in love with Dave Roberts. I think I have a chance of getting back together with him, and I don't want to screw it up with an affair with you that's not going anywhere."

"What are you talking about, Annie? I love you, and you know it."

"Maybe you do, Jim; but not enough to leave your wife. I'd be bad for your image, and to you, image takes precedence over everything, even love."

"What the hell do you see in that mamby-pamby Roberts? He's a weakling and an asshole" Spaulding said, his voice hardening. "Besides, he'll never leave Cindy for you."

"That's not true, Jim. I saw him earlier this month and although he denies it, he still has the same old feeling towards me. I've never stopped loving him, and I think he'll come around."

"Are you saying that he's better than I am?" Spaulding had raised his voice.

There was no response. "Is that what you're saying?" he asked again, with obvious fury in his voice this time.

"No" she replied softly. "But my decision is final. I can't see you anymore; and please don't try to persuade me to change my mind. I'm having dinner at my sister's tonight so I'll be home late. I just don't want to have a confrontation with you over this. You get upset very easily, and sometimes, you get a little rough."

Now, Spaulding was really angry, "Listen you bitch; nobody blows me off. If there's any breaking up to do, I'm the one who does it. Not you. Especially not you. Listen, you two bit whore, if you do this, you'll be sorry, very sorry."

"Don't you threaten me, you sanctimonious son of a bitch! Remember the Polaroids we took? You and me standing together, nude, fondling each other. If you try to see me or harm me, I'll send one to your wife, one to the Hartford Courant and spread a few more copies around in the right places. What's going to happen to your precious political career then, Mr. Family Values man?"

Anne continued, "and besides, what did you say to me a few minutes ago, 'I love you, Annie.'" She laughed. "Another one of your lies. Jim, the only person you love is yourself."

Spaulding slammed the phone down.

"December 24th, 5:15 p.m." the other male voice said.

My God, Becky thought. *Annie incriminates him from the grave.*

Suddenly there was a knock on the door. "Anybody in there?" a woman called.

Becky turned off the machine, shut the drawer quietly but quickly, grabbed her purse, ducked into the closet and closed the door.

She heard the door being unlocked, and then a woman's voice. "Hmph, I thought I heard voices in here" she said. "Must be the weather that's affecting my hearing."

Becky stayed quiet, huddled in the corner of the closet. She heard the woman start to clean the bathroom. *Good thing I didn't hide there* she thought. She stayed in the closet, not making a sound as the woman cleaned the rest of the office. She froze in place and stopped breathing every time she saw the woman's feet through the slats at the bottom of the door. Eventually, the woman left, and Becky returned to the drawer. She took her microcassette recorder out of her purse, rewound the tape in the machine and then played it back again, this time recording the conversation on her recorder. She checked to make sure she had gotten it. Then, she put the December tape back in the middle of the pile and replaced the original tape where it had been on the machine.

Why didn't he erase it? she wondered. *Probably, he forgot about it when it happened, he was so angry. Then, if he did remember it, he probably thought it would never be found; just like Nixon. He didn't burn the tapes. He was told he'd never have to surrender them. Who knows?*

Where are those Polaroids she talked about? That would really help if I could find them in Spaulding's possession. She put her hand into the drawer and tapped the bottom. It sounded hollow. False bottom. She picked up the tapes, took a paperclip, inserted it into the break midway on the bottom and pulled up the wood.

Voila. There are the Polaroids. She picked them up, and there was Spaulding in all his naked glory with his arm around a naked woman who was not Anne Tremaine. Damn it. It's not her; and this is probably where he would have put the photos if he got them back.

They may be here somewhere. She opened his other desk drawer and found a file labeled "Tremaine, Anne," but there was nothing in it except two American Express receipts for restaurants in New York City. She replaced the file.

I can't look through the entire office tonight; and I don't want to press my luck.

Becky put the photos back in the false bottom, replaced the wood, put everything back the way it had been, locked the bottom drawer just as she had unlocked it. She listened carefully at the door, then left the private office making sure the door was locked behind her. She moved hurriedly through the building, stopping and leaning flat against the wall as a cleaning lady walked through the hall heading in the other direction. Becky slipped out the back door of the LOB and walked quickly towards the Capitol. Her car was still parked on Trinity Street, on the other side of the Capitol. The street was now deserted. As she drove away, she thought, *some ladies man; but it may turn out to haunt him*.

38

"Attorney Powell, do you have a report as to why the medical examiner's addendum was not provided to defense counsel? It's clearly exculpatory material." Judge Bronner asked shortly after court opened Tuesday morning. It was 10:02. Bronner usually came on the bench right on time.

"Yes, your honor. I talked with everyone in my office earlier this morning. The secretary who usually opens the mail thinks she saw the addendum, but she's really not sure. She doesn't read the mail when it comes in other than to determine who should receive it or what file to put it in. It probably would have been put on either Mr. Smith's desk or mine. Mr. Smith doesn't recall seeing it when he read the report, and I didn't see it either.

I called Dr. Washington's secretary. She believes it was attached when she mailed it to us, but even she can't be sure.

The only thing I can say is that if it was attached, it must have come loose and fallen off. It probably was thrown out with the trash."

"Thrown out with the trash, Attorney Powell?" Judge Bronner asked. "Something this important thrown out with the trash?"

"We searched the office in all places where it might have fallen or been misplaced. We even looked through the trash we still had.

Essentially, we looked everywhere it might have been, and we came up empty. I'm sure it was an accident, if we in fact did receive it. I apologize to the Court and to the defense, but I don't see that there's much more I could have done or can do now."

She had had some heated words with Smith and Cassella over this she recalled. They had brushed it off, said that Washington's office had probably not attached it in the first place, and in any event, it was not a big deal. The defense was still able to use it, and we still had enough evidence to convict Roberts. There's no way he can explain his fingerprints on the glasses or the letter, and he's been placed at the scene at the time of the murder; and, he was caught in a lie. Still, she felt uncomfortable about the whole incident, and she had told Smith that. "You probably feel bad because you were embarrassed in open court, but it wasn't your fault. Don't worry about it; it will soon be forgotten. Now, go to court and chew them up" he had said. She still felt uneasy.

Judge Bronner looked down at her again. "I assume you went over the report with Dr. Washington in advance. Didn't it come up then?"

"Both Mr. Smith and I talked to him. We concentrated on the fingerprints. We didn't mention the addendum because we didn't know it existed. He didn't mention it because he probably assumed we had it, and didn't need to talk about it because it was self-explanatory; or maybe he thought Attorney Kelly would bring it up anyway. I really don't know what he was thinking."

"Your honor," Kelly spoke up. "I appreciate Attorney Powell's report; but, as your honor well knows, failure to turn over the report is failure to turn over exculpatory material to the defense. It's a violation of the Connecticut Constitution as well as the rule set forth by the U.S. Supreme Court in Brady v. Maryland. It's clearly Brady material, and I ask that the court impose severe monetary sanctions against the State's Attorney's office and advise the jury of the State's violation." The Governor had told him not to go for a dismissal on the basis of prosecutorial misconduct. If he wasn't cleared by the jury and the charges were dismissed on a technicality, most people would still believe him to be guilty.

"Mr. Kelly, it doesn't seem to me any harm was done to your client. You did receive the information in time to do an effective job of cross-examination; and, Dr. Washington can be recalled. Under the circumstances, if you call him as your witness, I will allow you to question him as if it were cross. In view of that, I'm not going to say anything to the jury, at least, at this time. As to sanctions, I think that's appropriate, but as to the amount, I'll reserve decision on that at this time.

Now, if there's nothing else, marshal, bring in the jury."

Powell's first witness of the day was Tony Cassella, the S.A.'s chief inspector. She took him through the crime scene with emphasis on the letter from Governor Malone. Then, she asked him about the conversation he and Detectives Shaw and Hopkins had with Governor Roberts at the Governor's office. Cassella acted very professionally and spoke well. Kelly still detected a gleam of satisfaction in his eyes.

"When Governor Roberts told you he hadn't seen the victim since the first week in December, what was your reaction?" Powell asked.

"I figured he was lying. We knew he had been there after December 23rd because we found the letter of that date with the defendant's fingerprints on it. Hopkins and Shaw felt the same way."

"Objection, your honor, move to strike the reference to Hopkins and Shaw. It's not only hearsay but non-responsive."

"Sustained. The remarks about Detective Hopkins and Shaw may be stricken. The jury is to disregard those remarks."

On cross-examination, Kelly sought to bring out Cassella's bias against Roberts because of Cassella's closeness to Smith and because Cassella didn't like Roberts' opinions on search warrants or the war on drugs. Cassella maintained that, regardless, he was not biased against the defendant, and that he had told the truth.

"Did you know about the letter from Governor Malone when you interviewed Governor Roberts?"

"Yes." Cassella had testified that he had seen the letter shortly after he first arrived at the crime scene.

"Did you mention the letter to the Governor?"

"No."

"Why not?"

"I wanted to see whether he would lie about his being there, and he did."

"Didn't you try to set him up, Inspector?"

"No, I didn't." Cassella replied.

"You never asked him for an explanation as to why the letter was there, did you?"

"No, because there couldn't have been any other explanation."

"There couldn't? What about other people who might have had access to the letter?"

"We interviewed them. We talked to everyone in the Governor's office, even the janitor. They all denied taking the letter."

"When did you ask them, before or after you interviewed Governor Roberts?"

"Afterwards."

"So, at the time of the interview for all you knew, there might have been another explanation?"

"I suppose there could have been, but there wasn't."

"Did you refrain from interviewing the staff first because you were afraid they might tip him off about the letter?"

"No" Cassella said.

"Isn't it possible that some visitor to his office that day could have taken the letter?"

"No. We interviewed everyone on his appointment list for that day, and they all denied taking the letter."

"Inspector, you've been at this business all your life. You're an experienced investigator. Do you really believe anyone you talked to would have admitted taking the letter, one that didn't belong to them?"

"I don't know" Cassella replied heatedly. "Look, counselor, all this talk about other people is a lot of baloney. Anyway you slice it. Roberts left it there, and he lied about it."

"But you can't rule out the possibility that someone else planted that letter, can you?"

"Objection, your honor." Powell was on her feet.

"Anything's possible, counselor" Judge Bronner commented.

"Question withdrawn" Kelly said.

"You'd like to see Governor Roberts go to jail, wouldn't you, inspector?" Kelly almost shouted.

Cassella's face was flushed. "Yeah, except jail's too good for him. He killed that woman. They should ask for the death penalty for this mamby-pamby excuse for a Governor. He deserves to die!" Cassella was breathing hard.

"Thank you Inspector. Thank you for letting us know exactly where you stand. Thank you for your unbiased testimony!" Kelly said.

"Objection" Powell said.

"Withdrawn" Kelly replied.

Kelly had scored some points against Cassella he thought. The jury probably doesn't like him, but there's still the letter and Roberts' statement to the investigators.

As expected Hopkins and Shaw confirmed what had been said when they interviewed the defendant with Cassella.

Next, Attorney Powell tried to establish motive. After a few preliminary questions, she asked Anne's sister about her conversation with Governor Roberts at her sister's wake.

"I told him that I knew Annie had still loved him, and that the first week in December she tried to renew their relationship."

"What else did you tell him?"

"That I knew he had turned her down, but that she was determined to change his mind."

"What did Governor Roberts reply to you?"

"He said 'I know she did. It's too bad it had to end this way.'"

"What was your reaction?"

"I was taken aback; I couldn't believe my ears."

"What did he mean by that?"

"Objection, your honor. That's pure speculation. How could she know what was in his mind?" Kelly was on his feet.

"Sustained," Judge Bronner said. "Rephrase the question, Ms. Powell."

"Certainly, your honor. When Governor Roberts said what he did to you, how did that make you feel?"

"I was shocked. I felt he had killed her to keep her quiet" she said. There was a gasp from the crowd.

Kelly didn't spend much time on cross.

"You loved your sister very much, didn't you?"

"Yes."

"And back when they were both single before she went to Hollywood, when they were having an affair, you hoped that she and Governor Roberts would get married, didn't you?"

"Yes. I told her she was foolish to go to Hollywood, that he might not be there for her when she got back."

"And, the night of the wake, you were upset about your sister's death, weren't you?"

"Yes, but I know what he said."

"You know what he said, but, think now, isn't it true that you don't really know what was in his mind at that moment, what he really meant when he said that? Think about it, please."

"Well, when you put it that way, yes. I don't know what he really meant."

"Did you consider Governor Roberts a friend of your sister even though they were no longer romantically involved?"

"Yes."

"Well, then, for all you know, he could have meant that he was sorry that their friendship had ended because she had died."

"I suppose he could have."

"And for all you know, he could simply have meant that it was too bad her life had to end so young and in the manner in which she died?"

"Yes, I suppose so."

"Then, would you agree with me that even though his choice of words may not have been the best, what he said could be subject to interpretation?"

"Yes," she sighed.

"And not necessarily sinister, isn't that true?"

"Yes."

"One final question. Did you ever hear your sister say or indicate that she had threatened David Roberts in any way, to expose their earlier affair, to say anything to his wife, or to make trouble for him in any way if he didn't come back to her?"

"No."

"Thank you. Thank you very much."

He had recovered some ground here too, Kelly thought, but, all in all, it was not a good day for the defense.

39

Promptly at 9 o'clock the next morning, Becky knocked on the door of Judge Bronner's chambers. "Come in" came the answer. Becky and State Police Lieutenant Paul Russo walked in. Bronner had taken off his jacket and was sitting in his high backed chair puffing on his pipe.

"Becky, it's good to see you again" Bronner said.

"Thank you, your honor. This is Lieutenant Paul Russo." Bronner leaned forward to shake hands.

"What can I do for you this morning" he said. "Sit down, sit down" he pointed to the two chairs in front of his desk.

"Your honor, we have a search warrant application for you to read; and in view of the subject matter, we'd like our presence here not to be disclosed at this time."

Judge Bronner smiled and said "Well, let's see what the big mystery is all about." He started reading and his face became serious. "I see what you mean." He got up and opened the door slightly. He called to a marshal. "Vinnie, would you please stand by the door and don't let anyone in. Tell them I don't want to be disturbed."

"Certainly, your honor" the marshal replied.

Judge Bronner closed the door, returned to his seat and resumed reading.

“This has Colonel Andrews’ blessing” Becky said. Andrews was Commander of the State Police. The State Police had jurisdiction over the State Legislative Office Building.

Becky made the application affidavit complete. They had to show that there was probable cause that Spaulding’s office contained evidence of a crime having been committed in order for the judge to authorize the warrant.

First, she had claimed the crime of threatening had been committed by Spaulding and had attached a transcript of the tape she had discovered in his office.

She also stated that the tape of Spaulding’s conversation with Anne made reference to photographs which could be exculpatory evidence by showing Spaulding’s relationship with the victim. She claimed the photos might be hidden in Spaulding’s office. She claimed that the tape was not only evidence of the crime of threatening by Spaulding, but that the conversation was further evidence of Spaulding’s relationship with the victim; and that all of this was exculpatory evidence because it pointed to Spaulding as a possible suspect. By the search, they expected to obtain the original tape, probably photos of Spaulding and Anne and other evidence incriminating Spaulding or supporting the charge of threatening.

Judge Bronner finished reading. “Are you two going to sign the application and affidavit?”

“Yes,” Becky replied. “I’m no longer a member of the state police, but I checked the statute, Sec. 54-33a, which allows the application and affidavit to be signed by any two credible persons.”

"I'm aware of that, and I certainly consider you credible" Bronner commented.

"Your honor." Becky continued. "I know this could be accomplished by an order to disclose in open court. Either way, it would tip off Senator Spaulding and he could destroy the tape and any other evidence he has not already destroyed."

"That's one of the reasons I didn't ask Attorney Kelly to join us. If we had him here, we'd have to have Attorney Powell here. I don't think we should inform her in advance of the search warrant. She might inadvertently say something to her boss, Frank Smith who, as you know, is a close personal friend of Senator Spaulding; and he might let something slip in his conversation with Senator Spaulding. Additionally, it might put her in a difficult position."

"I understand" Bronner said. "Do you have your copy of the tape with you?"

"Would you please play it for me?"

"Of course." Becky took the recorder out of her bag and pushed the play switch. The voices of Jim Spaulding and Anne Tremaine filled the air.

When the conversation concluded, Bronner said, "That's certainly Jim Spaulding's voice. Even the tone is threatening. I've seen and heard enough. Sign the affidavit and then I'll sign the authorization for the search. However, I'm also going to have the warrant sealed as to the media and public."

They signed and acknowledged their signatures, and then Bronner signed the warrant.

“Thank you, your honor” Russo said.

“I’d suggest that you leave separately through the public area so you don’t run into Smith or Powell; and do it quickly. It’s already 9:40 and they should be arriving any minute for trial.

“Good luck,” he said as they left.

40

Two hours later, eight state police officers led by Lieutenant Russo entered the Senator's office in the Legislative Office Building and asked for Senator Spaulding. He came out of his inner office. He approached Russo. "What's this all about?"

Russo looked at him, "Senator, I have here a warrant to search these premises signed by Judge Bronner."

"Let me see that" Spaulding replied. Russo handed him the warrant. Spaulding's face showed increased surprise and anger as he read through it. He just glanced at the transcript. He already knew the contents of the conversation between him and Anne Tremaine.

"You can't do this!" he exclaimed.

"Oh, yes we can. If you have a problem, take it up with Judge Bronner. Meanwhile, step aside" Russo ordered. He directed two officers to guard the entrance and not let anybody in or out. Then he stepped forward and announced to the staff what was happening, to continue with their work and ordered them not to interfere with the state police officers. They were not to leave the office.

He then went directly to the bottom right hand drawer of Spaulding's desk and directed Spaulding to open it or give him the key. Spaulding refused. Russo took out a set of keys; tried several and eventually opened the drawer. He took everything, answering machine, all the tapes, photos and other materials in the false bottom.

"I don't need you anymore, Senator. Please leave the office."

"You'll hear about this" Spaulding replied as Russo continued to search his desk.

This is NBC Nightly New with Brian Williams.

"Good evening. A startling event today that may or may not be related to the murder trial of Connecticut Governor David Roberts. In an unprecedented move, the Connecticut State Police executed a search warrant on the office of State Senator James Spaulding in the State's Legislative Office Building. This happened a little before noon today. For more on this unusual development, here's Roger O'Brian reporting from Hartford."

The screen showed O'Brian in a trench coat standing in front of the Legislative Office Building.

"Brian, this search of Senator Spaulding's office has the legal and political communities buzzing; actually it's more widespread than that. The story has already been broadcast on local radio and TV and there is rampant speculation as to what it means. This was the scene late this morning outside Senator Spaulding's office on videotape taken by our NBC affiliate, Channel 30."

The screen showed two state troopers standing guard at the door to Spaulding's office, and then Spaulding walking out with a look of rage on his face. The camera zoomed in, microphones were thrust in front of his face, and someone asked "Senator Spaulding, what's this all about?" Spaulding's face softened just a little as he looked into the camera. "No comment," he said, as he continued walking. "Is this related to the Roberts' case?" asked another reporter. "I said no comment." Spaulding replied. "The judge has sealed the warrant, and I'm not going to comment on it."

"But, . . ." began a reporter. Spaulding stopped and looked at the man. "What is it that you don't understand about 'no comment'?" he said and started to walk away again.

O'Brian came back on, chuckling, "He's got a point there, Brian. The warrant has been sealed by the judge. NBC news has learned that the search warrant was signed by Judge Alan Bronner, the judge who is presiding over the Roberts' murder trial, but that is the only connection to that trial. Other than that, it's a mystery.

"Roger, where does the Roberts' trial itself stand?" Williams asked.

"The prosecution is expected to wrap up its case in chief tomorrow. Right now most legal observers believe that despite some setbacks for the state, Governor Roberts is still in trouble; but, of course, we haven't heard any defense witnesses yet, and then, we don't know what the prosecution is planning for rebuttal. As you said, Brian "It ain't over 'til it's over'."

"Thank you Roger. That phrase is not original with me. Roger O'Brian reporting from Hartford."

41

The court reporter was already present as the lawyers filed into Judge Bronner's chambers the next morning. They sat around the conference table which was perpendicular to his desk. Attorneys Powell and Spivack on one side, Kelly and Allen on the other side. At the end was Attorney Mark Salois.

"Your honor," Powell began. "This is Attorney Mark Salois. He represents Senator Spaulding. He asked to join us this morning. I told him I would introduce him, but, of course, the decision would be yours."

"Thank you, Arlene. Good morning Attorney Salois. What brings you here this morning?"

"Well, your honor, as Attorney Powell said, I represent Senator Spaulding right now only as to the search warrant that was executed yesterday. He's told me what's in the affidavit, and he feels he needs legal representation regarding the warrant to protect his interests. Attorney Powell is filing a motion to suppress the tape of the telephone conversation, and I'd like to be heard on that."

Well, before I read the Motion to Suppress, let's go off the record for a moment. I'd like to tell you of an incident that took place in my courtroom last week. I think you'll find it interesting.

I was doing arraignments, and this defendant appeared before me on a charge of Sexual Assault 3. Now, as you know, Sexual Assault 1 is forcible intercourse, Sexual Assault 2 is sex with someone under sixteen and Sexual Assault 3 is forcible sexual contact. What do you think the defendant says to me?

"Your honor, why am I charged with Sexual Assault 3? This is only the second time I've done it."

There was an outburst of laughter from the attorneys.

"I explained to him the numbers reflected the seriousness of the crime, and told him: 'Trust me, sir, you don't want to be charged with Sexual Assault 2 which carries a nine month mandatory minimum.'"

Judge Bronner paused and then said: "All right, Counsel, let's get back to business."

Powell handed the Motion to Suppress to Judge Bronner. "Give me a moment to read this, please," he said. He quickly read the motion, looked up, and said to Salois, "Mr. Salois, your client hasn't been charged with anything, ... yet!" he emphasized; "and this is a separate case. However, I do understand your concern. If this evidence were to come in in the Roberts' trial, it might potentially harm your client if he is later charged. It certainly wouldn't help his reputation. Technically, you have no legal standing in this case. Nevertheless, I'm inclined to let you sit in this morning at least for reasons that will become apparent in a few minutes. Any objection, Attorney Kelly?"

"No, your honor."

"Well, that's settled. I presume the state has no objection since you seem to be on the same side on this. You can stay Mr. Salois."

"Thank you, your honor."

"Now, Arlene, the thrust of your argument is that the information about the tape being in Senator Spaulding's office was obtained illegally, is that correct?"

"Yes, your honor," Powell replied. "We believe that Becky Brown was committing burglary when she was in Spaulding's office obtaining a recording of the tape. We believe the evidence will show that although she had a right to be there initially because she was attending a party, she remained there after the party ended when she had no right to be there. While she was there, she was intending to commit a crime. She did just that by breaking into the drawer and recording the tape. That's at least criminal mischief and larceny. Remaining in a building illegally to commit a crime constitutes burglary under our statutes, as your honor well knows. If the information in the search warrant affidavit was illegally obtained, then the items seized must be excluded under the exclusionary rule," she said.

"Was there any damage to the drawer?" the judge asked. "If not, where's the criminal mischief?"

"Entering a locked drawer illegally even without damage is still criminal mischief," she replied; "and even though she didn't take the tape with her, the recording of it by her and the taking of it is the illegal taking or theft of something valuable, and that's larceny."

“You mean his words were valuable?”

“They were to him,” Powell replied. “It’s no different than taking a copy of a letter he wrote and photographing it.” She smiled. “That’s what they call espionage in slightly different circumstances.”

Judge Bronner returned the smile. “Very clever, Arlene” he said. “But don’t you have a problem with her not being a police officer?”

“Perhaps, but the information was still illegally obtained, and, under Connecticut Law, the fruits of the so-called poisonous tree should be excluded and suppressed.”

Bronner turned to Salois. “Does your client agree with that?”

“Yes, your honor.”

“Well, I must say,” Bronner replied. “I find this very ironic. As you all know, the U.S. Supreme Court has established an exception to the exclusionary rule; namely, that even though the affidavit for the search warrant may be defective, as long as the officers executing the warrant are acting in good faith, which they probably were here, the evidence is still admissible. However, that’s not the rule in Connecticut. Our Supreme Court has declared that under the Connecticut Constitution, there is no good faith exception to the exclusionary rule and the evidence must be suppressed.”

“What is ironic here is that Senator Spaulding has been pushing for a constitutional amendment so that the good faith exception would apply in Connecticut; yet he is now using the same Constitution he sees as hampering law enforcement to exclude evidence about himself. I suppose it’s whose ox is gored, isn’t it?”

Salois looked at him, "That may be, your honor; but under the law as it stands now in Connecticut, the evidence must be suppressed."

"I wonder what Governor Roberts would think of this? Admission of the evidence would probably help him in this case; yet he opposed Spaulding's efforts to change the law and wants the exclusionary rule to remain as it is in Connecticut which could mean that he could not use this evidence to help him" He turned to Kelly, "and I suppose you don't want the evidence suppressed?"

"That's correct, your honor." Kelly replied. "I recognize the irony, but in my client's best interest in this case, I want the evidence to come in."

"Very interesting" Bronner said. "But as for me it may be academic. I'm the one who signed the search warrant, and under our system, I cannot hear a motion to suppress claiming what I authorized is invalid.

I allowed this discussion to go on because it's so interesting, but we really should talk about timing. I'm referring the motion to suppress to Judge Amenta. I"ll put that on the record in open court when we convene later this morning. Judge Amenta, as presiding Judge, can either hear the motion to suppress herself or assign it to another judge. Are we close to finishing your case in chief, Arlene?" he asked.

"Yes, your honor. We have one more witness at this time."

"And I suppose you want to argue the motion yourself?"

"Yes, your honor."

"You too, Brian?" he turned to Kelly.

"I do also, your honor" he replied.

“Well, that means we’ll probably have to take a day or so during the defense case here to argue it. The judge who hears it may also want briefs on the motion so you might consider that too. Attorney Salois, the judge who hears the motion can decide whether you have standing. Maybe, you can come in as amicus curiae (a friend of the court).”

“Is there anything else, counsel?”

“No, your honor.” they replied.

“Then, I’d like to get started. Why don’t you see Judge Amenta after we finish with this next witness.”

42

"The State calls Mr. Robert Forrester to the stand," Attorney Powell announced. Judge Bronner had opened court and stated his referral of the Motion to Suppress on the record.

Robert Forrester entered the courtroom from a side door escorted by two officers from the Hartford Correctional Institution. He was dressed neatly in a suit and tie. He was clean shaven and his thinning hair was neatly combed back. He hardly looked like a prisoner. After he was sworn and seated, the guards moved away, one sitting against the wall behind him, the other sitting in the aisle next to the audience and nearest to the witness stand. Forrester was not handcuffed, and at that point looked like an ordinary middle aged businessman.

Powell took him through the same story that was contained in the statement he had signed after talking to Cassella. When he identified Governor Roberts, she asked, "Do you see the man you saw entering and leaving the condo last Christmas morning in this courtroom?"

"That's him; right over there, the one with red hair seated at the table." He pointed to Roberts.

"May the record reflect that the witness has identified the defendant," Powell said.

"The record may so reflect," Judge Bronner declared.

"No further questions," Powell said.

"Cross-exam, Mr. Kelly?" Judge Bronner asked.

"Thank you, your honor" Kelly said as he got up and approached Forrester. He smiled at him.

"Good morning, Mr. Forrester. You look very nice this morning. I'm Attorney Brian Kelly, and I represent Governor Roberts. Is it all right with you if I ask you a few questions?" Kelly smiled again as he looked at the jury.

"Of course, and thank you for the compliment." Forrester replied.

Suddenly, Kelly turned toward Forrester, his smile gone and he said, "Did you discuss your testimony with anyone before you took the witness stand this morning?" he asked in a stern voice.

Forrester moved back in his chair as if afraid of Kelly, "No, of course not."

You mean the first time you knew what questions Attorney Powell was going to ask you was when she started asking them of you in this courtroom?"

"That's right." Forrester responded.

I should have warned him, Powell thought. *The oldest trick in the book. He's denying it because he doesn't want it to look as if he was rehearsed; and the jury doesn't believe him.*

"I object to this line of questioning, your honor."

"Overruled. It's proper cross examination."

"Mr. Forrester," Kelly continued to bore in, "don't you think its unusual, even foolish of Attorney Powell not to know what you're going to say before you take the witness stand?"

"Objection, your honor. That calls for speculation. Also, Mr. Forrester is not qualified to give an opinion. He's not an expert on cross-exam." Powell was on her feet.

"Well, I'd certainly agree with that last statement," Kelly said. The courtroom erupted in laughter.

"Order, order" Judge Bronner said. "Objection sustained."

Kelly kept on, "How do you think she knew what questions to ask you if you didn't talk to her in advance of your testimony?"

"Objection"

"Overruled. Answer the question, Mr. Forrester."

Forrester looked at Kelly, "Nobody told me what to say."

Kelly turned to another line of questioning.

"What kind of car do you own, Mr. Forrester?"

He's not going to get me on that one, Forrester thought. "I don't own no car." he said.

"Did you own one on December 25th of last year?"

"No."

"Then, how did you get the one you drove to River View Condominiums on Christmas morning?"

"I borrowed one from a friend."

"Who was that friend?"

"I don't remember."

"Did you keep the car or did you return it?"

"Of course I returned it. It didn't belong to me. I wouldn't hold on to something that don't belong to me."

"How did you return it if you don't remember the friend who loaned it to you?"

"Objection, argumentative."

"Overruled."

Forrester looked confused. "Would you repeat that, please?"

"Certainly," Kelly said. "How did you return the car to the person who owned it if you didn't remember who loaned it to you?" Kelly said slowly and patiently.

"I don't know. I must have remembered him then."

"But, you don't remember him now?"

"That's right. I don't."

"Do you remember what the car looked like? Was it a four door? What color was it? What make was it? How old was it?"

"I don't remember" Forrester said. "I was a little fuzzy that night as I said."

Kelly held up a photograph to Forrester. "Did it look like this car?" he asked.

"Yeah, something like that."

"Your honor, may the record reflect that this is a photograph of my car!" There was more laughter from the audience.

"It may not!" Judge Bronner said angrily, "and the question and answer before it are stricken. You know better than that, Mr. Kelly. Move on."

"I'm sorry, your honor." Kelly said.

"Mr. Forrester, you said you left a party next door to Angelo's Place, and then you went home, correct?"

"Yeah." Forrester was sullen, now.

"And, Angelo's Place is at 1150 Wethersfield Avenue, isn't it?"

"I guess so. I'm not sure."

Kelly went back to the counsel table and picked up a Hartford telephone book. "Let me show this phone book to you and ask you to look at this page next to the red check mark. Does that refresh your memory?"

"Objection."

"Overruled."

"Yea, Angelo's Place is at 1150 Wethersfield Avenue, so what?" Forrester said.

"And, at the time of the party you lived at 1170 Wethersfield Avenue, didn't you?"

Kelly had obtained Forrester's address from his police record.

"Do you want me to show you some records to refresh your memory as to where you lived last December?"

"No. So I lived at 1170 Wethersfield Avenue. I had a room there. So what? Is that a crime?"

"No, Mr. Forrester, it isn't. But answer me this. Your room is only 2 blocks from the party you attended and on the same side of the street. Why did you have to borrow a friend's car to drive home if you lived only 2 blocks away?"

"Objection, your honor. The question states facts not in evidence."

"Overruled. Answer the question, Mr. Forrester." Judge Bronner looked at him.

Forrester shrunk back a little. "I don't know. As I said, I wasn't thinking too clearly that night."

"As a matter of fact, you didn't drive home that night, you didn't drive to the condominiums and you never saw Governor Roberts, isn't that true, Mr. Forrester?"

Forrester thought, *I still want the deal.*

"No, that's not true." he said.

Kelly wanted to ask him if he were color blind, but he didn't know whether he was. If he wasn't it would only highlight Forrester's identification of Robert's red hair. Don't ask a question when you don't know the answer; a basic rule of cross.

"You don't live at 1170 Wethersfield Avenue anymore, do you?" Kelly asked.

"No."

"Where do you live now?"

"On Weston Street."

"Where on Weston Street?"

"Objection, your honor. May the jury be excused?" Powell asked.

"Of course. Ladies and gentlemen, would you excuse us for a few minutes?" The jury filed into the jury deliberation room.

Kelly could see what was coming. "Your honor, may the witness be excused? I don't think he should hear this discussion. Further, I would ask that he be placed in a room that is guarded and no one be allowed to talk to him, especially anyone from the prosecution."

"I resent that!" Powell said. "That's a slur against our integrity."

"Resent it all you want. I just don't want him coached any more than he has been. If he hasn't been coached or if no one intends to coach him, then there should be no problem in no one being allowed to talk to him" Kelly retorted.

"All right, all right. That's enough, both of you." Judge Bronner said. "There's certainly no harm in sequestering him for a few minutes. Marshal, have the corrections officers take him to the nearest empty room outside the courtroom. The corrections people can stay with him, but no one is to talk to him, and keep your eyes on him.

Forrester left the courtroom with the marshal and two guards.

"Now, what's your objection, Ms. Powell?"

"Your honor, Attorney Kelly is about to go into the fact that the witness is a prisoner. However, he's not a sentenced prisoner. He's being held on bond. He hasn't been convicted. He's only been arrested. That's proof of nothing. It's not relevant. It's more prejudicial than probative. It shouldn't be allowed. Further, I'm sure Mr. Kelly is going to go into his record, and I would like the court to caution him in advance that he can only go into felony convictions, not misdemeanors; and I don't want him waving the record in front of the jury. It is, of course, a lengthy record, but a lot of the convictions were misdemeanors; and if he waves around the whole list, it will mislead the jury into believing they're all felony convictions."

"Mr. Kelly?"

"Yes, your honor. I will ask only about felonies and I do not intend to wave his record in front of the jury. I do know better than that.

But, as far as where he's being held now and why he was arrested, I want to ask him if he made a deal to testify, explore what sentences, if any, have been promised to him. It goes to his credibility, his bias and his motive for testifying. If he hasn't been offered a deal, he can deny it; but I have a right to test his credibility in this regard."

"Bias and motivation as it relates to the credibility of a witness is always relevant" Judge Bronner said. "Objection is overruled. Marshal, bring back the witness, and once he's settled in as he was before, bring in the jury."

Once again Kelly approached Forrester being sure to stay a little to Forrester's right so he would not block the jury's view of the witness. Kelly always spoke up so there was no danger of the jury not hearing him. Sometimes, he questioned from the far end of the jury box, especially with a friendly witness, but here he wanted his presence menacing or not, to be close to Forrester.

Forrester again looked sullen and afraid, his earlier confidence gone. *I've got to be careful with this guy.* he thought. *I don't want him to catch me lying. If I don't do well, Powell and Cassella ain't going to stick to their deal.*

"Now, Mr. Forrester," Kelly began. "Just before we took a break, you said you lived on Weston Street. Be more specific. In what building on Weston Street?"

"The Hartford Correctional Institution."

"You're a prisoner there, right?"

"Yes."

"And why are you there?"

"Because I can't make bail."

"What is your bond?"

"$20,000.00."

"You must have done something serious to warrant that kind of bond," Kelly saw Powell started to get up, and then he said "Withdraw that. Mr. Forrester, what are you presently charged with?"

"Sale of marijuana."

"And, this nice suit and tie, your sartorial splendor, about which I complimented you earlier, that's not your customary mode of dress, is it?"

"I don't understand the question."

"Well, let me rephrase it. You usually don't wear those clothes in jail. You usually wear a prison suit, an orange jump suit, isn't that correct?"

"I suppose so."

"Well, is it correct or not?"

"Yes."

"Who gave you the suit, shirt and tie you're wearing?"

"No one gave it to me. They loaned it to me."

"And who loaned it to you?"

"Mr. Cassella."

"You mean Chief Inspector Tony Cassella of the State's Attorney's Office, is that right?"

"Yeah"

"And where did they loan it to you?"

“In Mr. Cassella’s office this morning. He told me to change.”

“Wasn’t that nice of them, to make you look more presentable?”

“I suppose so.”

“And how does it fit?”

“O.K., I guess, but I feel more comfortable in the jump suit.”

There was a ripple of laughter from the audience.

“Is that because you wear the jump suit more often?”

“Yeah.”

“As a matter of fact, when you’re not in jail, you rarely, if anytime, wear a suit, isn’t that true?”

“Yeah.”

“You don’t wear a business suit, but you’re still in business, aren’t you?”

“What do you mean?”

“Well, in addition to doing odd jobs now and then, you’re in the business of stealing, aren’t you?”

“Objection, your honor, to the use of the word business.” Powell interrupted.

“Your honor, I claim it. I’m prepared to show that stealing is his main occupation, and that he works for himself. The word ‘business’ is appropriate. That’s why he’s dressed in a business suit.”

“There’s no need for sarcasm when addressing the court. Mr. Kelly.”

“Sorry, your honor. I got carried away.”

"Don't let it happen again. The use of the word is proper. Objection overruled." Bronner said.

"I ask you again, are you in the business of stealing?"

"No."

"Well, let's see about that" Kelly said as he returned to the counsel table. He picked up the pile of papers containing Forrester's arrest record hoping the jury would see its thickness. He put the pile down again. He didn't want to be accused of waving the record in front of the jury. He remained standing behind the counsel table, and picked up the first sheet.

"Are you the same Robert Forrester who was convicted of robbing a package store on Franklin Avenue in 1997?"

"Yes."

"The same Robert Forrester who was convicted of burglary of a residential home in 1995 on Woodside Circle?"

"Yes."

The questions were coming rapid fire now.

"The same Robert Forrester who was convicted of robbing a convenience store on Capitol Avenue in 1994?"

"Yes."

"And robbing a gas station in 1993?"

"Yes."

"And burglarizing a house on Kenyon Street in 1992?"

"Yes, but I didn't do that one alone. I had to take the fall for the others."

Kelly continued with more convictions until Judge Bronner stopped him.

"I think we have the point, Mr. Kelly. How far back are you planning to go?"

"Just one more, your honor. Are you the same Robert Forrester who was convicted of selling cocaine in 1988?"

"Yes."

"And you served 4 years in prison for that, didn't you?"

"Yes."

"So you've gotten very used to wearing a jump suit over the years, haven't you?"

"I guess so" Forrester sighed.

"Do you still say you haven't been in the business of crime, Mr. Forrester?"

"Yeah."

"What would you call it. Making ends meet?"

"I suppose so."

"And now you're charged with the sale of marijuana that carries a penalty of seven years, doesn't it?"

"Yes" Forrester was looking more and more uncomfortable.

"And you could be facing a much stiffer sentence, couldn't you?"

"What do you mean, stiffer sentence?"

"I mean you could now be charged as a persistent serious felony offender and be sentenced to up to 30 years; that's what I mean. You're facing 30 years?"

"Objection, your honor, he's not an expert on sentencing." Powell interrupted.

'He's been around, your honor. He knows. He can say he doesn't know if he doesn't know."

"Objection overruled."

"Mr. Forrester," Kelly continued. "You've served time in Hartford, correct?"

"Yes."

"Enfield Correctional?"

"Yes."

"Somers Correctional?"

"Yes."

"And other prisons, too?"

"Yes."

"Do you understand that if you lie here today, you're subject to a charge of perjury?"

"Yes."

"And that's another felony, correct?"

"Yes."

"You're not only familiar with the jail system, but you've entered into many plea bargains with prosecutors, haven't you?"

"Yes."

"So, I ask you again. Do you understand that you're now facing 30 years in prison?"

"Yes."

"As a matter of fact, Mr. Cassella told you that, didn't he?"

How does he know that? Forrester wondered. *I don't want to be charged with perjury. I've got enough problems.*

"Yes, he did," he replied.

"You were arrested in early January, after the murder of Anne Tremaine. Isn't that true?"

"I think so."

"Well, you say you were free in Hartford the morning she was murdered, so it had to be after that, right?"

"Yes."

"Where did you talk with Mr. Cassella?"

"At his office."

"Just the two of you?"

"Yeah. Mr. Cassella told the guard to wait outside."

"Is that when he told you that you could be charged as a serious felony offender and could get 30 years?"

"Yeah."

"And did he tell you that possession of less than 4 oz. of marijuana is a misdemeanor carrying a maximum of one year in jail?"

"Objection, hearsay!" Powell was on her feet.

"I claim it, your honor. I'm not asking whether what Mr. Cassella said was true, but rather to establish the effect of what he said upon the hearer, namely Mr. Forrester."

"I agree" said Judge Bronner. "It's not hearsay, but ladies and gentlemen" he looked at the jury, "the question is not to show that what

Mr. Cassella told Mr. Forrester was true, but only to show what effect the statement had on Mr. Forrester; so you should consider his answer only in that regard. The objection is overruled. Repeat the question, Mr. Kelly."

Kelly repeated it.

"Yeah, he told me that, but I already knew that," Forrester said with a touch of pride in his voice.

"So, it was a choice of 30 years or one year, right?"

"Well, I suppose so, but we didn't make no deal. I'm still charged with sale of marijuana."

"But that could be changed at any time by Mr. Smith or Attorney Powell; higher or lower?"

"Yeah, I guess so."

"Depending upon what you say today?"

"No, no. there weren't no deals."

"Then you want us to believe that you volunteered to Mr. Cassella what you testified to today?"

"Yeah."

"But, you told us earlier that you hadn't discussed your testimony today previously with anyone. That wasn't the truth. was it?"

"I forgot about Mr. Cassella. I thought you meant this morning."

"Well, then, you either didn't remember seeing Governor Roberts Christmas morning or you lied about that, too."

"No, no that's the truth. I saw him."

"Mr. Cassella had you brought to his office when you volunteered this information. Isn't that true?"

"Yes."

"You didn't call him up and say you had some information you wanted to share with him, did you?"

"No."

"Then, why do you think he had you brought to his office?"

"I don't know. Ask him."

"You wanted to make a deal with him for your testimony, and he knew that didn't he?"

"No, no. There weren't no deal, I told you."

"Why did you come forward, Mr. Forrester?"

"Well, it was my civic duty. I heard about the murder and I thought I should tell what I saw."

"You're 53 years old, aren't you?"

"Yeah."

"So if you were to serve the full 30 years, you'll get out when you're 83, or you'll die in prison, right?"

Forrester's face turned white. "I suppose so."

"But if the charge is changed to simple possession, you'll get no more than a year, and considering the time you've been held on bond with good behavior, you could be released 2 or 3 months from now?"

"Yeah."

"Thirty years versus 2 months. That's not a hard choice, is it?"

Forrester didn't answer. He was starting to perspire. He pulled on the back collar of his shirt.

"That's not a hard choice, is it Mr. Forrester?" Kelly repeated.

"No, I guess not."

"And they offered to change the charge to simple possession if you came in and lied about Governor Roberts, didn't they?"

"No, no. There weren't no deal."

Kelly picked up the pile of sheets and walked toward Forrester. "So you want the jury to believe that after a life of crime, you suddenly became a public spirited citizen who came forward only because you wanted to see justice done."

"Yes" Forrester replied. This time in a weak voice.

"I have no more questions of this public spirited witness." Kelly said.

Powell was on her feet, "One question, Mr. Forrester, do you know what public spirited citizen means?"

"No," he replied. There was laughter from the audience.

Kelly got up again.

"Mr. Forrester, do you know what civic duty means?"

"I'm not sure."

"If I were to tell you that being a public spirited citizen means working for the betterment of your community and doing your civic duty is essentially the same thing, do you think you would qualify?"

Before Forrester could answer, Kelly raised his voice and said, "Do you think a person who spends his entire adult life breaking laws is a public spirited citizen who is doing his civic duty? You don't have to answer that!"

Kelly gave Forrester a look of contempt, returned to the counsel table, threw down the papers in disgust and sat down. He put his hands behind his head and looked at the ceiling.

Judge Bronner adjourned court.

43

"Sorry we're late." said Cindy Roberts as she and Governor Roberts sat down at the table in the private room at the Mill on the River Restaurant. It was 8:30 p.m. the evening of Forrester's testimony, and the defense strategy group had gone out for dinner.

The Governor had suggested that they meet away from the Capitol, the Executive Mansion and Kelly's office, the likely places the media would find them. Present, in addition to the first couple, were Kelly, his assistant Barbara Allen, Becky Brown and Chief of Staff Bill Donovan.

The Mill on the River was Kelly's favorite restaurant. It was located in South Windsor, a Hartford suburb just northeast of the Capital City, on the bank of the Podunk River, named after the Podunk Indians. It was a charming old, colonial structure complete with wooden beams and walls inside, and a covered "kissing bridge" from the parking area to the main entrance. The group was in a private room in a corner of the lower level looking up at the large waterfall that started below the bridge at the northerly end of a wide expanse of the river which was in the shape of a lake. A fire in the fireplace at the other end of the room cast a reflection on the windows.

"Two scotch on the rocks." Governor Roberts said to the waitress. "It looks as if Cindy and I have some catching up to do." he said.

"We stopped to visit Ed Lincoln at St. Francis Hospital and we felt we should stay to the end of visiting hours at 8:00." Cindy declared.

"How is our lieutenant governor doing?" asked Donovan.

"Well," replied Cindy, "His heart attack was serious. It looks as if they will have to do bypass surgery. They're still doing tests. Other than that, he seems to be taking it well."

"He's no spring chicken." said Donovan. "That's one of the reasons we put him on the ticket, remember. To sort of mix the young and the old," he laughed.

"Ed's been a loyal member of the team." the Governor said. "He's a good guy; and somewhat of a bulldog. He'll come through. Let's talk about something else. What's everybody ordering?" The waitress was standing next to the table, pad and pen in hand.

They each ordered a shrimp cocktail with 8 large shrimp in a tangy cocktail sauce.

Barbara ordered the tuna steak au poivre, Cindy the rosemary and garlic roasted chicken; and Becky, trying to remind herself of Martha's Vineyard, ordered baked Maine lobster with crabmeat stuffing. Governor Roberts had jagershnitzel with pfifferlingen, Donovan the duck a l'orange and Kelly the veal chatelaine, marinated with sweet chestnuts, his favorite at and a specialty of the Mill. He ordered a bottle of white chateau and a bottle of red sonoma wine to go with the meals. They each had a salad of watercress and Belgian endive with a 40 year old balsamic vinaigrette dressing.

"Let's have another round while we're waiting for dinner." the Governor said to the waitress.

"Brian, you did a great job on Forrester today. You really destroyed their so-called eyewitness. Powell and Cassella didn't look too good either. But, I don't feel like celebrating. It's still an uphill battle."

Cindy chimed in, "But, we've got to get some relaxation. We're all exhausted, and we've got to be in top shape the next few days."

"Agreed" the Governor said, "but let's talk strategy after dinner."

An hour and a half later, after the dishes had been cleared, and they were drinking coffee, the Governor looked at Kelly, "All right, Brian, where do we stand?"

"Judge Amenta will hear the Motion to Suppress tomorrow morning.

As for the trial itself, I think we've scored some points. Forrester has no credibility with the jury, and I don't think Anne's sister hurt us. The best thing we have going for us is the tape of the Spaulding-Tremaine phone conversation. If it comes in, that gives someone else, namely Spaulding, a motive."

"Did the search warrant turn up anything else?" The Governor asked.

"Unfortunately no." Kelly replied. "We're lucky, as it is, that Spaulding didn't erase the tape.

The problem is that even with the tape we can't place Spaulding at the scene, and I doubt if the Judge will order Spaulding to submit to a saliva test, especially if the taped conversation is suppressed. Spaulding certainly won't agree to such a test, and, without the tape, it'll probably be considered too remote. Even with the tape, we may not get a saliva test."

"That's the bad news." Governor Roberts smiled, "What's the good news?"

"Wait." Kelly replied. "There's more bad news. Your fingerprints are on the glasses, and most importantly, on the letter found in the victim's bathroom. Right now, if the jury believes the letter, they'll believe you were there Christmas morning or eve, and that you lied about it. I believe Spaulding probably killed her, or maybe Cassella, and somehow planted the glasses and letter; but I don't know how we can prove it. The only reasonable doubt is the possibility that someone else did it. That's not much in light of the glasses and the letter. And don't forget you were in the area at the time of the murder. Our one hope is that a test of your saliva will show that it doesn't match the saliva on Anne's chest; but that depends on how impressed the jury is with DNA evidence. It's highly technical and some juries don't buy it. But it could create enough reasonable doubt to overcome the letter and the glasses. Overall, though, it doesn't look good."

"Well, I wasn't in the condo, so someone must have planted that evidence." the Governor declared.

"Dave, I believe you. We all do; but, we're not the jury."

"Also, I don't want to hang my hat on reasonable doubt. If I'm acquitted on that basis, many people will still believe I did it; and there goes my political career, down the tubes," Roberts replied. "Bill, what do you think?" he turned to his chief of staff.

"Oh, I agree completely as to your political career," he said, "and . . . ."

"Gentlemen," Kelly interrupted. He stood up, his face flushed. "Hold it! Hold it! You're getting your priorities mixed up. Right now, your political future is the least of your worries, Dave. Unless we pull this one out in the next few days, you'll be spending the rest of your life in prison." Cindy let out a little cry. "Oh, no!" she said. The others gasped.

"I realize that." Roberts said, "But what are we going to do about it?"

Kelly turned towards Becky. "Becky's going to have to dig deeper. Spaulding or Cassella killed her, and whoever it is, they're trying to frame you. So far, he's done a pretty good job. Becky's the best there is, and she'll do whatever has to be done."

"Where do we stand on timing?" Roberts asked.

"The state has completed its case in chief. We're going to start our defense tomorrow afternoon. We have the Motion to Suppress in the morning. We're going to put on Margaret Halleck, the next door neighbor first, and by late afternoon or the next morning, you'll be on the stand, Dave. If we don't get the tape in, that'll be it." Kelly said.

"Have we decided that David will testify?" Cindy asked.

“I don’t see any choice. With the way things stand now, we have to pull out all the stops. Dave, this will be the biggest performance of your life. You’ve got to pour on the sincerity and the charm; but don’t flash that famous Roberts’ grin too much. This is serious business. The jury might be offended if they think you’re taking this too lightly.”

“I understand” Roberts said.

“What about cross-exam?” Cindy asked.

“There’s nothing in Dave’s background that will hurt him. He’s Mr. Clean. As a matter of fact, he has a very impressive background. That will help him, not hurt him; but Dave, you’re going to have to exude sincerity and integrity. Don’t try to give a reason for the glasses and the fingerprints. Just say you don’t know how they got there. At this point, the only thing you’ve got is your honesty. They have to believe you when you tell them you didn’t do it. This is the most important election you’ve ever faced. You only need 12 votes, but you’ve got to get them all. Be yourself but use everything you have of your personal appeal.”

Everyone was serious now. The pre-dinner laugher was gone.

“O.K. let’s do it!” Roberts said as they all got up to leave.

44

It was 2 o'clock the next day when the trial reconvened. The hearing before Judge Amenta on the Motion to Suppress had taken the entire morning. She had promised to have a decision as soon as possible. The prosecution had rested its case in chief, and Kelly had called Margaret Halleck as his first witness.

She identified herself as Anne's neighbor in the condominium complex. Kelly had a drawing of the buildings and surrounding areas and large photographs of the area pinned up on a board.

Kelly's questioning brought out the events that had taken place. She described how she had seen a man drive up in a black car, how he had parked in front of Anne's front door, slammed the car door and entered the condo. She established the time at just about 7:00 a.m., describing the church bells playing Christmas carols. Then, she talked about taking her dog, Horatio, out for a walk and coming around the back of her row of condos, so she was in a position to see the man drive up and get out of the car.

"It's too bad Horatio can't talk" she said. "He'd agree with everything I've said."

"What kind of dog is he?" Kelly asked.

"An English Setter; and I'm sure if he could talk he'd talk perfect English."

There was a ripple of laughter from the audience.

"Does he have a last name?"

"Of course he does. His full name is Horatio Hornblower, after the British naval hero. I told you he's an English setter."

This time the crowd laughed heartily. Even the jury smiled at her. She smiled back. They seemed to like her. She was homespun and down to earth.

"Now, Mrs. Halleck, what did the man look like?"

"He was sort of short, and a little bent over. He had on a trench coat and gloves. I couldn't see his face too well. He had his hat pulled down low, and he was wearing sunglasses."

Kelly walked over behind Roberts and put his hands on his shoulders. "Is this the man?" he asked.

"Oh my heavens, no. That's Governor Roberts. I'd recognize him anywhere, especially with the red hair. No, no, it wasn't him."

"Did you see Governor Roberts at all that day?"

"No, but I wish I had. He's such a nice man and he has such a pretty wife."

Powell let that pass without objection.

Kelly then showed her a photo of Cassella's car. He had previously interrupted the testimony to put on the photographer who had taken the photo with the license plate showing. Powell had stipulated that it was Cassella's car.

"Is this the car you saw the man driving?" he asked Mrs. Halleck.

"Why, it looks exactly like it, although I can't be positive it's the same car. That's what I told Inspector Cassella."

"When was that?"

"The day after they found poor Anne's body. He came by and asked me if I'd seen anything. I told him what I saw."

"Do you see that man in the courtroom?"

"Yes," she said, and she pointed to Cassella sitting int he front row. "The one with the beard."

"Let the record reflect that the witness has identified Inspector Anthony Cassella of the State's Attorney's office." Kelly said.

"The record shall so reflect" replied Judge Bronner.

"What did you tell him?" Kelly asked.

Mrs. Halleck then went on to describe the man she had seen and the car. She described how Cassella had shown her a picture of Governor Roberts, and that she told Cassella the man she saw was not Governor Roberts.

Powell objected to replies from Cassella in the conversation as hearsay. Judge Bronner overruled her saying that Cassella was in court and that under the circumstances, the state could call him as a witness in rebuttal.

"I told him about the car and the man who was driving; that it looked just like the car he was in when they drove away the day the body was found. I told him I had seen that on the TV news, too."

"What did he tell you to do?"

"He told me not to say anything about this to anyone and not to tell anyone he had talked to me. He said something about the media would misquote me."

"When did you see him next?"

"Well, I saw him when he and Attorney Powell drove away from the courthouse in Hartford in the same car. You know, the one with the wire pulled back. I saw him on the TV news."

"When did you see him again in person?"

"Not until I saw him in this courtroom today." she replied.

The jury was looking at Cassella with a very unfriendly look.

The court took its afternoon recess, and when they returned before the jury came in, Kelly was on his feet.

"Your honor, we've just heard another incident in which the prosecution has blatantly violated the Brady v. Maryland rule by again failing to disclose exculpatory material to the defendant. What could be more exculpatory than a witness at the scene at the time of the murder who states that the defendant was not there and that a man of a different description in a car very likely belonging to Mr. Cassella was there at that time. And we were never told about Mrs. Halleck. Our investigator had to track her to Martha's Vineyard to persuade her to talk to her, which was not easy in view of Mr. Cassella telling her not to talk to anyone. This smacks of a coverup."

"Your honor," Powell said. "I assure you this has come as a complete surprise to me. I had no knowledge of it."

"Well," Judge Bronner said, "Inspector Cassella is part of your staff, and you're responsible for him. I appreciate your integrity, Attorney Powell. However, Mr. Cassella's apparent lack of it and his withholding of exculpatory evidence is charged to the state. Mr. Kelly, I'm not sure your client has been hurt. You did find it out in time to use it effectively.

Attorney Powell, I'll reserve decision until after cross and any rebuttal with Inspector Cassella; but, I warn you, if nothing changes, I will impose substantial financial penalties, and I will even entertain a motion to dismiss. Now, let's bring in the jury."

Powell approached Mrs. Halleck with a feeling of trepidation.

"How old are you, Mrs. Halleck?"

"Do I have to answer that, your honor?" She looked at Judge Bronner.

"I'm afraid you do, Mrs. Halleck" Bronner replied.

"I'm 72 years old" she said.

"I see you wear glasses, Mrs. Halleck."

"What are you saying, Attorney Powell? That just because I'm in my seventies, I have to wear glasses! That's age discrimination, you know!"

A few of the older jurors nodded their heads and smiled at her.

"No, no, I didn't mean that," Powell replied hurriedly. "Let me put it this way, what is your eyesight with your glasses?"

"20-20"

"And you're sure you were wearing them both times?"

"Absolutely. As you may have noticed, I wear bifocals, so I wear them all the time."

"Except when you're in bed. Did you put them on when you got up?"

"Well, of course I don't wear them when I'm sleeping, but I do wear them in bed when I'm watching TV or reading. But I did see what I've described. I saw it from the window and outside after I'd gotten cleaned up and eaten breakfast. I put my glasses on as soon as I woke up and kept them on."

Arlene was feeling frustrated. She was still upset from learning that Cassella withheld evidence. *I'm not getting too far here. I'd better wind this up.*

"But, you can't be sure who got out of the car and went into the condo, isn't that right?"

"That's what I said; but it wasn't Governor Roberts. I saw the man's hair, and it was dark hair. He was wearing a fedora so it didn't cover all of his hair."

"Could he have been wearing a wig?"

"Objection, calls for speculation" Kelly said.

"Sustained. Do you have any more questions for this witness, Attorney Powell?" Judge Bronner was suggesting to her that she should drop it or she'd get into more trouble.

"And, there's one more thing," Mrs. Halleck said.

There was no question pending, but Arlene thought she'd better not appear to be trying to shut her up. Besides, Kelly would ask her anyway.

"Oh, and what's that, Mrs. Halleck?"

"I could see a little bit of his hair. I"m pretty sure it was his hair, or maybe it was the stubble on his chin and cheeks as if he hadn't shaved yet; and it was dark. I've never seen someone with red hair on top and a black beard" Mrs. Halleck smiled.

Powell sat down. "No more questions."

"Redirect, Mr. Kelly?" Bronner asked.

"No, your honor, Attorney Powell asked all the questions I would have asked and got the same answers. There's nothing left for me to ask. She did a good job." (*for the defense*, he thought)

"Never mind the commentary, Attorney Kelly. You'll get your chance at final argument." Judge Bronner admonished him.

"It's almost 5 o'clock. We'll adjourn court for the day."

"All rise!" said the marshal. "Court is adjourned until 10:00 a.m. tomorrow.

Becky walked up to the counsel table. Cassella looked at her with a menacing look! *If looks could kill*, she thought.

"We've got to have a strategy meeting," she said.

45

Becky looked around the table. "Well, I talked with Spaulding's kids this morning, Russell and Nancy. I caught up with them outside Litchfield High School. They told me what they got for Christmas; and guess who wasn't home early Christmas morning? Their father, the good Senator. Their mother told them he had business in Hartford and had to stay overnight." She held up her hand. "That doesn't mean he was with Anne Tremaine. He could have been sleeping with another one of his bimbos, but unless she'd be willing to come forward, he doesn't have an alibi. I suppose we could subpoena his wife and him" she said.

"I'll get them right away." Kelly said. "I'll subpoena the wife, too. Spaulding will go through the ceiling," he said with a smile.

"As for Cassella, he lives alone. He was divorced a long time ago, and his kids all live out of state. He was probably home alone. That's not much of an alibi. I'm still checking some leads on where he was.

And as I told you before, Tom Price was at the State Police Barracks in Westbrook from early Christmas Eve until after noon time on Christmas Day.

As for the possibility of a hit man from the people backing the Stratford casino proposal, I haven't been able to dig up anything on that. My sources so far have come up with a big fat zero."

Governor Roberts looked at Becky. "Good work, Becky, but without the tape coming in, Judge Bronner probably won't let this testimony in. We have to have at least the tape for a motive for Spaulding to kill Annie before we can show he has no alibi and was in a position to take things from my office and plant them at the condo.

Even with the tape, that's not proof that Spaulding did it or planted the evidence. Mrs. Halleck wasn't able to I.D. him. All of this may, and I emphasize the word 'may', give the jury reasonable doubt; but I wouldn't want to bet my life on it."

"For a guy who hasn't practiced criminal law for a while, you haven't lost your touch," Kelly said. "Dave's right, it's still too 'iffy'; and if that's all we have, we are taking a chance on his life, life in prison, that is."

"We simply have to get more," Cindy declared. "We've got to place Spaulding or Cassella at the condo."

"What about testing their saliva?" Barbara Allen asked.

"I still don't think we have enough to persuade the judge to order a test; and neither of them are going to volunteer. I suppose, Becky, as to Spaulding, you could try to get into his office again and get a glass with his saliva; or if he kissed you again you might get traces of saliva," Kelly smiled at her with a twinkle in his eye.

"Once is enough. Thank you. That was above and beyond the call of duty. Anyway, after I snookered him once, he's not going to let me get within ten feet of him or his office." Becky replied. "Besides, we'd have to get it tested in the state lab where the saliva from Anne's chest is, so we could show a match and we can't get a court order on their saliva or the lab with what we have now."

"You're right" Kelly said. "We have to place one of them at the condo. Becky, have you talked to the trooper who was on duty at the Capitol Christmas morning? We should know who might have been there with the opportunity to get the glasses and the letter from David's office."

"I've been trying to catch up to him. He works odd shifts, and I can't seem to find him at home. I'll give it another try this weekend" Becky replied.

Kelly followed up. "You should also go back to Anne's condo and make a thorough search. Maybe, you'll find the photo Anne mentioned, although the police and forensic people didn't find it. You're just going to have to go there and find something they didn't find. That's the best we can do at the moment."

"All right. I'll do it as soon as I can. Brian, you've got to stall a little, give me some time. If I find something I might have to follow it up," Becky said.

"I realize we're all frustrated," David remarked, "but we've got to keep looking."

"That's it then," Kelly said. "By the way, we're not the only ones who are frustrated. I'll bet Arlene Powell is frustrated because she's not getting straight answers from Cassella."

46

Frustrated was an understatement. Arlene Powell was getting more and more angry as she engaged in a heated conversation with Smith and Cassella. She had gone straight to the office after court and found Smith and Cassella sitting in Smith's office passing each other a bottle of scotch. She had demanded to know why Cassella hadn't told her about talking to Margaret Halleck. Cassella had denied Mrs. Halleck's story, and Arlene didn't believe him.

"What are you listening to some old broad like that for? Sure I talked to her. She told me she didn't see nothing. What she said was part of her fantasy world, or she's just looking for attention. She's probably led a dull life, and this is her chance to be in the spotlight. You put me on the stand, and I'll tell what really happened. Then no one will believe her."

"What about her identifying the car?" Arlene asked.

"She probably did see us drive away in it when we left the crime scene, but that don't mean that she saw it the day of the murder. She couldn't have because it wasn't there. I had it home with me on Christmas Day," Cassella said.

Smith laughed, "Maybe, Tony killed her, right Tony? Look Arlene, Tony will testify he had the car at his home. What are you worrying about? Roberts killed her, we've got a good case against hm, and we're going to get a conviction. He'll never be able to explain the fingerprints on the glasses or the presence of the letter."

"Here, have a drink, Arlene. It'll calm you down."

"No, thanks, Frank. It's been a long day, and I have to get home."

She walked out to her car. *Frank seems to make sense*, she thought. Still she didn't totally trust Cassella. She thought about it all the way home. Her uneasy feeling returned.

47

It was a cold and mostly cloudy Sunday morning as Becky drove her jeep on Rte. 44 toward Hartford. When the sun was not behind the large puffy clouds, it was very bright as it rose in the east. Becky wore her sunglasses continuously and had pulled her visor down. The sun glinted on the hood reflecting toward her below the visor. Fortunately, there wasn't much traffic on the road at 7:00 a.m.

Ben had decided to go with her. He had some legislative work to do, and they wanted each other's company. "This will enable us to push each other, if necessary" she had said, "So we can get an early start back." The weather forecast was for snow coming in from New York State hitting Litchfield County first. At the same time there was a nor'easter moving up the east coast expected to spread far enough west to meet the snow coming in from the west. The nor'easter had already reached New York City. The wind was growing stronger in the Hartford area in advance of the storm.

Becky had learned that Officer Krieger of the Capitol Police was on duty Christmas day from 7:00 a.m to 3:00 p.m. There were no entries on the sign-in log, but Becky knew something was wrong. *Access* she thought. *Access. The killer must have had access that day to the Governor's office. That's the only way he could have stolen the two glasses and the letter from Governor Malone to plant in Anne Tremaine's condo.*

If I can't find out who that was, then that leaves only one prime suspect, Governor Roberts, she thought. She tried to put that thought away. *It couldn't have been Dave,* but lingering doubt remained.

Becky had mentioned this possibility to Ben on the ride in. He had poo-poohed it, but had to admit that if she couldn't learn anything from Krieger, they didn't have any real options left; and time was running out.

Becky drove up Capitol Avenue and turned left into the driveway of the huge Legislative Office Building to drop Ben off at his office.

"I'll call your cell phone when I'm ready" he said "and vice-versa. Good luck with Krieger."

Becky then drove out onto Capitol Avenue and turned left into the circular driveway leading to the south entrance of the State Capitol building. The sky was totally filled with darkening clouds, and a light cover of snow had already accumulated on the ground.

She parked opposite the parking space reserved for the Speaker of the House and got out of the jeep. She had had a tough time tracking Krieger down, but she had learned he was on duty this morning. She hadn't made an appointment. She wanted to surprise him.

A tall, blonde man in the uniform of the Capitol Police came out of the building walking toward her. "The building is closed today," he said. "There's no one here."

She looked at him. He was wearing one way sunglasses that hid his eyes. *He was an imposing figure* she thought. She smiled as she approached him. "Officer Krieger?" she asked.

"Yes," he replied.

"I'm Becky Brown" she said. "I used to be with the State Police, Western District, Troop L in Litchfield. Could I talk to you for a minute inside, out of the cold? I've been looking forward to meeting you."

He looked at her as he shifted his feet. She couldn't tell his reaction because of the sunglasses, but he wasn't smiling. "Let me see some I.D." he said.

Becky took out her wallet, and pulled out her State Police identification card, which she had kept, showing her photograph and rank as a Lieutenant. She handed it to him. He studied it as she took off her glasses. He compared her to the photo, handed it back to her and said "All right, Lieutenant, come with me."

Krieger turned and walked with her around the grey stone barrier that set off the drive through area, up three steps and through large varnished oak doors into the lobby of the Capitol building. He held the door open for her. *A model of courtesy* she thought. He took off his sunglasses revealing bright blue eyes and a light complexion. He escorted her over to a large bench. He smiled. *Finally*, she thought as he offered her a cup of coffee.

Becky took off her hat and scarf, opened her parka and shook out her hair. She removed her sunglasses. Krieger handed her the coffee and sat down on the bench. He took off his hat revealing thick blond hair. As she leaned back against the bench, he asked, "What can I do for you, Lieutenant Brown?"

"Well, as I said, I'm no longer with the State Police. I'm now a private investigator working for Governor Roberts and Attorney Brian Kelly on the Anne Tremaine murder." She held out her P.I. identification.

The smile vanished from his face. "What does that have to do with me?" he asked.

Becky explained that the murder occurred Christmas morning about 7:00 a.m. and that someone had entered the Governor's office at the Capitol sometime that morning. I"ve checked the records, and you were on duty, the only officer here from 7:00 a.m. to 3:00 p.m. Now who was it who came here to enter the Governor's office that morning?"

"I'd have to check the sign-in log for that day" Krieger replied.

"I've already checked it. There were no sign-ins" she said.

"Well, if there weren't any sign-in, then nobody came. I keep good records" he declared proudly.

"Look, Officer Krieger, let's stop playing games here. The person who went into the Governor's office that morning stole two glasses and a letter to the Governor, all of which had Governor Roberts' fingerprints on them. They were then planted at the murder scene to frame Governor Roberts. That's why it's critical that we know who entered his office that morning."

"Well, assuming I was distracted and didn't get the name and some-one did come in, how am I supposed to remember that far back?" Krieger said.

Becky was getting angry. She stood up and faced Krieger, her face flushed. Even standing she was just about eye level with him. "Having duty here Christmas morning is not a time you would forget" she said. "Now, who was it?" she demanded, her voice raised.

"Now, take it easy, little lady. How do you know the governor didn't have these items when he killed her? The State had him arrested, and according to the papers, they have a pretty good case."

"Don't you dare call me little lady, you male chauvinist!" Becky shouted. "If you don't answer me here, you'll have to answer Attorney Kelly, in court and under oath. Would you prefer that?"

Krieger thought back to Christmas morning. *That son of a bitch put me in the middle on this; and for a lousy $2,500. He wanted me to cover up a murder for him. That's got to be worth at least 50 grand* he thought, *if I don't remember; but I'm not even sure who he is*.

He got up, towering over Becky. He pointed his finger at her. "Are you threatening me?" he asked. "You'd better not be. If I said I don't remember, then I don't remember anyone coming here."

"Let's calm down a minute" Becky said. She sat down, and Krieger joined her. "Is it possible someone could have gotten in here without going through you?" she asked.

"I don't see how," he replied. "This place is guarded 24 hours a day, and after hours, like on Sunday or holidays, the doors are locked. The capitol police have the only key, except possibly the Governor."

"He's not likely to come here to frame himself" Becky retorted. "How about through the tunnel from the Legislative Office Building?"

"Unlikely" Krieger said. "That area is closed on both ends on Sundays and holidays, and there's a 24 hour guard at the LOB. The doors to the LOB are always locked. The same with the entrances to the tunnel." Krieger immediately regretted telling her this. It might have sent her down to the LOB to investigate and out of his hair.

"I'm getting a little tired of this, Officer Krieger. I'm convinced that someone came into this building Christmas morning" Becky said wearily.

"We'll find out who, one way or the other. We'll also subpoena you as a witness. If you don't tell the truth, you'll be charged with perjury and obstruction of justice. Next Christmas, you won't be here. You'll be sitting in a cell in state prison in Somers" Becky stated quietly but with determination.

Krieger though, *This broad is serious. This isn't worth going to jail. Thank God the $2,500 was delivered in cash and that I deposited it in a Massachusetts bank. Besides, that bastard took advantage of me paying me only $2,500. He won't dare tell anyone about the payoff. This cheapskate deserves what's coming to him.*

Becky was getting up buttoning her coat. "Wait a minute" Krieger said. "The reason I haven't said anything is that I'm trying to remember. Sit down a minute, will you?"

Becky resumed her seat.

"Thinking back, there was a guy who came here with a briefcase. He said he'd only be a minute, that he had left important papers in the Governor's office. That's probably why I didn't have him sign in. It was cold, he was in a hurry and besides, he flashed his credentials at me.

I didn't get a close look, but they seemed to be the real thing." Krieger paused. "He asked me not to say anything because it would be embarrassing to him to have to admit he left confidential papers in the Governor's office" Krieger added.

"Who was he?" Becky asked.

"I don't know. He didn't give his name. He looked familiar, but I couldn't tell who he was."

"Well, now that your memory has suddenly miraculously returned, is it good enough to recognize him from a picture?" she asked.

"I suppose so" Krieger replied.

Becky took an envelope out of her bag and pulled out six pictures. One was of Senator Spaulding, one of Mark Price, one of Tony Cassella and three mug shots of known Mafia hit men she'd received from Chad Burnham. She laid them on the bench. "Take a look at these" she said.

Krieger bent over. "This one is Senator Spaulding. I've seen him around the Capitol. He looked at the photo of Price. "I don't recognize him. Besides he's too heavy." He flipped through the three mug shots and then stared at the last picture. "That's him" he pointed. "That's the guy."

Becky's heart started to race. "And you're sure?" she asked.

"Yeah, that's him" he said placing his finger on the picture. "I'm positive."

"Absolutely?"

“Absolutely” Krieger said. “He was here about 7:45 that morning.” Krieger smiled and thought *screw him. The lousy bastard. He don’t deserve no better.*

Becky almost couldn’t contain her excitement. “You wait right here, Officer Krieger. I’ll get my laptop computer from the Jeep and type up an affidavit for you to sign.”

48

By the time she picked Ben up, it was already snowing steadily. Becky was smiling, eager to tell him what she had learned. Even while he was fastening his seat belt, she was already talking to him excitedly and rapidly. Ben interrupted "Wait a minute. Slow down" he said; "Let's talk here for a few minutes, Becky" he said. "Leave the motor on so we can still stay warm and the wipers will work."

Becky described the conversation, showed him the pictures and the statement she had taken from Krieger. Ben interrupted several time with questions. When she had finished, he clapped his hands and leaned over to give her a kiss. "Congratulations, darling, you've done it again" Ben said. "If these seat belts weren't so confining, I'd give you a big hug, too" he added.

As Becky pulled out onto Capitol Avenue again to head toward the entrance to I-84 West, they were engrossed in an animated conversation as to what they would do next. Whether it was that or the thickly falling snow, they didn't notice the white Chevy Blazer that had been idling on Oak Street facing the Capitol. It pulled onto Capitol Avenue and followed them onto I-84 West. Two men were in the four-wheel drive, heavily dressed wearing black jackets with fur around the collar and heavy boots. They each had a cigar in their mouth, although the driver's had gone out. The driver was short and stocky with a crew cut and a beard. The other man in the passenger seat was clean shaven, taller but with a dark complexion. His name was Sal, and he turned to Rudy: "She must have gotten something from the cop. We've got to get our hands on it" he said.

"Yea!" the driver grunted as he settled the Blazer into a 40 mph steady speed careful to stay far enough behind the Jeep not to be seen, but close enough to catch up to it if it suddenly picked up speed or turned off the highway. Both cars were being buffeted by high winds. The drivers had limited visibility because the heavy snow was coming right at them.

"We picked a great day" Ben said. They had briefly talked about stopping off at a hotel in downtown Hartford or the Farmington Marriott when they got through West Hartford, but had decided against it. Adam and Alice were both home and Ben and Becky didn't want them to be alone if the storm were to get worse. After several times, Ben had reached Alice on the car phone and apprised her of their situation.

Becky turned off I-84 at exit 39 and headed northwest onto Route 4 into Farmington, an affluent suburb of Hartford which was nearly deserted on this snowy Sunday morning.

Ben had suggested they stop at the Governor's residence in Hartford to bring Roberts up to date on what Becky had learned. They had decided against that, too, when they heard the weather forecast over the Jeep's radio. "They're predicting blizzard conditions and a wind chill of -16°" Ben told Becky who was busy concentrating on driving and didn't hear most of what was coming over the radio. "We can't stop" she said.

"The kids are home alone. They're resourceful, but what happens if they lose power?" she said. "They've never needed the emergency generator before. It could be a nightmare for them."

"You're right" Ben said. "But be careful. If you go too fast on this road, we can end up in the Farmington River, and then we'd both have a nightmare" he said.

Becky slowed down as they went through the Unionville section of Farmington. This area had been devastated by a hurricane and major flooding during the summer of 1955. Many of the buildings along this same route had been flattened or carried away when the river roared over its banks.

Bang!! There was a huge crashing noise as Becky and Ben jolted forward. "What the hell was that?" Ben yelled as he turned back and saw the white Blazer up against the rear of the Jeep. He felt a sharp pain in his neck. The Blazer fell back and then came up and hit them again. Becky struggled with the wheel as she tried to retain control of the Jeep. "Son of a bitch" she exclaimed. "Just when we least expect it."

"They've probably been following us since we started driving into Hartford" Ben said. "Maybe they think you got something important from Krieger" he added.

Just then the Blazer pulled alongside them and rammed Becky's side of the Jeep. She could feel the jolt on her side and the sound of scraping metal on the right as the jeep hit the guardrail. Again, she was hit on the left side slamming the Jeep into the guardrail.

"If they keep this up" Ben said, "they'll knock us into the river!"

Becky gripped the wheel hard and gritted her teeth just as hard. "Not if I can help it" she said.

The Blazer hit them again, and just as it pulled away, Becky slammed on the brakes of the Jeep. It skidded to the left, the right rear bouncing off the guardrail. The Jeep came to a full stop diagonally across the road. The Blazer, which had moved ahead of them, continued straight down the road. Becky could see the brake lights flashing, but they were soon lost in the swirling snow.

Becky straightened out the Jeep; her hair and face were wet with perspiration. The defroster was going full blast. She quickly moved ahead and then turned left onto Burlington Road. She shifted gear for the long steep climb and pressed harder on the gas. The rear of the Jeep swung back and forth. As it stopped swaying and began the climb to the top, it settled into a slow but steady advance up the steep hill.

"How'd you know to turn there?" Ben asked. "I couldn't even see the road with all the snow coming down."

Becky laughed, "Instinct, I guess. I've traveled this way home so many times I can almost sense it when I reach this turnoff. Besides," she said "I had to get away from them. It was perfect timing. By the time they turn around, if they find Burlington Road, they won't know whether we've taken it or gone back toward Hartford. The plows have been through here, but it's still coming down. Add the wind, and I'm sure our tracks are quickly covered."

Ben sighed "I hope so" he said wearily. He picked up the car phone to call the state police and then Alice and Adam. "Damn it" he said, “the phone is dead. It may have been knocked out by the crashes or the weather or both” he said.

Ben looked at Becky. “You must be exhausted” he commented.

She smiled “My arms do ache. Actually, now that you ask, they’re killing me” Becky said.

“Let’s switch drivers when we reach the top” Ben replied.

Becky nodded her head up and down. “You talked me into it” she said.

A short time later, they reached the crest of the hill. On their left was the Johnny Cake Airport, a private facility with several small airplanes parked. Snow drifts had almost covered up some of the planes. The open space of the runway allowed almost hurricane force winds to blow the length of the field onto Route 4. Becky had stopped the Jeep. They had tried to get out to change seats, but it was too windy. Becky climbed into the back as Ben slid into the driver’s seat. Then she climbed into the front passenger seat. She fastened her seat belt, turned to her husband and said with a grin “O.K. Mario Andretti, show me what you can do.” In his younger days, Ben had driven race cars at Lime Rock.

Ben put the Jeep in gear for the slow ride down the hill. They proceeded cautiously, the snow still coming down in front of them. Just before the intersection of Route 4 and Route 118 which would take them into Litchfield, they went through Harwinton where there was a very large sweeping turn in the road. As Ben completed the turn, Becky looked back. The wind direction had changed and she could see the Blazer hurtling down the road toward them.

"Ben," she said. "They're here, they're catching up to us. They must have had a map and know we live in Litchfield."

Ben immediately changed gears and started to increase his speed. The Jeep swayed and skidded on the road. Ben was able to maneuver the Jeep out of skids before it spun out of control. His experience was paying off. The Blazer, careening wildly across the road was still catching up. As Ben raced through the overpass over Route 8, a shot rang out. The rear window of the Jeep shattered throwing broken glass around the inside. The bullet had gone through the rear window on a trajectory that also took it through the front window shattering the glass there too. Becky had leaned forward and covered her head with her hat and her face with her hands. She felt blood on the back of her hands and a sharp pain in each hand. She looked up and saw pieces of glass inbedded in her hands. Otherwise she was unhurt. She was shaky. "Ben, pull off. This isn't going to work" she said.

They were approaching the center of Litchfield. The Blazer had fallen back a little, but was starting to catch up again. Ben veered to the right and took a driveway that sloped down into a gas station. He pulled to the right of the building and stopped.

"Now we've got them." snorted Sal. He opened the passenger window as the Blazer started down the driveway, stuck his head out, the rifle in his hands. Becky and Ben were crouched on either side of the rear of the Jeep, each with a 22 rifle they had retrieved from the back seat. "Now!" Becky shouted, and they opened fire. They both aimed for the driver's side. Sal started to shoot back. He heard a grunt, and saw Rudy slump over the wheel, blood spurting out of his neck. Sal tried to grab the wheel, but it was too late. He couldn't turn away from the gas pumps.

"Run!" Ben shouted. "Run to the back." As they reached the front end of the Jeep, Ben grabbed Becky's hand, and they surged forward fighting the snow drifts. They had reached an area behind the building when they heard a tremendous explosion. The Blazer and the gas tanks erupted into a ball of fire totally demolishing the Blazer and everything in it. The building caught on fire. Becky and Ben pulled themselves out of the snow drift into which they had leaped head first. "Ben, your back's on fire-your coat's on fire." She pushed him backwards into the snow snuffing out the fire that was smoldering on the back of his jacket. There was debris scattered around the snow, burning pieces of wood and metal. Becky felt blood on her forehead. She pulled Ben up and they held each other tightly. He was kissing her. "But, there's blood on my face" she said.

"I don't care" he replied. "I'll take you anyway you are." He clutched her to him. Then, his eyes widened. The Jeep had caught on fire.

"Let's get out of here before that goes" he said. Together, they plowed their way through the snow, moving away from the Jeep, heading north. When they reached a row of evergreens, they turned and fought their way through to the road. As they reached it, there was another explosion.

"That must be the Jeep" Ben said. He turned toward Becky and started to say something.

She held up her hand. “Don’t worry dear, I have Krieger’s statement and the photos in my inside jacket pocket” Becky laughed. “Women don’t carry everything in their purses” she said.

They were walking up the road. The only way they could recognize it was because there was less snow on it. The snow was lessening, and the visibility had increased.

“The State Police barracks are just up ahead” Becky said as they walked holding hands, as much for support as anything else.

49

"The defense calls the defendant, Governor David Roberts, to the stand" Kelly announced. It was 10:15 in the morning. Judge Bronner had had to sign an important search warrant, so he had opened court a little late.

The courtroom was packed, and a stir arose from the audience when the Governor of Connecticut got up and walked to the witness stand. The national media was there in anticipation of Roberts' testimony. "This is a first, I'll bet" said the New York Times correspondent. "Oh, I agree with that. We've had it researched" replied the A.P. correspondent. "This is the first time a sitting governor charged with murder has taken the witness stand in his own defense. As a matter of fact this is the first time a sitting governor of any state has been charged with murder."

Kelly walked forward. "May I approach the witness, your honor?"

"Of course, Mr. Kelly" responded Judge Bronner.

Kelly stood to Roberts' right facing him and the jury.

"Governor Roberts, why did you agree to testify today?"

"Because I am innocent, and I have nothing to hide. I am not concerned about being cross-examined" Roberts said as he looked squarely at the jury with the most sincere and honest look he could muster.

"We'll get into the details later" Kelly said, "but first I'd like you to tell us a little about your background" Kelly said.

Kelly then led Roberts through his schooling, service in Vietnam as an Air Force pilot, his prisoner of war experience, his college basketball career, his experience as a federal prosecutor and his progression up the political ladder in Connecticut. He questioned him about his family, his divorce and his marriage to Senator Cynthia Stevens. He had him describe his prior relationship with Anne Tremaine.

By the time he was finished with the background, Roberts came across as bright, courageous, charismatic, a loving father and husband, and most of all, a man of the highest sincerity and integrity.

That was exactly how Kelly wanted him to appear. He turned to Roberts.

"What was your reaction to being arrested for Anne Tremaine's murder?"

"I was shocked. I was already feeling bad enough about her death, but to be accused of her murder? I was stunned. This is a woman I may have loved once, and although it didn't work out, we still remained good friends."

"Did you kill her?"

"Of course not. I swear on everything that is sacred to me that I did not kill her." Roberts' eyes started to tear. He looked straight at the jury, making eye contact, pleading with his expression for them to believe him.

"The only time I ever killed anyone was in Vietnam from an F-4 fighter, in combat, fighting for my country," he said.

"Then, how do you explain the letter from Governor Malone in Anne Tremaine's bathroom and the glasses with your fingerprints?"

"I can't explain it. At least I have no proof of how they got there. I certainly didn't put them there. When I told Inspector Cassella I hadn't been there since the first week in December, that was the truth then, and it's the truth now" Roberts said again with emotion and his head held high.

Powell's cross-examination was brief, focusing on Roberts' affair with Anne Tremaine.

Just then Becky walked up the aisle. Kelly looked at Judge Bronner, "May I have a moment, your honor?"

"Of course" Bronner replied.

Kelly returned to the counsel table, and talked quietly with Becky. He turned to Judge Bronner. "May counsel approach the bench, your honor?"

"Come forward" the Judge replied. Judge Bronner pushed the microphone aside.

"Your honor, something very important has come up. I have to do some investigation that is crucial to our case. I need the rest of the week and the following two weeks. I'm requesting a recess until two weeks from next Tuesday" Kelly said.

"I object, your honor" replied Attorney Powell. "This is highly unusual. You should have done your investigation before" she said.

Kelly looked partly at her and partly at Judge Bronner. "Your honor, I realize this is an unusual request, but we just learned of this new information. As you well know, this is a murder case with the governor of the state on trial. This information could be crucial to a verdict of not guilty.

What is the rush when it could make the difference in the outcome? After all, this is a search for the truth. How would it look if Governor Roberts is convicted, and then proof of the real killer comes out in three weeks? It would undermine faith in our criminal justice system and put our state government into chaos. Connecticut would be the laughing stock of the country."

"What is this so-called crucial evidence?" Powell asked.

"I can't go into that at this time" Kelly replied. "I don't have it all yet. If I can use it, you'll know. If I can't, I'll tell you both after the trial."

Kelly looked straight at Judge Bronner. "Judge, you've known me for more than ten years. You've never had a reason to question my integrity." He looked at Powell. "Nor have you, Arlene." He looked at Judge Bronner again. "I'm asking you to trust me on this. I am not making this request lightly."

"All right, Brian" Bronner said. "I'll grant your request. Make it on the record without too much detail. Arlene, you can put your objection on the record as well. Now, please step back."

A few minutes later, after Kelly and Powell had briefly spoken on the record, Judge Bronner announced. "Motion granted. This case is in recess until Tuesday, February 23rd at 10 o'clock.

As Bronner left the bench, Becky said to Kelly "We've got a lot to do, and just a little time in which to do it." She turned to Roberts, "I hope both of you still have some favors to pull in."

50

During the approximately three week recess, speculation was rampant throughout the state as to the "real" reason for the delay. Reporters and investigators from the state's attorney's office tried to follow Kelly and Becky but all to no avail.

"The defense calls State's Attorney Frank Smith to the stand." Kelly announced. There were loud murmurs throughout the audience. It was 10:05 a.m. February 23rd.

"Quiet" Judge Bronner said in a sharp voice," We must have order if we're going to proceed."

By this time, Powell was on her feet. "I object to the calling of this witness, your honor. He's a member of the prosecution team, and he has nothing relevant to say."

Kelly, too, was on his feet: "He's not one of the courtroom attorneys who are trying this case, your honor; I don't intend to ask him about the state's courtroom strategy."

"Will counsel please approach." Judge Bronner said as he beckoned the two lawyers to the front of the bench. He put his hand over the microphone and turned toward Kelly. "What's this all about Mr. Kelly? Do you want to put on an offer of proof outside the presence of the jury?"

"No, your honor. First, I intend to get into the issue of the missing addendum to Dr. Washington's earlier report. I want him to tell the jury what he knows about why it was missing; and I may want to ask him other questions as well." Kelly said.

Powell leaned toward the bench "What other questions? Why can't we have an offer of proof?"

Kelly turned toward her: "Because I don't want him to prepare his responses to look better before the jury. There's no rule that requires me to make an offer of proof. It's discretionary with the court. I assure you, the questions are relevant. If you don't think so, you can always object to the question." He turned to Judge Bronner: "Your honor, as you well know this is a murder case. A conviction would not only be crushing to Governor Roberts but devastating to the State as well. I ask you to give me a little latitude here."

"All right, counsel, please step back. We're back on the record. The objection is overruled. In view of the seriousness of the charges, I will grant defense counsel some latitude. Just don't overdo it, Mr. Kelly."

"Thank you, your honor. Would you please take the stand Mr. Smith" Kelly responded.

Frank Smith strode to the witness chair without hesitation and with a broad smile on his face; and was sworn in by the clerk.

"Good afternoon, Mr. Smith" said Kelly.

"Good afternoon to you, Mr. Kelly, long time, no see." Smith replied.

"Mr. Smith, are you here in response to a subpoena signed by me?" Kelly asked.

"Yes, I am."

"You are State's Attorney for Hartford County, are you not?"

"Yes."

"In overall charge of this prosecution, is that right?"

"Yes; although Assistant State's Attorney Powell is trying the case as you know."

"How long have you held the position of State's Attorney for Hartford County?"

"Eleven years."

"So, you're very familiar then with office procedures and duties; correct?"

"That's true, but only on an overall basis. I leave the details to others." Smith replied with a slightly satisfied smirk on his face.

"What is the procedure for handling the mail when it arrives?" Kelly asked.

"When it comes in, the receptionist takes it and puts it in a special box in the file room. Then, one of the secretaries distributes the mail by placing it on the desk of the person to whom it is addressed. The secretaries alternate the distribution on a daily basis."

"What about mail addressed just to the office?"

"Those would be opened, and if it concerned a particular case, it would be given to the attorney in charge."

"So, when the report from Dr. Washington came in regarding this case it would be placed on Attorney Powell's desk, correct?"

"Correct."

"Probably opened?"

"Probably; the secretary would have to open it to learn what's in it."

"The mail on her desk, would that be opened before she gets it?"

"Generally, yes. The secretaries are instructed to slit open all mail unless it's marked personal or confidential."

"So, Dr. Washington's report would have been available to anyone in the office who wanted to read it?"

"Available? I suppose so; but highly unlikely unless someone were snooping in her office. I don't expect that any member of the state's attorneys office would do that."

"How about Inspector Cassella? He worked on this case, didn't he?" Kelly asked.

"Yes, but I doubt if he'd do something like that. You'd have to ask him" Smith replied.

"Did you look at the report before it was reviewed by Attorney Powell?"

"No, not that I remember."

"Well, let me refresh your memory. Would it surprise you to know that your fingerprint was found on the outside of the envelope and that Attorney Powell threw the envelope out when she took the report from the envelope?"

Smith stopped smiling and began to look uncomfortable. Powell was on her feet: "Objection, your honor, he's citing facts, I should say alleged facts, not in evidence."

"I'll rephrase the question, your honor." Kelly said.

"Mr. Smith, did you have possession of Dr. Washington's report before Attorney Powell did?"

"No, not unless it was misdirected to me first."

"Was it misdirected to you first?" Kelly asked.

"I don't recall, it might have been, it might not." Smith's voice rose. "Look, Mr. Kelly, if the addendum to Dr. Washington's report was missing, it's because he didn't attach it in the first place."

Kelly took an envelope out of his pocket. "Does this envelope look familiar to you, Mr. Smith?"

"Yes, it looks like an envelope we generally receive from Dr. Washington. It has his name and return address and it's addressed to our office. What did you do Mr. Kelly, look through our trash?" Smith replied with a slight sneer on his face.

"As a matter of fact, that's exactly what we did." Kelly retorted.

"I object, your honor, and move to strike the remarks about the trash" Powell said, walking toward the bench.

"He's the one who asked the question" Kelly replied.

"Motion to strike denied. Let's move on Attorney Kelly." Bronner said.

Good, Kelly thought. *I've gotten Smith upset. He's no longer your friendly and smiling state's attorney.*

"How well did you know Anne Tremaine, Mr. Smith?" Kelly asked.

Powell was on her feet again, but Smith waved her back. "That's all right. I'll be happy to answer the question." he had regained his composure. "Hardly at all," he said. "Of course, I knew who she was. She was well known at the Capitol. I think I was introduced to her once a few years ago when I was there testifying on anti-crime legislation."

"So you hardly knew her? She was basically a stranger to you personally other than you're having heard of her, is that correct?"

"Yes."

Kelly went back to his table and picked up a pink piece of stationery which was folded in threes.

"Permission to approach the witness, your honor?"

"Granted," said Judge Bronner.

Kelly handed the paper to Smith. "Can you identify this letter?" he asked.

Smith studied the letter. It was on Anne Tremaine's stationery addressed to her sister. It said that Anne was fearful for her life, that she had recently gotten into serious arguments with two men with whom she'd been having affairs. Smith's name was mentioned along with that of Senator James Spaulding. *He's trying to trap me* Smith thought.

"What are you trying to do here, Mr. Kelly? This letter is a fake. It's not even in her handwriting."

"Mr. Smith," Kelly replied, in slowly paced words, his voice a little elevated. "How would you recognize her handwriting if the only time you met her was a brief, one time introduction?"

Smith didn't say anything. He seemed surprised and frustrated. He realized he'd made a mistake.

Kelly asked again: "Mr. Smith, may I have an answer please? Or would you like the question read back by the court reporter?"

Smith glared at Kelly. "No, no, that's all right. I must have recognized her handwriting from the letters the police found in her condo."

"Why would letters from her, signed by her, be in her possession? Isn't it more logical that the letters signed by her would be in the possession of the people who received the letters?" Kelly asked.

"Well, then, I must have seen her signature on other documents, like canceled checks, that the police took as evidence" Smith replied.

"Do you really want this jury to believe that you, personally, studied her cancelled checks or other documents to the point where you became so familiar with Anne Tremaine's handwriting that you were able to distinguish it from her signature on this letter?"

Powell was on her feet again. "Your honor, I've been pretty patient here with Mr. Kelly, but now he's gone too far. He's trying to impeach his own witness. He's the one who called Mr. Smith, and therefore, vouches for his credibility. Further, the questions are leading, argumentative, based on hearsay and on facts not in evidence."

Kelly stood up: "Your honor, as far as the handwriting is concerned, the witness opened up the door to that. I merely asked him if he recognized the document. He's the one who described the handwriting. As for impeaching my own witness, I ask the court to find Mr. Smith a hostile witness for the purpose of allowing me the latitude of cross examination."

"The witness may be considered hostile to the defense based upon his responses to questions as well as the fact that he is the states attorney, the person in overall charge of this prosecution. The objection is overruled" Judge Bronner said. "You may proceed Mr. Kelly."

"Thank you, your honor. Mr. Smith, do you have any education or training that would qualify you as an expert in the field of handwriting analysis?"

"No."

"Who does your office use when you need a handwriting expert?"

"Lieutenant Rogers of the Connecticut State Police."

Kelly turned to the audience: "Will you please stand, Lieutenant Rogers?" A man in a State Police uniform with the insignia of a lieutenant stood up in the back of the audience.

"Is that man standing the same Lieutenant Rogers who is your handwriting expert?"

"Yes" Smith replied. *My God* Smith thought. *He's going to call him as his expert. The letter is still hearsay, but the way Bronner is going, he may let it in anyway.*

"Let me repeat the question I previously posed, that you didn't answer" Kelly said. "Mr. Smith, do you really want this jury to believe that you, personally, studied Anne Tremaine's cancelled checks or other documents to the point where you became so familiar with her handwriting that you were able to distinguish it from the signature on this letter? Yes or no?"

"Yes." Smith replied.

"Did you know that the State has not introduced into evidence any documents showing the signature of Anne Tremaine?"

"I don't know."

"Well, the record will show that the state hasn't. If her signature is so irrelevant to this case, — up until now —, then why on earth would you have studied her signature on items that were not to be introduced?"

Smith replied: "Routine. We routinely study all the evidence."

Kelly looked intently at Smith: "Isn't it true, Mr. Smith, that you, in fact, knew Anne Tremaine very well, that you'd been having an affair with her and received several pieces of correspondence from her; that's why you thought you could recognize her handwriting?"

"Objection, your honor." Powell called out.

"That's all right. I'll withdraw the question" Kelly said.

"No," shouted Smith.

"There's no question pending, Mr. Smith" Kelly replied.

Powell stepped forward again: "Your honor, this is simply not fair. Mr. Kelly makes a false allegation in the form of a question; and then withdraws it before your honor can even rule on my objection. I think in all fairness, Attorney Smith should be allowed to answer the question now, when this so called scenario was placed in front of the jury, and not wait until much later when I have an opportunity to question the witness. This scurrilous attack should not be allowed to sit in the minds of the jury without an immediate opportunity to respond. Attorney Kelly is very clever, your honor, but I think the state is also entitled to some latitude here" she said.

Kelly started to reply, but Judge Bronner interrupted him, "Never mind Attorney Kelly. I realize it's technically proper procedure for Attorney Powell to wait, but in light of the circumstances, I'm going to allow Mr. Smith to answer the question. Mr. Smith, do you recall the question?"

"I certainly do, your honor" Smith replied, his face flushed. "I've never heard such a false, misleading and outrageous question before."

He turned to Kelly and glared at him. With a deliberate and defiant voice, he stated, "The answer to your question is no, Mr. Kelly. I did not have an affair with her, I did not know her well. However, now that I recall, Miss Tremaine frequently sent me memos supporting anti-crime legislation; and as a lobbyist for Citizens Against Casinos, she sent me letters warning of the high potential of a sharp increase in crime if additional casinos in the state were approved. She even sent me statistics supporting her argument" Smith added.

"Do you have possession of those documents?" Kelly asked.

"Certainly not with me." Smith answered. "They may be in my office, at least some of them, but some of them may have already been thrown out."

"At the recess, would you go downstairs to your office, find them and bring them back to this courtroom?" Kelly asked.

"Of course." Smith replied now with a smile on his face. "I'll do anything to help."

"Thank you, Mr. Smith. I must say you have a very resourceful and convenient memory" Kelly started to reply.

"Objection, your honor." Powell was on her feet. "Those comments are totally improper. I move they be stricken."

Bronner looked at Kelly. "Everything after Thank you may be stricken. The jury will disregard those comments. Mr. Kelly, you know better than that. Save your comments for final argument. I suggest you move on to another subject, Mr. Kelly."

"Sorry, your honor. I will move on" Kelly responded.

Kelly returned to the counsel table, looked at his notes, and then looked at Smith. "Where were you, Mr. Smith, last Christmas morning at about 7:00 a.m. at about the time of Anne Tremaine's death?"

"Objection, your honor." Powell rose from her chair. "This goes beyond the question of Dr. Washington's report. States Attorney Smith is not on trial here. The question is irrelevant as to the guilt or innocence of Governor Roberts."

"Your honor," Kelly replied. "As you well know a trial is supposed to be a search for the truth. It seems to me that in defending my client, I have a right and even a duty to show that someone else committed this crime. My client is on trial for murder. Whether he is found guilty or not guilty is crucial to him, and in light of the office he holds, of vital importance to the citizens of this state. Again, I ask you to give me some latitude here."

"This defendant should not be treated any differently because he is the Governor of Connecticut. Justice is supposed to be equal, your honor," Powell declared.

Judge Bronner looked down at her with a frown: "I'm well aware that equal justice is an important tenant of our judicial system; and Governor

Roberts will be given no special consideration because of his office. However, Mr. Kelly is correct. This is a search for the truth and it is a murder case. Governor Roberts is entitled to the same rights as anyone on trial for murder. He should not be denied his rights because he is Governor of Connecticut. Mr. Kelly, do you have any evidence to support your claim or is this just a fishing expedition?"

"I do have evidence, your honor." Kelly looked at Smith who was glaring back at him. "You've already seen Lieutenant Rogers, who will testify; and there are other witnesses whose identities will become apparent in a few moments. I assure you, your honor, I will be able to tie this all together."

"All right," Judge Bronner said. "I'll give you the latitude you need. The objection is overruled. Go ahead, Mr. Kelly. But tie it in quickly, please."

"Thank you, your honor. Mr. Smith, let me repeat the question, where were you at the time of Anne Tremaine's murder, last Christmas morning, December 25th at 7:00 a.m.?"

"I was home, of course. We opened Christmas presents with our kids."

"At 7:00 a.m.?"

"Yes."

"How long did it take to open the presents?"

"About an hour."

"Are you sure?"

"Yes."

"No mistake about it?"

"No. I may be slightly off on the timing, but what I said is essentially correct."

"You're absolutely sure that you and your family opened the presents together?"

"Yes, of course. I've said it three times."

"Do you know my private investigator, Becky Brown, seated behind me here?" Kelly asked as he pointed at Becky.

"Sure. I've seen her around. She used to be a state police lieutenant."

"A competent one?"

"Yes, in my dealings with her, she was competent."

"What if I told you that your two children, Heather and Jimmy, told Becky that you were not home to open the Christmas presents that morning; that Becky learned this from talking to them recently where they go to school?"

"What?" Smith shouted. "You leave my kids out of this." His face got red; he was sputtering he was so angry. He leaped out of the witness chair and approached Kelly in a rage. "How dare you involve my family." he shouted. The courtroom erupted in noise, spectator's standing to see the confrontation.

Crack!! Judge Bronner slammed down his gavel. "Mr. Smith" he shouted. "Stop!!" Two marshals ran up to Smith one on either side and grabbed his arms. "Mr. Smith, settle down, get back on the witness chair now, and behave yourself. You're an officer of the court, for God's sake."

Smith stopped struggling. He turned around, walked back to the witness chair and sat down. "Sorry, your honor, but I love my kids, and I'm outraged by Mr. Kelly dragging two innocent children into this trial. I understand that he has to defend his client, but this is going too far." He took a sip of water. "I realize Mr. Kelly is desperate, but interfering with my family is unacceptable, no matter how desperate he may be."

Powell considered asking for a recess, but she was still annoyed with Smith over the incident with Dr. Washington's report. *Let's see how he does on his own* she thought.

"Mr. Kelly" Smith said. "My kids were correct. Before they came downstairs, I did go to my office, in this building, as a matter of fact, to check something. I did get back in time to go over their presents with them."

"You mean when I asked you questions before about being there to open the presents, you totally forgot that you had gone to your office?" Kelly asked. "Or is this answer an example of your selective memory?"

"Objection!"

"Sustained. You're pushing your luck with the comment about his memory, Mr. Kelly. That may be stricken. The jury will disregard it" Judge Bronner said.

Smith looked at Kelly. "Well, it's true. I have a lot on my mind right now."

"I'll bet you do." Kelly replied. "Now, search your memory for that morning. Did you go right home from the office?"

"Yes."

"Did you stop on the way going to the office from your home?"

"No."

"Why did you go to your office on a Christmas morning?"

"There was something on my mind concerning a particular piece of evidence in another case, and I wanted to check it out."

"What was so important that it couldn't wait to the next day or at least later on Christmas Day?" Kelly asked.

"I can't tell you about the case. It's confidential. It was important to me; and when something like that is bugging me, I'm not comfortable unless I check it out right away. I thought I'd be home in time to open the presents."

"Did you stop at the State Capitol that morning?"

"No. I've already told you that I didn't stop between my home and my office."

"Well, I just want to be sure. I don't want you to tell me later that you went to the Capitol at some other time that day. So let me ask you this: at any time between midnight of Christmas eve/Christmas day and midnight of Christmas day, did you go to the Capitol?"

"No."

"Are you sure?"

"Yes, I'm sure."

"No other loss of memory as to what happened that day?" Kelly asked.

"No. I did not go the Capitol December 24th or December 25th." Smith replied, smacking his fist into his other hand for emphasis.

"Mr. Smith," Kelly continued. "You know, from previous statements that the defense contends that the killer of Anne Tremaine went to the Governor's office in the Capitol that same morning and took away two of Governor Roberts' glasses and the letter from Governor Malone of Massachusetts, all of which had Governor Roberts' fingerprints on them and planted them in Miss Tremaine's condo in order to frame Governor Roberts for this murder?"

"Yes, I've heard that; but it's a lot of fantasy and poppycock. Your client committed the murder, Mr. Kelly."

"Fantasy, you say, Mr. Smith." Kelly looked thoughtful, and then, still in a calm tone of voice, said: "Mr. Smith do you know Officer Henry Krieger of the State Capitol Police?"

"I don't believe so" Smith replied.

"You mean you're not sure?"

"Well, yes, I can't really remember if I ever met him or not."

"Let me try to refresh your memory." Kelly turned toward the audience and said: "Officer Krieger, would you please stand up?"

Halfway back in the audience, a tall man wearing sunglasses and civilian clothes stood up. "Please take off your sunglasses, officer." The man removed his sunglasses and looked at Smith.

"Does that refresh your recollection, Mr. Smith?"

"Not really. I don't recognize him. I don't believe I've ever seen him before."

"What if I told you that Officer Krieger was on duty at the Capitol last Christmas morning from 7:00 a.m. to 3:00 p.m. and that he's prepared to testify that you came to the Capitol Christmas morning at 7:40 a.m., identified yourself with your credentials, and with his permission, you entered Governor Roberts' office to, as you put it, get something you left there the day before."

A gasp rippled through the audience. Attorney Powell put her head in her hand.

"He must be mistaken or it was someone impersonating me." Smith replied. "It wasn't me."

"Even if he shows you his official log checking you in at 7:40 a.m. and checking you out at 7:52 a.m.?"

"Same answer. It must have been someone impersonating me." Smith said.

He's a real cool character Kelly thought, *but I'm not finished yet.*

"Could we take a recess, your honor?" Smith asked.

"I object, your honor. I only have a few questions left, and I'm at a crucial point."

Powell didn't say anything. Smith glared at her.

"Request denied. If we keep going we might finish today. Go ahead, Mr. Kelly." Judge Bronner ruled.

"Thank you, your honor. Now, Mr. Smith, I understand that you strongly support the use of DNA evidence in trials, that you believe them to be accurate. Is that true?"

"Yes, that's correct."

"You are, of course aware of Dr. Washington's report and testimony in this case, in which he stated that the drop of saliva found on Anne

Tremaine's chest was not hers, and in his opinion, it was that of the killer, remember that, Mr. Smith?"

"Yes, of course."

Kelly went back to his counsel table and picked up a paper. He walked toward Smith holding the paper. It had the name of the Connecticut Medical Examiner's Office and Dr. Washington printed on the top.

"What would you say, Mr. Smith, if I told you Dr. Washington had found that the saliva on Anne Tremaine's chest is not a match with that of Governor Roberts' but is a DNA match with your saliva? And that he's prepared to testify to that. Dr. Washington, would you please stand up."

There were more gasps from the audience. The reporters were on the edge of their seats, ready to rush to the telephones.

Dr. Washington stood up from the far side of the audience and removed his sunglasses.

"You remember Dr. Washington, the Chief Medical Examiner, don't you Mr. Smith?"

Smith was beginning to perspire. He loosened his tie. "Of course I do; but you're bluffing Mr. Kelly. What you said is impossible. I never gave a sample of my saliva to anyone."

"Do you smoke cigars, Mr. Smith?"

"Yes."

"And do you sometimes put them down in an ashtray after you've smoked part of a cigar?"

Smith looked shocked. He stammered. "I suppose so."

"As a matter of fact you have, and your saliva was on the half used cigar. Have you been missing a few lately, Mr. Smith? Say at a Bar Association dinner?"

Smith stared back, wide-eyed, and astonished when he realized what he had done.

Powell was on her feet again. "Your honor, may we approach?"

"Of course" said Judge Bronner.

When the two attorneys reached the bench, Powell whispered "I think we've reached the point where Mr. Smith should formally be advised of his rights under the Fifth amendment."

"I agree" Kelly said.

There was a sudden rise in the noise level from the audience. Someone shouted: "He's got a gun!"

Smith had taken out a nine millimeter pistol and pointed it at the crowd as he stepped down from the witness chair.

"Don't anyone move!" he shouted.

In the same motion, he swung around and pointed the gun at the marshal guarding the rear door from the courtroom into the non-public corridor used by judges and staff. Smith walked up behind the marshal and put the gun against his head. "Back up into the corridor with me." They moved back, and then Smith shoved him away toward his right.

"Move down the corridor away from me" he ordered. "MOVE!" He pointed the gun at the marshal. "I'll give you ten seconds to get to the end of the corridor" he shouted.

The marshal, who was unarmed, started running down the corridor. Smith leaned into the courtroom, and shouted "Stay where you are!" Then, he fired a bullet toward the ceiling. Most of the crowd went to the floor to avoid any more shooting.

Smith raced down the corridor to the north end of the building.

51

Smith ran to one of the elevators in the rear of the building, got in and closed the doors before anyone saw him. He had to move quickly before word of his escape spread too far. He took the elevator to the garage, hurried to his black sedan, and pulled out of the garage onto Oak Street headed north. At the intersection of Capitol Avenue, one block away, he turned left and then drove to the parking area in front of the Legislative Office Building. He walked casually through the main entrance, greeted the guard and continued on to the corridor that led to the underground passageway to the Capitol building. When the LOB had been built, a subterranean tunnel had been constructed from the LOB ending at an escalator that took people up to the first floor lobby of the Capitol near the stairs. By using this route, Smith could get into the building without having to face the guards outside the Capitol. He walked quickly along the corridor, then hopped onto the moving walkway. Instead of remaining stationery on the walkway, he walked forward on it, faster where there were no people and quickly went up the escalator. There were no guards in the lobby as he arrived there. He climbed the stairs, walked a few feet to the Governor's office and burst in brandishing a 9 millimeter pistol. There were people in the waiting area, who looked up startled as he walked through the swinging doors, past the receptionist and turned right towards the Governor's private office. He grabbed the arm of one of the secretaries, Jody Bradley, a redhead in her mid-twenties, held the gun to her head and pushed her into the Governor's private office. He turned to the people watching, pointed the gun toward a window and fired shattering the glass. "Everybody out of here, now if you don't want to get hurt." He closed and locked the door behind him being sure to also lock the deadbolt. He told Jody to sit on the couch. "Don't move, or I'll blow your head off. What's your name?"

"Jody . . . Jody Bradley" she stammered with tears in her eyes. "What do you want?"

"Well, Jody. Here's the way it's going to play out. I'm State's Attorney Frank Smith. I'm wanted for the murder of Anne Tremaine last Christmas. That's right. Roberts didn't do it. I did, and they know it. You're my hostage, you're going to stay with me until I get what I want, a helicopter to take me to Bradley Airport and a jet to take me to Brazil. I've got money there, and I can be safe there. No way am I going to prison!

By now, the cops realize where I am and that I've taken you as a hostage." He got up and closed the drapes on the already locked windows, with just enough room for him to see out. "They're probably moving in a SWAT team, a hostage negotiating team, and surrounding the building with state troopers. They're going to try to talk me into releasing you and giving myself up."

"Will you let me go?"

"Yes, but only when I get what I want. In a few minutes, that phone will ring, and there'll be a hostage negotiator on the other end."

Just then the phone range. “See, what did I tell you,” Smith smiled as he picked up the phone but kept his gun trained on Jody.

“This is Captain Pickett of the Connecticut State Police, Mr. Smith. We have a SWAT team here, and the building is completely surrounded. You have no chance of escape. Why don’t you give yourself up so no one, including you, will be hurt? There’s no other way out.”

“You’ve been watching too many cop shows,” Smith replied. “Who do you think you’re talking to? Some dumb dumb who just got off the boat. I’m the State’s Attorney for Christ’s sake!”

“I’m in the outer office” Pickett said. “Your Deputy, Attorney Powell, is here, Becky Brown is here and Governor Roberts is here. They want you to give yourself up. We’ve contacted your wife, and she’s coming down to talk with you. In the meantime, how about if I come in to talk to you? I won’t have a weapon, and we can talk this over.”

“Captain, maybe it’s you who just got off the boat. Now, listen to me and listen to me good! Without interruption!” Smith said. “You are not to bring my wife down here. You keep her out of this.”

What Smith didn’t know was that microphones had been raised to just below the open transom. Other microphones were picking up what Captain Pickett was saying, and their conversation was being broadcast over all radio and TV outlets even though video cameras had been barred from the Governor’s office. TV cameras and a crowd of local and national media people were outside the building which was in the process of being evacuated. People throughout the nation were listening to the conversation with cameras showing the outside of the building.

"Second," Smith continued, "I've got this young, pretty hostage here, Jody Bradley. I've got a 9 millimeter pistol pointed at her head. If you try to rush me, if you don't do exactly as I say, I'll blow her brains out; and you'd better believe that. I have nothing to lose" he added.

"What do you want?" asked Pickett.

"I thought you'd never ask" Smith replied.

I want a state police helicopter to land in 15 minutes on the north lawn. You're to withdraw the police from around the building and let me get to the helicopter with my hostage.

The helicopter is to fly to Bradley Airport where you will have an air force or National Guard jet, fully fueled with an experienced crew ready to fly me to Brazil non-stop. Any deviation from this plan, and the hostage will die. That's it. End of discussion." He hung up the phone.

Smith told Jody to sit on the Governor's desk. He sat in the Governor's chair, and held the gun close to her.

The Governor's desk was at the far end of the room facing the door 21 feet away. There was a window behind the desk facing the Legislative Office Building to the west. Another window was to the left of the desk facing out southerly onto Capitol Avenue. There was a plush blue rug throughout the room. The couch against the north wall and the visitor's chairs were all covered in a light blue fabric. Photographs of former governors hung from the walls as well as paintings of landscapes which had been selected by Cindy. Most of the remaining wall space had mahogany bookcases filled with a variety of books including the Connecticut State Statutes.

In the outer office, Colonel Lewis, the head of the State Police had arrived. He and Pickett were discussing the situation with Governor Roberts.

"We can get a helicopter here that quickly," Lewis said; "but we can't let him get aboard. He won't release the girl. Either she'll be killed or the pilot will be or both, and if we give in, we'll only inspire another hostage situation somewhere else."

"We can't rush him. He'll kill the girl for sure then" Pickett said.

"Sharpshooters won't do it. He's got the drapes closed" Lewis added.

"Maybe, Arlene can talk to him. If she can change places with Jody, she'll have a better chance of convincing him to give up. Besides, he likes Arlene and is less likely to kill her," Governor Roberts commented.

"Arlene," Roberts said. "Why don't you try talking to him?"

Arlene Powell picked up the phone and buzzed the inner office. Smith answered.

"Frank, this is Arlene. Why don't you let the girl go? She's totally innocent in this whole thing. She doesn't deserve to be hurt or killed."

Smith relented, "O.K., I'll let her go if you take her place."

Arlene gave Roberts the thumbs up sign; but Smith wasn't through.

"On condition, that you bring Becky with you" he said. "I want two for one."

"Let me check" she said. She put her hand on the receiver and looked at Becky, "He wants you and me in exchange for Jody."

Becky looked at Roberts.

"Absolutely not, Becky. He doesn't like you very much right now. You brought him down. If you go in there, he's likely to try to kill you for revenge." Roberts warned.

"He won't kill me. He knows that once he kills someone, he'll be taken out even if it means rushing him. Also, I have some training that may help us in a pinch; and watching two of us is more difficult than keeping his eyes just on Jody." she said. "I'll give it a try." Becky smiled at Roberts.

"No, Becky. You're still not going in there. You've taken enough risks already." Roberts said. "Let Arlene go in alone." He started to move toward Becky.

Smith unlocked the door and opened it to let Arlene in. Arlene walked in and suddenly Becky ducked under Roberts and pushed in after her, closing the door behind her.

Roberts cursed: "Dammit, Becky, what do you think your doing?"

The door was already closed. It opened quickly and Jodi walked out. Then Smith double locked the door again using the deadbolt.

Becky looked at Smith and said: "I am in here against the Governor's orders." she said, "But, Frank, I wouldn't miss this for the world."

"Where the hell is that chopper?" Smith demanded.

"It'll be another 15 minutes," Becky said. "They have to bring it in from Bradley. You know how it is."

"Yeah, I do," Smith said. Suddenly, he slapped Becky hard across the face. "That's for talking to my kids" he said. "You had no right to get them involved."

He hit her across the other side of her face. "And you deserve that for showing my picture to the Capitol Police Officer. You were trying to do me in, Becky, just to save that miserable excuse for a man and a Governor."

"Frank, stop!" said Arlene. "That's over." He walked closer to Becky.

"I was only doing my job, Frank."

"Yeah, well was it your job to steal one of my cigars; or were you so thorough just so you could stick it to me?" He put the gun in his left hand and with his right, he punched Becky hard in her stomach causing her to double over. She fell back onto the couch gasping for breath. He had knocked the wind out of her.

"Frank," Arlene said, trying to get his attention away from Becky, "Why did you kill Anne?" She was sitting in Roberts' chair.

Smith turned toward her and yelled, "Get out of my chair!! That's my chair," he paused, "or at least it should be!"

Is he a little crazy from all of this? Arlene Thought. She quickly got up and walked over to Frank who was now facing the desk and looking at Becky on the couch.

"Why did you kill Anne?" Arlene asked again.

"I didn't really mean to go that far," he said. "I got angry when she called me and tried to blow me off Christmas Eve, and then when she threatened to send a photo of the two of us, nude together, to my wife and the press, I really got ticked off. I went there the next morning to get the picture back and to try to keep us together. She gave me a hard time, practically spit in my face; and when she kneed me in the groin, I really lost it."

"That doesn't sound like murder," Arlene replied. "You were under extreme emotional distress. You could probably get manslaughter one," she said. "You'd end up serving less than ten years."

"Maybe so," Smith replied. "But can you imagine an ex-prosecutor in prison with the same people he prosecuted? I wouldn't last a week."

"They could probably make arrangements for you to do your time in a federal prison."

"Are you kidding me?" Smith raised his voice. "What do you take me for, Arlene? Do you think I just got off the boat?" he demanded. "Even if I did survive in federal prison, what's the future for an ex-state's attorney, a convicted felon no one would hire?"

Smith moved around the room, his voice rising and his face flushed. "I'd be disbarred. I wouldn't be able to support my family, who probably would be ashamed to have a well-known convicted felon for a husband or a father."

He slammed his fist on the desk: "No, my life is over here, and it's all your fault, Becky, and Annie's fault, you bitches." He was screaming now and moved toward Becky as if he were about to hit her again. Becky flinched and moved back. *He's hysterical* she thought. *The gun could go off if he loses it completely*. Smith continued: "In Brazil I can start over where they can't get me!" Smith yelled. "I have some Swiss accounts. Don't sell me short you bitch. I'll do all right there," he said. "And I can even send for my family to join me."

"Why did you try to frame Roberts?" Becky asked.

"Because he's a mamby-pamby crud who's in the office I should be in. Besides, he's a logical perp. He had an affair with Anne even though it was quite a while ago; I knew that he jogged every morning near Anne's condo; and it was a cinch to talk my way into his office, take the letter and glasses from his desk and go back and plant them in the condo. I even planted Annie's fingerprints. It almost worked. If you hadn't shown my picture to Krieger, it would have worked. When Kelly destroyed Forrester's credibility, it was no great loss. We made a deal with him and told him what to say, but he blew it. I did try to hide the report on the saliva test, and that would have worked if you hadn't stumbled into it, Arlene. I think the jurors' eyes were glazing over on that one anyway.

Hey, what are you unhappy about Arlene? You're going to be acting State's Attorney."

He turned to Becky. "What I want to know is how you first got on to me. I didn't leave anything that would lead to me. What made you show my picture to Krieger?"

"Actually, I didn't intend to show it to him" Becky replied. "The only photo I could get of Cassella was a newspaper photo of you presenting Cassella with an award. Instead of identifying Cassella, Krieger identified you as the one who'd been there Christmas morning. It was a lucky break." she said.

"For you, maybe; but not for me. Even then, I had a chance. I paid Krieger $2,500 to keep his mouth shut. Just goes to show, no on keeps their word anymore."

"What about my cigar? How'd you get that?"

"Once I found out you were at the Capitol, we tried to find other evidence. Remember the Bar Association dinner at the Hilton?" Becky asked. "You and Inspector Cassella were both smoking cigars."

"Yea, but how did you get them?"

"Frank, I'm a little hurt that you didn't recognize me. I wore a blonde wig, shaded glasses and a cute little waitress's outfit. I managed to get assigned to your table. Remember how I kept offering you more wine? Once you were somewhat sloshed, it was easy to take the half used cigars from the ashtrays. Cassella's saliva didn't match; yours did."

"Very clever" Smith said; "but it won't do you any good. You're going to Brazil with me."

"Another affair, Frank?" Becky asked. "But you're a married man. What ever happened to the family values and sanctity of marriage you're always talking about?"

"Don't be a wise ass, Becky, or you might not make it to Brazil" Smith said. "You don't know what it was like with Annie. It's almost as if she cast a spell over me. I couldn't stay away from her. She became an obsession with me."

"Seems to me I've heard that before from Tom Price" Becky replied. "But why you, Frank? Why did Annie pick you?"

"It is possible, you know, that she might have been attracted to me. Maybe, she was setting me up to drop charges against friends of hers; but she never asked."

52

In the outer office, Governor Roberts, Captain Pickett, Colonel Lewis, Brian Kelly and Cindy Roberts were standing around a desk that had, by now, become a mini-command center. The Governor's Chief of Staff, Bill Donovan, was also there with the press secretary, Bob Sweeney. Additional state troopers and gubernatorial aides were standing in the back of the room.

"We're at a stand-off" Colonel Lewis said. He sounded frustrated. "Smith has the upper hand. We can't let him get on the helicopter but if we rush him, we're going to end up with at least one dead hostage."

"We've got our SWAT team in place" Captain Pickett said. "We could just wait him out."

Roberts held up his hand. "No. Smith won't allow that. If things don't move soon, he'll shoot one of the hostages to show he means business, and once he takes that first shot, anything can happen. I've got to go in there and negotiate with him one on one" he said.

"What?" Colonel Lewis, Cindy and Brian Kelly shouted almost in unison.

Cindy moved closer to him. "David, don't. He's just waiting for a chance to kill you."

"If anyone can reach him at this point, I can. He may not like me. . . ."

"That's the understatement of the year" Kelly interrupted. "He hates you. He'll take you hostage, and even if he gets away, he'll kill you first. You'll only add fuel to the fire."

Roberts looked around the room. "We wouldn't be in this mess if it weren't for me."

"That's ridiculous" Cindy replied vehemently. "It's not your fault. It's the fault of that deranged man in there."

"Well, it's certainly not Becky's fault or Arlene's."

"I still remember what a political columnist for the Courant, Jack Zaiman, once told me. The function of leadership is to lead. He was right. I was elected to lead. This is something I have to do" Roberts declared.

"Colonel, get him on the phone" he ordered.

Lewis buzzed Smith on the intercom. "The Governor wants to talk to you" he said. Roberts picked up the phone.

"Frank?"

"Where the hell is that helicopter?" Smith asked. "You're the man at the top, Roberts. You have the power to get it here right away. Let's stop the stalling and passing the buck."

"Frank, I give you my word. It's on its way" Roberts replied. "We can still work this out. I'm coming in so we can talk face to face. Unlock the door."

"Are you kidding? I'm going to let you in with your army right behind? Why don't you get real?"

"Frank" Roberts said. "I assure you. . . ."

"I spoke too soon" Smith interjected. "But to make sure you'll come in alone and unarmed, I want you to hear from Becky." Smith had Becky up against the wall, with his right hand holding the pistol against her head. He held the phone up to her.

"Governor, he's holding his gun right up against my head, just behind my ear. He's on the side away from the door. There's no way you could rush him without his killing me and probably Arlene, first. But don't come in or he'll kill you, too."

"Shut up!" Smith shouted. He hit her in the head with the phone and slammed her against the bookcase. She slumped to the floor, blood trickling down her forehead.

"Your people have always been loyal to you, Roberts" Smith said. "See what it got her — a hit in the head! You better bring some bandages with you. And be prepared to offer me something worthwhile. Like a pardon" he laughed.

"Anything's possible, Frank."

"O.K." Smith said "The door is already unlocked. Take your jacket off before you come in."

Roberts took off his jacket and tie. He moved toward the door. Colonel Lewis blocked his way. "Sorry, Governor, I can't let you go in there. We're charged with protecting you. It's too dangerous. You'll either be taken hostage yourself or be killed." Lewis paused. "Or both." He stood squarely in front of the door. "I would not be doing my duty, sir, if I allowed you to go in there."

Roberts gave him a determined look. “Colonel, have you forgotten? As chief executive of this state, I outrank you. Now, please! Step aside!” Colonel Lewis hesitated, so Roberts looked at him and in a steely tone of voice said, “That’s an order, Colonel!”

Lewis handed him a first aid kit and then moved away.

“I’m coming in, Frank” Roberts said in a raised voice. He opened the door, walked through and closed it behind him.

“Up against the wall” Smith said pointing at Roberts with the gun. “But, first, lock the door.”

Roberts moved to the door and slammed the deadbolt to the right. Then, he put his hands against the wall. Smith moved behind him. “Spread ‘em” he said. Roberts spread his legs. Smith moved in behind him and put his left foot in front of Robert’s left leg, ready to trip him from his precarious position. He held the gun against Roberts as he patted him down with his right hand, being careful to feel his ankles.

“All right” he said as he backed away. He motioned to the couch. “Sit over there” he said to Roberts. Smith had taken the first aid kit and tossed it to Arlene. “Pick up Becky and then the two of you sit next to him.” He motioned towards Roberts who was now sitting on the couch.

“Why not let Arlene and Becky go, Frank? One hostage is enough and you’ll only have me to watch.”

Smith looked at him, his face flushed. “I’m still giving the orders here,” he said in a menacing voice; “but O.K., you’ve got a point. I’ll let Arlene go, but not Becky. I need someone I can handle who’s smaller than I am.”

He turned to Arlene who had finished putting a bandage on Becky's wound. "Go ahead. You can let them know how serious I am. Tell them to back off." He raised his voice and shouted toward the door. "Arlene's coming out. Back away from the door!" Smith didn't realize that his every word was being picked up by microphones feeding his voice into radio and TV stations. "Let them know, in detail, how dangerous this is" he said to Arlene. Arlene opened the door and walked out closing the door behind her. Smith quickly re-locked the door, all the time keeping his gun trained on Becky and Roberts.

"How does it feel sitting next to your hero?" Smith asked sarcastically. "See how easy I am?" he added with a grin.

Smith moved a chair to the middle of the room and sat down facing them. "O.K." he said. "Let's get down to business."

"Frank, you know a pardon is out of the question. Even if I promised it to you, someone would go to court to stop it, claiming it was promised under duress."

"I know, I know" Smith replied.

"I can guarantee you won't get the death penalty. I heard you describe what happened. It came over the radio. They've got microphones picking up this conversation. A case could be made for your being under extreme emotional disturbance. Manslaughter is a 20 year maximum; and we can have you housed in federal prison to keep you away from prisoners you've prosecuted."

Smith leaned forward: "What about kidnaping and assault?" he shouted, "and perjury? You know I denied what Kelly said under oath.

If these sentences are consecutive or even on the kidnaping, I could go away for life."

"Frank, you're a prosecutor; you know all about plea bargains. Those sentences, or even the charges can be reduced to under 20, and they could run concurrently with the manslaughter. You're still looking at a max of 20 years. With good behavior, you could get parole after 12. You're still in your mid-forties. You could be out while you're still in your fifties. You can resume your life with your wife and children."

Smith didn't reply immediately. "It doesn't sound bad" he conceded, "but it's too risky. The judge may not go along with it. They'll still say the deal was made under pressure. And, what about when I do get out. I can't work as a lawyer anymore. I suppose there's always a book deal, but 12 years from now, this whole thing will be forgotten. Besides, the alternative is better. Living in Brazil with the money I've got stashed away; sending for my family and just think" he grinned. "No more snow."

Becky was watching Smith closely. *He must be bipolar* she thought. *One minute he's hysterical and the next minute he's calm, cool and collected.*

"But, Frank," Roberts began. He was suddenly interrupted by the sound of helicopter blades. The phone rang. Smith picked it up. "It's on the lawn" he said more to Becky and Roberts.

"I'm coming out with two hostages" he said to Captain Pickett. I'm going to use the window. It's close enough to the ground. Is the jet at Bradley yet?"

"We're still working on clearance from the Air Force" Pickett replied.

"That jet better be there or a lot of people will die, Captain" Smith threatened.

He pulled Becky to the window with his arm around her neck. "Open your mouth" he ordered, and quickly put the barrel of his 9mm pistol inside. He told Roberts to open the drapes. Then, he looked out the window toward the Legislative Office Building. The clouds had cleared and the sun was shining. Smith instructed Roberts to put the telephone speaker on. "Just as I thought" he said to Pickett. "You've got troopers out there behind the trees. Tell them to unload their rifles and pistols, drop them in the snow and move to the other side of the building. My gun is in Becky's mouth with the safety off. Do it now or she and Roberts are history."

A minute later, the troopers dropped the rifles and pistols and moved from behind the trees toward the north side of the building.

"Is that all of them?" Smith asked Pickett.

"It is."

Smith told Becky to sit on the windowsill facing out with her legs together. He was placing her in position while keeping an eye on Roberts. Suddenly, his face got red. He pulled Becky back and shouted through the speaker to Pickett. "You son of a bitch. You lied to me. You've got a sniper on the deck outside the LOB, crouched behind a post. I can see the reflection of his rifle in the sun. Tell him to stand up, throw his rifle away and walk toward the LOB. Don't worry, my pistol won't shoot that far; but if he doesn't do it, I'll shoot Becky. Do it now!" he screamed.

Smith looked out the window, saw the trooper stand up, throw his gun away with his hands in the air.

"Sorry, Mr. Smith" Pickett said. "He must not have heard the message. Just a communications problem, I assure you."

"Communications problem, my ass. You just got caught lying. If you do it again, I'll kill Becky and still have Roberts as a hostage.

Now, I want you to drop two pair of handcuffs with keys through the transom. Move it!"

He told Roberts to pick them up.

"Put a set on her wrists in front of her" Smith instructed.

Smith ordered Becky to do the same to Roberts' wrists but to put his left wrist inside her right wrist first.

"This way, I not only have both wrists handcuffed, but I have you handcuffed to each other. Perfect fit" he added.

"Tell them what I've done" he directed Roberts. "And tell them we're coming out the door. The window escape isn't going to work." Roberts spoke into the speaker. "Captain, he's got our wrists handcuffed and to each other. He's very dangerous right now. His gun is in Becky's mouth. Don't make any sudden moves or the gun will surely go off even if he doesn't want it to. Do what he says for now. Maybe something will happen along the way. We're coming out through the door. Smith wants everybody to step back out of the way."

Roberts opened the door. They moved forward, Smith behind Becky with his left hand around her neck and his right hand holding the gun in her mouth.

On the other side of the second floor, the press had been allowed to gather with radio and television crews. Bob Schieffer: "I've just gotten word that Governor Roberts and Becky Brown are being brought out of the Governor's office with State's Attorney Frank Smith holding them hostage. For more from inside the Capitol, we go live, now, to CBS correspondent Ted Baker."

Baker's image appeared on the side of the screen. Tall, handsome and with graying hair, he had been with CBS news for 20 years. He talked in a low voice, "Bob, this is the scene on the second floor of this historic state capitol. That's the door to Governor Roberts' office. It's expected to open momentarily. We're standing behind a railing in front of offices on the north side of the building looking southerly across a large open area. The governor's office is on the other side. The open area looks down upon the first floor. The door to the governor's office is opening now. On the left as you look at them is Becky Brown. She is the governor's private investigator. Behind her as they turn right toward the stairs is Frank Smith, the state's attorney. His left arm is around Mrs. Brown's neck tilting her backwards, and his right hand is holding a firearm, a 9mm pistol we're told, against her head behind her right ear. On their right is Governor Roberts. Brown and Roberts appear to have handcuffs on their wrists in front of them. Mrs. Brown has a bandage on her forehead." The camera zoomed in on Becky's forehead. "Governor Roberts is in shirt sleeves without a tie. The police have moved out of the way, but you can be sure their guns are trained on Smith from behind the columns. Smith and the hostages have now reached the top of the stairs."

Suddenly Smith shouted "Everybody stay back. One slip and this gun goes off!" They started down the stairs out of the view of the cameras. Reporters tried to follow them, but were restrained by state police. Becky, Smith and Roberts moved slowly down the grey concrete steps, reached a landing and turned down more steps leading to the southerly side of the building. As they came into view at the bottom of the steps, their movements were picked up by another TV camera.

"This is Dave Conlin of CBS news" a voice came through the television set as the camera focused on the group moving steadily toward the door. "There are two state police officers moving toward them." "Stay back" Smith shouted.

"He means it." Roberts said. "Move back, Colonel; you, too, Captain Pickett" he ordered.

"Everyone, inside and outside, take out your guns, unload them and kick them away" Smith shouted; he turned slightly toward Roberts. "Order them to do it."

"Do what he says" Roberts ordered. "We'll deal with him later." The troopers complied.

Smith, Becky and Roberts then moved quickly through the outer doors of the capitol, down the steps and along the line of state police cars parked in front. Smith stopped at the head of the line, and looked at the trooper behind the wheel. The window was open.

"What's your name, trooper?" he asked.

"Trooper Kenneth L. Davis," he replied.

"Well, Trooper Davis, unlock the doors, put your hand brake on, and look straight ahead. We're going for a little ride. If you don't do exactly as I tell you, I'm going to kill Mrs. Brown here and your commander in chief, Governor Roberts. Turn around, and look at them. You can see the gun in her mouth, and the handcuffs. So, do what I say, understood?"

"Yes, Sir" Davis replied as he turned his head forward again.

Smith spoke to Roberts. "Open the back door. You get in first."

Roberts opened the door, and moving sideways, they all slipped into the backseat. Smith pulled Becky along sitting her on his lap.

"Now, both of you slide forward."

Smith opened up his legs and Becky slid down so she was half sitting on the edge of the seat, Smith's legs holding her in place. Roberts, handcuffed to Becky, had moved down to the edge of the seat. Smith ordered him to lean back. Then, he shut the back door and ordered Davis to lock the doors. During all this time Smith held the gun in Becky's mouth.

"One more thing, Trooper," Smith said. "Very carefully, now, remove your weapon from your holster and hold it up in the air . . . . with the barrel forward. Hold it by the barrel handle, keep your fingers away from the trigger. Get it ready to fire, and push the safety off."

Davis hesitated. Smith grabbed Roberts by the hair "Governor, issue an order to Trooper Davis, here. I don't want any misunderstandings as to who's in charge."

"Do what he says, Trooper" Roberts commanded. "That's an order. And don't hesitate. Mr. Smith's a little trigger happy."

"Yes, Governor!" Davis said as he released the safety on his 9mm pistol and handed it over his shoulder to Smith.

"That's it, handle first." Smith grabbed the gun and quickly placed the barrel under the left side of Roberts' jaw pointed up. "Now, get Colonel Lewis or Captain Pickett on the radio."

Captain Pickett's voice came over the speaker. "Attorney Smith, this is Captain Pickett. It's not too late to put a stop to this. We have you completely surrounded. Give yourself up, now, and no one will be hurt."

"God damn it, Captain, cut out that crap. For all I know, you've got a sniper who'll take me out as soon as I release these two."

"I give you my word . . . ."

"Your word? That's as good as your promise to move troopers away from the window. Of course, you didn't mention the sniper at the LOB.

Listen, Captain. We'll get along just fine if you shut up and do as I say. No more debate. Just follow my orders.

Governor, tell him what's happening." Roberts described the scene in the backseat emphasizing the gun in Becky's mouth and the gun pressed against his jaw.

"Give him some slack, captain" Roberts ordered. "This will still work out."

"Captain" Smith said. "We're going to Bradley Airport. I want an escort. I want the side streets blocked off. I don't want any unavoidable accidents" he said. "Trooper Davis, take I-84 to I-91 north. You know the way. Captain, that military jet better be there" he said. "If it's not, you'd better have at least 4 hearses in its place. Now, enough talk. Let's move."

Brian Williams of NBC was summarizing the conversation.

"So, that's where we are. Now, let's switch to NBC correspondent Jim Doyle. He's in an NBC news helicopter hovering over the Connecticut state capitol. What are we looking at?"

"Brian, this is an overview of the state capitol. The state police car carrying Governor Roberts, Becky Brown and Frank Smith is just about to leave the Capitol grounds. Two state police cruisers with their red and blue lights flashing have just gone west on Capitol Avenue followed by a Hartford police car. Here's the hostage car moving in behind them. Now here comes another Hartford cruiser followed by two more state police cars moving parallel to each other. Lights are flashing and sirens have been activated. Hartford police have blocked off intersections and pulled other vehicles to the sides of the streets. Now, this caravan, if you will, is turning right onto Broad Street, moving north, past the State Armory and the Hartford Courant. An entrance ramp to I-84 East is just ahead. As you can see, they're now taking that ramp. All eastbound traffic has been stopped on I-84 just before this ramp. Traffic is moving slowly in the other direction. Many people are rubbernecking as they listen to this chase scene on their car radios. People are standing on the overpasses. Now, the caravan is taking the exit leading to I-91 north. There they go, up the ramp, crossing over I-84 headed north along the westerly side of the Connecticut River. The State Police have blocked off the entrance ramps onto I-91 north. The caravan is traveling at about 70 mph. The roads are clear. In a few minutes they'll be passing through Windsor. We'll continue to follow them. Back to you, Brian."

Meanwhile, the state police helicopter had taken off from the north lawn of the State Capitol. Colonel Lewis, Captain Pickett and several armed SWAT team troopers were on board. They were flying a little ahead of the NBC news helicopter.

"Captain, what do you think Smith will do when he realizes there's no Air Force jet at Bradley?" the leader of the SWAT team asked.

"He could go crazy. That's one very frustrated man down there. He's counting on a jet to Brazil as the only way to get out of this mess" Pickett replied.

"We're going to have to stall him. Tell him its on its way" Colonel Lewis remarked. "And find some way to free those hostages. One thing's for sure. We can't let him leave the airport with the hostages. I've got Lieutenant Briggs of the SWAT team devising some options for us."

The caravan had picked up additional police cars and news helicopter flying overhead. As the hostage car took the exit to Bradley Airport, Smith ordered Trooper Davis to contact Captain Pickett. Davis held the microphone over the back of the front seat.

"Captain, I want you to open the gate that allows us to go right onto the runway area. Keep the car traffic away from that gate and clear our way to it. Shut down all air traffic in or out. NOW!" Smith ordered.

"What about planes on final approach?" Pickett asked.

"You can let them land, but have them taxi to the other side of the field and stay there. All other incoming traffic is to be diverted to other airports. They can easily make Boston or Providence.

And get that military jet over near the gate we're using."

The state police helicopter had landed. Colonel Lewis was in the control tower, and Captain Pickett was on the balcony in front of the window of the passenger terminal. Communications equipment was in place that allowed them to communicate with each other and Smith as well as to another state police command post nearby. The conversations with Smith were being fed to the radio and television pool. Troopers with rifles were on the balcony as well as the roof of the terminal building. Three ambulances had pulled up to the area beneath the balcony.

Trooper Davis drove through the gate and stopped, at Smith's direction, far enough away from the balcony to be able to see the entire terminal building.

"Get rid of all these police cars, the troopers on the balcony and the roof" Smith spoke into the microphone to Captain Pickett. "Do it now or you'll be part of the first assassination of a Connecticut Governor."

The cars drove away, the troopers left the balcony and the ones on the roof moved out of sight.

"Where the hell is that Air Force jet?" Smith shouted to Pickett.

"It's on its way" Pickett replied. "We just got clearance from the Air Force. It should be leaving Westover as we speak."

"Bullshit!" Smith exploded His face was flushed and distorted with rage. "You're a Goddam liar" he screamed. "Davis, lower the front window and put your arm out, now."

Davis complied. Smith shot him in the arm.

"I just put your trooper on the disabled list, Captain!" Smith's voice was now high pitched. He seemed almost out of control. "Zoom in with that TV camera on the balcony. You can see the blood dripping!

You don't think I'm serious? Next time you'll have at least two bodies for the morgue. I'm not going to put up with any more stalling. You hear me?"

"Mr. Smith, this is Colonel Lewis. Take it easy. We'll do whatever you say."

"We'll see about that, Colonel. Patch me through to the American Airlines supervisor."

"We can't do that. . . ."

"What?" Smith interrupted.

"But, we'll bring him out on the balcony. Please, calm down. We can't connect directly to the counter. Here's Mr. Grenier, now."

A medium size man with thinning hair, dressed in an American Airlines jacket, picked up the microphone. "Yes, sir" he said in a nervous voice.

"Listen to me, Grenier. Don't lie to me, or you'll be responsible for the killing of Governor Roberts. Understood?"

"Yes, sir."

"Where's that DC-10 headed for? The one over there to your left at the terminal?"

"Puerto Rico."

"How many passengers?"

"Ah, let me think. Two hundred forty one."

"Are they all on board?"

"Yes, sir. It was just about to pull away from the terminal."

"How many flight attendants?"

"Eight."

"All right, Mr. Grenier. Close the doors. Have the plane pull away from the terminal and bring it out here where I am."

"But, sir. I don't have the authority. . . ."

"Colonel Lewis. You want another demonstration? Talk to him. Don't worry, I'll let the passengers go."

Smith could see Grenier talking to Captain Pickett. Then, he returned to the terminal.

"All right, Mr. Smith" Colonel Lewis said. "It'll be done."

The DC-10 engines, already running turned up to a higher pitch, and the huge aircraft started to back away from the terminal. It stopped about 100 feet beyond the state police cruiser with its side facing the terminal.

"All right, Colonel" Smith said. "Move the ramp up to the door, and bring the passengers out two at a time. Follow them with the flight attendants, also two at a time. They can go right to the terminal. I want to see two hundred forty one passengers and eight flight attendants come down that ramp. Do it now, before I change my mind."

Smith directed Davis to move the car closer to the airplane. Darkness had set in, but there were enough lights from the terminal building to illuminate the area. The passengers and flight attendants came down the stairs. Smith counted two hundred forty one plus eight.

By this time, Colonel Lewis had joined Captain Pickett on the balcony.

"Good job, Colonel. I guess you're finally getting the message. Leave the stairs in place" Smith said.

Davis pulled the cruiser up in front of the stairs, and at Smith's direction, had turned off the motor. Smith leaned forward and opened the door to his left. He kept the pistol against Becky's head with his left hand and the pistol in his right hand held against the Governor's neck.

"This is going to be awkward. Follow my instructions carefully; otherwise these guns will go off."

Directing Becky and David to sit up and where to move their feet, Smith and Becky struggled out of the cruiser with Roberts right behind. They stood at the bottom of the stairs facing the cruiser which acted as a shield. With Becky in front of him and Roberts to his right, they started to back up the stairs one at a time.

Colonel Lewis had directed two snipers onto the roof of the building, spread apart but facing the DC-10.

"Stay low" Lewis instructed. "On my command to fire, Hardy you shoot out the front right tires. Burke, you knock out the ones on the left. This aircraft is not going to leave."

"What about the hostages, Colonel?" Captain Pickett asked. "If you shoot out the tires, that could set Smith off. He could kill Becky and Governor Roberts. Is it worth the risk?"

Lewis looked at him, "It's riskier to let them go" he said.

Smith, Becky and Roberts had reached the top of the stairs. Schieffer, Williams and ABC News were describing the scene to millions of viewers.

Quietly, but suddenly, two troopers in SWAT team gear came out of the plane. The first one put his right arm around Smith's neck and pulled back hard while using his left thumb to press Smith's nerve in an attempt to paralyze him. At the same time Roberts lifted his hands and quickly grabbed the pistol and Smith's left hand and pulled the gun away from Becky's head and toward him a split second before it fired. Almost simultaneously the other trooper grabbed Smith's right arm and the other pistol pulling them down and away from Roberts' neck. That gun also discharged. Blood was coming out of Roberts' left cheek just below and midway between his left eye and left ear.

"Oh, my God!" someone cried. Becky and Roberts, dizzy from their wounds, struggled to keep their balance. With the handcuffs neither could reach the railing. They swayed back and forth. Roberts fell backwards his feet going out from under him. His heavier weight brought Becky down the same way. They slid down the steps. Trooper Davis, his left arm still bleeding, raced up the steps and stopped their slide about halfway down.

EPILOGUE

Governor Roberts and Becky Brown suffered flesh wounds to their cheeks. When the wounds healed, they each underwent plastic surgery and were pronounced good as new. Their spouses commented that it was an improvement over the original. Roberts' Chief of Staff, Bill Donovan, had suggested that Roberts carry the scar as a badge of heroism at least until after the next election. Roberts said no. "Most people would like to forget what happened" he remarked.

Frank Smith was unhurt aside from some bruises. He was charged with murder, assault and kidnaping. His defense to murder was extreme emotional disturbance. He asked Brian Kelly to defend him. Kelly declined. A plea bargain was being considered. Governor Roberts, true to his word, offered to have his imprisonment served in a federal prison.

Arlene Powell was named acting State's Attorney. She disqualified her office from prosecuting former State's Attorney Smith. His case was transferred to another Judicial District. Powell resigned a few months later and became a well known criminal defense attorney.

State Trooper Davis became Governor Roberts' driver and bodyguard.

Chad Burnham was never able to pin down the Mafia connection. The proposed casino was defeated in the Legislature. It's backers vowed to reintroduce the bill in the next session.

When Ben and Becky Brown returned form a Bahamas' vacation, she continued to work as an investigator with Brian Kelly.

Robert Forrester was sentenced to five years in prison for the sale of marijuana. He was not prosecuted as a persistent felony offender.

Inspector Anthony Cassella was convicted after a trial of bribery of a witness and sentenced to five years in prison. He was placed in the same cellblock as Forrester. For Robert Forrester returning to prison was like old home week. "Tony" Cassella had a very unpleasant time in prison.

Judge Patricia Amenta was elevated to the State Supreme Court. Declaring the issue moot, she had declined to rule on the Motion to Suppress the phone recording.

Judge Alan Bronner remained, by choice, on the Superior Court bench continuing to try cases.

Edwin Lincoln resigned as Lieutenant Governor following quadruple bypass surgery, on advice of his doctor. The President of the State Senate, Cynthia Stevens Roberts became Lieutenant Governor. It was the first time in history that a governor and lieutenant governor were married to each other. Time and Newsweek both ran cover stories on "Connecticut's First Couple."

They considered filling the vacant U.S. Senate seat. Cindy suggested David resign as Governor making her Governor, and she would appoint him to the Senate. He suggested his appointing her to the Senate. In the end, they did neither. They wanted to stay together in the Executive Residence as governor and lieutenant governor.

The night of the day Cindy was sworn in as Lieutenant Governor, she and David, as usual, got into bed together in the master bedroom. David looked at her, "This is the first time a governor and lieutenant governor have slept in the same bed together." "Another historic first" they said in unison. They started to laugh.